Witcha Gonna Do?

Witcha Gonna Do?

AVERY FLYNN

BERKLEY ROMANCE ✦ NEW YORK

BERKLEY ROMANCE
Published by Berkley
An imprint of Penguin Random House LLC
penguinrandomhouse.com

Copyright © 2022 by Avery Flynn
Excerpt from *Resting Witch Face* copyright © 2022 by Avery Flynn
Penguin Random House supports copyright. Copyright fuels creativity,
encourages diverse voices, promotes free speech, and creates a vibrant culture.
Thank you for buying an authorized edition of this book and for complying
with copyright laws by not reproducing, scanning, or distributing any part of it
in any form without permission. You are supporting writers and allowing
Penguin Random House to continue to publish books for every reader.

BERKLEY is a registered trademark and Berkley Romance
with B colophon is a trademark of Penguin Random House LLC.

Library of Congress Cataloging-in-Publication Data

Names: Flynn, Avery, author.
Title: Witcha gonna do? / Avery Flynn.
Description: First edition. | New York: Berkley Romance, 2022.
Identifiers: LCCN 2022023149 (print) | LCCN 2022023150 (ebook) |
ISBN 9780593335215 (trade paperback) | ISBN 9780593335222 (ebook)
Subjects: LCGFT: Witch fiction. | Romance fiction. | Humorous fiction. | Novels.
Classification: LCC PS3606.L93 W58 2022 (print) | LCC PS3606.L93 (ebook) |
DDC 813/.6—dc23/eng/202200603
LC record available at https://lccn.loc.gov/2022023149
LC ebook record available at https://lccn.loc.gov/2022023150

First Edition: December 2022

Printed in the United States of America
1st Printing

Book design by Elke Sigal

To Rachel.
You really are magic, you know.
Xoxo, Avery.

Magic happens outside of your comfort zone.

—Jayde Adams, *Serious Black Jumper*

Witcha Gonna Do?

Chapter One

Tilda . . .

Among the magical sects who run the country, one family has been among the power brokers since it was only the thirteen colonies—the Sherwoods of Virginia. Unto every family, however, there is a black sheep. In the Sherwood family, that person is Matilda Grace Sherwood who, despite being from one of the most magical families in the entire Witchingdom, couldn't even pull a rabbit from her favorite baseball hat.

Hi. *Waves.* That's me. Please don't call me Matilda, it's Tilda—or Tillie if you're my oldest sister, Effie. Of course, she only gets away with that because she could turn me into a can of seltzer in a WitchyGram live video and she's annoyed enough some days to do it. You, however, can stick with Tilda.

Welcome to the Salem's Bakery and Coffee Shoppe right in the heart of downtown Wrightsville, where, in an act of naïveté or straight-up foolishness (take your pick), I'm waiting for my date. No wait, don't look over there. I'm not the gorgeous blonde standing at the counter ordering a double half-caf soy latte with one shot of sugar-free hazelnut and a warmed-up eye of newt muffin. Nope, sorry. I'm also not the fresh-faced cutie sitting by the window with auburn hair that falls down her back in waves that just go to show that somewhere on her family tree was a mermaid. I'm the short one with the practically glow-in-the-dark red hair, pasty pale skin, and glasses sitting at the corner table in the back under a dragon's blood tree.

Ugh. I hate these trees. Why? Let's just say that my chair is shoved as far forward as the tiny bistro table will allow because you only need to get the tree's sticky, bloodred sap in your hair once to learn that lesson. Ever had gum in your hair? This is worse. Imagine if that gum smelled *awful* and had a mind of its own. Yeah. Definitely not an ideal situation, to put it mildly. Even worse, the dragon's blood trees seem to desperately love me. Their branches lengthen when I'm near and twist to get closer. If I didn't know any better, I'd say they were totally crushing on me, but that's bizarre even for my life.

Maybe it has something to do with the fact that I'm an outré. That's what we call the rare breed of witch that has absolutely no powers.

Zero.

Zip.

Zilch.

Lucky me, right? Not only do I have the magical ability of your basic couch cushion, I attract nasty-smelling trees. And okay, that would be fine if I was really into trees (OMG, is that a real kink? If so, please don't tell me. My brain is a weird enough place as it is without that information.), but I'm not.

What happened and why I'm sitting here setting myself up for probable disappointment is this: A few months ago, I was going on a year without a date of any kind and I made up my mind to do something about it. Not because I think my life is pointless without a man, but because sometimes I just want a hand to hold, a person to joke with, and all of the other amazing (and okay, orgasmic) things that go along with falling in love and having someone you love who loves you too.

Is that so wrong? If it is, well then that just fits right in with the rest of me, because according to many of the people in the Witchingdom, I'm a magicless freak who isn't worth talking to, let alone dating.

So that brings us back to the reason why I'm at the bakery this morning in my cutest going-out top and casual (yet deadly awesome) jeans with the hidden elastic waistband because no one needs to spend their life with their eye-of-newt-muffin-padded gut getting pinched. I have a date. Ideally, I'd be sitting over where mermaid hair is by the window to check the possibilities as people pass by, but the instructions from the matchmaker were explicit.

Await a tall, dark, and handsome man beneath the dragon's blood tree.

Ugh. Really, I'd rather not be sitting anywhere near this tree (trust me, it smells so much like fetid dragon's breath that taking a deep, calming breath is not an option). But desperate times call for desperate measures and all that. My last three dates Griselda set up were ... well ... let's just say, they didn't go well.

You know how everyone has a nemesis in their life? I got set up on a blind date with mine not once, not twice, but three times, so yeah, you could say in addition to being about as magical as a dried-up tree stump, I'm also dating impaired. That's why I went with the matchmaker. I believed with all my heart that Griselda would pick better; she is a three-hundred-year-old sprite, after all. They are beyond lucky in love. Some of that has to have rubbed off on her pick of dates for me.

Right?

So my latest date is a few minutes late. That happens. Life in the Witchingdom can be uncertain. You never know when a troll is going to block your path under the overpass and demand you solve three riddles or dance the Macarena ten times in a row. Then there are the builder gnomes, who love to be helpful whether you ask for it or not. The other week, a gnome added a bay window to Mrs. Stuckley's house while she was napping. She'd never asked for it, let alone hired the gnomes for the job. Still, the gnome crew wouldn't leave until she paid the bill in M&Ms, but never the red ones.

It is wild out there. Trust me.

While waiting for my mystery date, I decide to scan Witchy-Gram to see how my efforts are going to bring my family, the Sherwoods, into the modern world of social media and make one of the most powerful (okay, and snobbiest) families in the Witchingdom more relatable.

Social media manager isn't exactly the job most people would expect a Sherwood to have. My family is basically the Tom Bradys of witchery—really good for a really long time. Jealous people are always accusing us of having cheated to gain political power, and yeah, Deflategate shenanigans did not help that belief, but still, it was a constant public image battle, which meant that for once my no-magic-having skills came in handy.

So while the rest of my family does the big magical things to make sure everything happens according to society's rules, I run the family social media account on WitchyGram under the watchful eye of my parents. Like really watchful, uber-controlling, all-seeing eye, because they are always expecting me to mess up. Okay, so that *has* happened a time or twenty—hello, posted pic of Mom mid-spell with her face making the most hysterical expression where her cheeks were puffed out and her eyes crossed. Sure, it wasn't exactly flattering, but it is our most viral post to date, and that is the whole point—making the most powerful family in Witchingdom a little more relatable and showcasing how awesome the Sherwoods *are* while I stay as far out of the photo frame as possible.

It's not that my family doesn't love me, it's just that having an outré in their midst doesn't exactly prop up the whole superpowerful-witches image my family wants everyone to have of us. An outré isn't seen as an exception that proves the rule of the Sherwood power, it is seen by some as the crack in the family lineage that proves the rot within.

That's something I'm reminded of every time I have to go through and clean up the comments people make in response to the family social media posts. Today's bit of ugly snark wasn't any different from the usual.

"A real witch of power would be able to spell a child out of being an outré."

"The Sherwoods should be ashamed of letting that Matilda monstrosity out in the world. Hiding away outrés was good enough for my generation, it should be good enough for this generation."

"Freaks and Cheats: The Sherwood Family History."

I may not be magic, but my delete-and-block reaction time is faster than you can say abracadabra—which no one really does anymore (a total pity, because it is such a fun word to say). I had to get quick with my see-ya-asshole reflexes because it makes up about fifty percent of my job. Everyone's a brave jerk from the safety of the Internet.

It used to be that each one of the poisoned-prick comments would leave me raw with my heart scraped up. I wish I could say that they don't bother me at all anymore, but that would be a lie. The reality is somewhere in the middle. The truth is, I'm a dud and the whole world loves to point that out as if I'm confused about it.

Hate to break it to those folks, but I have been aware of my shortcomings since birth. They're pretty impossible to miss.

I get to work under the power of my feet, not the snap, crackle, pop of magic like everyone else. I can't spell cast or read the tarot cards properly or hop from cloud to cloud across the horizon. I'm a freak, a weirdo, an outré. I'm the lone deviant in the entire city of Wrightsville, the whole of the Sherwood family tree, and (as far as I know) all of Virginia.

However, if I think about that too much, my skin gets hot, my palms sweat, and I'm looking for the closest exit so I won't do something even more un-Sherwood-like than being an outré—crying in public.

Instead, I exhale all the negativity and remember the good things in my life, such as my magical misfits support group, movie nights with my sisters, and the taste of warm eye of newt muffins—really, if they don't have them at your coffee shop, you sooooooo need to request them.

Per usual, once my lungs are empty of oxygen, I've pushed all that hate away as much as I can. I'm again ready to ignore the sometimes curious and sometimes cruel stares from people on the street and hold tight to my hope that there is a place for me in this world, even if it's just a small spot on the edge of being acceptable.

It's that little nugget of hope that explains why I'm here at Salem's, sitting at an awkward angle to avoid the dragon's blood tree sap and hoping that maybe this date will be the one that changes everything. As if the universe is listening in on my thoughts, the bell over the bakery's door jingles. The air around me shivers.

It could be him!

Keeping my eyes on my phone, I exit out of the WitchyGram app and inhale a long, calming, please-let-this-be-the-real-thing deep breath.

Realizing too late the mistake I've just made.

The foul stench of the dragon's blood tree fills my lungs. The scent of moldy leftovers and rancid milk is palpable enough I can taste it on my tongue. I gag. I cough. All the oxygen flees my lungs, leaving me spluttering for breath. My eyes water so much I can barely see. All I can make out of the blurry figure rushing toward me is that he has broad shoulders and is really tall.

He grabs me by the arm—hello, Mr. Firm, Strong Hands—and hauls me up from my chair and away from the tree. From the impact of him thwacking me on the back with his palm as I continue to fight for breath, I have no doubt that the size of his hands matches the rest of him. It takes a minute—and garners the attention of every witch in the bakery (many of whom have their phone cameras trained on me, oh yay, Mom's gonna love that)—but thanks to the help of my date, I finally catch my breath and regain my vision.

"Thank you so much," I say as I start to turn around and thank my date. "I know better than to take a deep breath around—"

The words "a dragon's blood tree" die on my lips as soon as I see my date—check that—my nemesis.

"And yet, you still did," Gil Connolly says in that rumbly, judgy voice of his that does absolutely nothing to detract from his absolute—and most infuriating—sexy-archeology-professor-with-a-perma-snarl hotness. "Please say you aren't waiting here for me. Again."

Getting set up on a date with my nemesis once? Weird.

Twice? An accident.

Three times? Serious bad luck.

Four times in one month? There is only one explanation.

I am most definitely cursed.

Chapter Two

Gil . . .

*F*ine. My research methods are rather unorthodox—that *is* the reason why I was banished on this fool's errand of a secret, undercover project by the Council—but they work.

In less than a month, I've had three opportunities (what some might call dates) to observe Matilda Grace Sherwood in her usual habitats and study her reactions to low-level cunning magic. We aren't talking floating teacups or corporeal transformation (what most witches call body swaps), but tactile reverberations and misdirections. These are the kinds of basic magic that even a newborn infant picks up on, the indescribable ghost fingers of something being out there that the child cannot see but can feel.

Tilda, however, tested true null at every turn. It was extraordinary. Not only is she an outré, she is the most flatlining nonmagical being on the record books. I've spent enough time with her to keep my handler from getting suspicious about whose team I'm really on—the Council's or the Resistance's.

Of course, the only team I belong to is my own.

It's a dangerous game, but I'm more than up for it.

I'll play both sides for as long as I need to in order to get what I really want—the Council releasing my parents from exile or the Resistance smuggling them out. I could care less who actually makes it happen, I'm just going to do whatever it takes to make sure it does.

So here I am working my contacts with the Resistance while doing the work of the Council, which for the past hundred years has managed to convince the regular citizens of the Witchingdom that it's nothing but an urban legend. But the truth of it is that they are very real, very powerful, and very determined to make sure that any magical threats to its power are eliminated. And *that* is why the Council sent me here deep into Resistance territory to figure out if Tilda Sherwood is faking being an outré as a cover for something more detrimental to the Council's existence.

Something, however, always seemed to come up that cut short my efforts to answer that question. That's why I've been forced to set up yet another date. It is as if anytime I start to get close to the third and fourth level of tests, something extraordinary happens and the so-called date ends abruptly.

The first date ended when she knocked over her mug of elderberry tea into my lap. If it hadn't been for the fact that she'd chosen the iced version, I would be speaking in a much higher octave right now.

A swarm of flying monkeys called an abrupt stop to our second date when they swooped down from out of nowhere and carried her off. If it hadn't been for the fact that she was laughing at the absurdity of it, I would have gone after her, but there was just something about the absolute joy in her giggles that struck me momentarily dumb.

Last week, I was just about to launch into the third level when her grande dame of a mother marched into the Museum of Drastic Spells fuming about some unflattering social media post. Smoke was literally wafting after Izzy Sherwood, little plumes of black and gray whirling around the few hairs that had broken free from her tight bun. I stepped between them to block Tilda from attack before I realized what I'd done. For her part, Tilda just nonchalantly stepped around me and rolled her eyes, totally unimpressed with the fury of one of the most powerful witches in the entire Witchingdom.

This time is going to be different though. This time the ridiculous and unexpected have already happened. It will begin our date—correction, opportunity to observe—not end it.

Tilda's purple glasses have gone wonky while I was patting her on the back to clear her lungs. She should look ridiculous.

Instead, I can't stop noticing that the cockeyed frames make her already big blue eyes seem even larger. It must be an optical illusion due to the thickness of her glasses since it isn't as if she has actual magic to create the perception, and there is no way just looking into her eyes would be this interesting without some form of illusion.

"Of course I'm not here for you." Tilda raises her middle finger—slowly and with intent—and then pushes and straightens her glasses in one smooth movement. All while glaring at me. "I have a date."

Of course she does. I've set it up, just like I arranged all the other dates.

"One scheduled by Griselda?" I manage not to smirk as I sit down at her table while sending out a subtle wave of feeler magic to start today's test.

My plan to date my way into answering the Council's question about Tilda Sherwood is also the perfect cover for meeting with my contact in the Resistance. You see, Griselda is not only the town matchmaker, she's also one of the canniest secret agents the Resistance has—not that the woman in front of me has any idea about all of that.

Tilda sinks down into her chair, barely missing getting her wavy red hair caught in the dragon's blood tree's branches. "Why does this keep happening?"

"You say that like you don't enjoy having tea with me." Rubbing the tip of my thumb against my pinky, I amp up the spell just enough to make the couple at the next table look around to see where it is coming from. However, Tilda shows no reaction. "There has to be something about our encounters that has you going to great lengths to make them happen."

"I would never," she says with a huff that sends her red bangs flying upward.

"And yet we're still meeting." I flash a smile her way and am rewarded with a distinct blush that brightens her cheek.

Perfect. We are right on course for today's test.

As every witch knows, strong emotions increase magic's power—something I learned the hard way. It is the reason why my family was exiled; a power like ours not kept in check was seen as too dangerous for the Council, which values control above all else. Luckily for me, emotions have no value or point beyond fucking everything up.

Teasing Tilda always seems to get to her emotions fastest, and with the clock ticking on the Council's deadline, I don't have time to waste. "How did you manage it? Did you offer to transcribe Griselda's biography?"

Her cheeks turn even more pink. "Yes, but that was for her to work her matchmaking magic, not for her to set me up with *you*."

Out of the corner of my eye, I catch a shimmer in the air near the dragon's blood tree. Using the movement for cover, I straighten the cuffs of my custom-made shirt and watch the interplay between Tilda and the flora. It only takes a few seconds to realize the damned tree has taken a liking to her. She leans forward and it moves with her. At one point, the end of a twig-sized branch curls around a stray lock of her red hair. When she unwinds it, barely seeming to realize what's happening, and moves her chair farther away from the branch, it seems to hang down in dejection.

Odd. So very odd.

Caught up in working out what that could mean, it takes me a moment to realize she's about to leave, ending the date—observation—scientific research opportunity.

Yeah, one you spent extra time getting ready for in front of the mirror because she's just an assignment.

Some days I really despise that voice of reason inside my head.

Tilda opens her purse and picks up the phone on the table, the rainbow-hued notebook with the fuzzy pink pen attached, as well as the bits and bobs scattered about and tosses them inside. "Anyway, you are the last man I'd ask to be set up with."

"What's wrong with me? I'm tall, handsome, a noted expert in the field of historical magic." Not a lie, every Council agent needed a rock-solid cover. "Women absolutely love me."

Not this one.

Tilda rolls her eyes as she shoves the last of her stuff into her huge purse. "You forgot full of yourself, snobby, and annoying."

I shrug off her stinging words that aren't even close to the worst anyone has ever said about me. "The salt balances out the sweetness."

"And the arsenic ruins the whole dish." Tilda stands up,

glaring at me, and pushes in her chair, signaling that the date is officially over. "You are the most odious man in the entire Witchingdom."

Damn it. I've come here for one reason and have failed—again—to conduct the third and fourth tests required to prove she is a true null because Tilda is a most distracting woman. One who is walking away from me without a goodbye or a single look back while I sit here like an eejit, unable to look away from her.

"Damned distracting," I mumble to myself.

Then, the air shimmers like the horizon in the desert half a second before the dragon's blood tree makes its move, sending branches shooting out after her with lightning speed. I don't think, don't even breathe, I just jump up, race across the bakery, and grab Tilda, yanking her out of the way. It would be a neat rescue if her feet didn't tangle with mine, sending us both tumbling backward toward the glass bakery case that will slice us to ribbons if we crash into it.

"Sarsum," I yell out, calling up the simple spell that will save us from falling.

My magic snaps like a whip, sending us flying in the opposite direction, spinning us with a power I hadn't intended. We sail through the air above the tables and the gawking witches. It is as if I were a teen again, unable to control the power coursing through me as my family's own magic escaped.

A vibrating humming fills me, and in an instant, all of my

senses are heightened to a nearly impossible level. Every single one is focused on Tilda as the magic that has been my family's curse escapes from my tight control as soon as I wrap my arms around her to protect her as we fly through the air.

Suddenly, her every reaction to me comes into focus. The way her pulse quickens with desire as she wets her full bottom lip. The intoxicating sweetness of her scent as her body responds to mine. The curve of her tits, the dip of her waist, the round curve of her ass all mesmerize me.

Grinding my teeth, I try to pull it all back, stuff the duíl attraction magic back into the mental lockbox I spent years developing, but I can't. The connection with Tilda is too strong. Check that. It's the most powerful thing I've ever felt in my life.

This has never happened with anyone else. Holding my breath, I concentrate on the tips for control my mother taught me when she helped me understand that our duíl magic does not manifest false attraction, it only emphasizes the truth that's already there. I try the deep breathing, the visualizations, and the meditation chants—none of it works.

It's not just that this connection feels as amazing as hunger and energy—wanting and fulfilling, lusting and satisfaction are all wrapped up into a spell I never summoned but has been cast anyway—it is Tilda. The power we Connollys have at the center of our magical abilities doesn't just call out the desires of others for knowledge or power or wealth or people, it calls our own as well.

Unleashed at last, the magic revs a tangible touch that teases and tempts until every fantasy, every wish, every desperate need that Tilda has ever had comes to me at once, filling my mind and becoming my own.

Damn, I love the way this woman thinks.

She reaches out, touching me back. Her fingertips glide over the buttons of my shirt, leaving an aching craving in their wake. As we whirl around in the air, she strains to bring herself close until we are pressed against each other, her soft, pliant body fitting perfectly against mine, feeling like the answer to a question I've never asked. Resisting the addicting tug of my magic, of Tilda, I fist my hands, determined to protect her from what has grown beyond my control.

"Gil," she says, her voice heady with lust. "Kiss me."

A better man would hold back, remember it isn't real, that it is just magic.

I break.

As I lean down and reach for her, every lightbulb in the bakery brightens as magic's electric buzz hums around us, growing louder and louder until every other witch in the bakery covers their ears and flees. The noise, the power, the sparks showering down from the bulbs hold me in place though. My hand cups Tilda's face and my lips are only millimeters from hers as the air sizzles around us, alive like I've never felt before.

This is more than just power breaking free.

It is more than losing control.

This is something altogether different.

In that moment, I realize *exactly* why Tilda has tested as a true magical null. She isn't an outré. She is something altogether more.

And if the Council finds out what she really is, the Sherwoods will have hell to pay.

Chapter Three

Tilda . . .

*W*hat's more humiliating than asking—okay, fine, begging, demanding, going all hey-big-wizard-that's-a-big-wand-you've-got sex kitten—my absolute most hated archenemy to kiss me?

The fact that he doesn't.

That's right, folks. Here I am all warm and melty, wrapped around Gil like an octopus in heat (Do they go into heat? I don't know, that's not the point here.), sparks are literally flying around me, and I'm experiencing the biggest adrenaline rush of my life. Seriously, I am riding a thunderbolt of let's-strip-right-now and all of it comes crashing to a halt the second Gil sets me down on my feet and steps back.

Everything changes in a second, as if some magical faucet

of overwhelming attraction is turned off (not that I would notice the feel of any magic, because that's not something us nonmagical witches get to experience beyond a little charge of static electricity). Instead of hot, I'm icicle cold. Instead of electricity lighting up the air, it's just a bit of lingering burnt-popcorn-smelling smoke. Instead of riding the wave of ultimate bliss, I'm wiped out on the beach of humiliation with sand up my bathing suit bottom.

Gil, his perfect dark hair all mussed for once, glares at me and takes another step back. "Cut the shit, Sherwood. What are you up to?"

"Honestly?" My voice cracks on the single word question because the universe isn't done showing me yet that I'm a dud in magic *and* basic attraction. "Trying to find a guy that isn't a total shithead, but I keep getting set up with you, and you obviously must have just pulled some bullshit spell on an outré that can't detect it. You don't have to do something like that to show me what a loser I am. I already know that!"

And now there are tears pricking my eyes and I'm clenching my molars together to keep my chin from trembling. I will *not* bawl in front of this smug-faced jerk.

I.

Will.

Not.

That means I have to get my ass in gear and get out of here, because the countdown to cry time has begun. Holding on to the slight bit of dignity I have left, I lean over and grab my tote from the floor where it fell. It's covered in sticky tree sap because of course it is, but damn it, I'm still a Sherwood, so I sling it over my shoulder as if I'm above all that and march out the door, leaving Gil the Git behind me.

Outside in the bright sunshine, I ignore the small crowd of witches who are all watching and tittering behind their hands. Several are straight up filming me on their phones. There is no way I'll get home in time to warn Mom of the incoming bad publicity and spin it so she/I/we can continue to ignore the fact that I am the least Sherwood to have ever Sherwooded.

Hell, she probably already knows about whatever happened back in the coffee shop. Bitch witches work hard, but Izzy Sherwood works harder, and her sources are as legendary as they are numerous.

That's why, instead of going right and catching the trolly up to Charmstone to the rambling house that has been the Sherwood family headquarters for the past two hundred years, I go left. Within the first block, the street goes from sunshiny and sweet with white picket fences and monarch butterflies floating on the breeze to twisting ivy covering dark stone fences, with the occasional bat hanging from the mossy oaks that span the width of the narrow cobblestone street.

Griselda's house sits back from the street, the iron gate rising up six feet high with ornate scrollwork that curls and curves into a sign that reads "Madame G's Tarot and Witchery, LLC." Below that is a no-soliciting warning and a smidge below that is another line, underlined three times, that states "By Appointment Only!!!!!"

Yeah, well, an exception is about to be made.

I push open the heavy gate and march down the cracked cement path crowded by overgrown shrubs that seem to whisper and giggle as I storm up to the two-story house that looks like you could tear off a piece of the latticework for a quick snack.

Trust me, don't try it. No, I won't tell you how I know that bit of information. Don't give me that look, I was eight and gullible.

The black cat door knocker hisses at me the moment I step foot on the front porch.

"Oh, deal with it," I say, yanking on its tail and setting off the *bing*s and *bong*s of Griselda's doorbell.

"Go away," comes the all too familiar baby-sweet voice.

"You did it again," I holler through the thick door. "I want a refund."

The door swings open and I lower my gaze and lower it some more to land on the old woman herself, with her wild white hair intermixed with strands of neon pink that she has twisted into two braids that go all the way down to the small of her back. Hands on her generous hips, she looks me up and down. Her top lip is curled up into a snarl that just might be her friendliest look—the kind she gives her favorite god-daughter, in other words, me. Even at nearly three hundred, the most respected sage in Virginia looks like she could take me in a bar fight armed with only a corkscrew and a bad attitude.

Griselda wipes her hands on her bright patchwork apron. "I didn't even charge you."

"But you keep setting me up with the same guy." Was I whining? Yes. Did knowing that stop me? Hard no. "Something has to be wrong."

"With *my* magic?" She straightens to her full five feet zero inches and lets out a little snarl. "Sherwood or not, you better watch yourself, girl."

"Please," I say, all but making puppy-dog eyes—fine, attempting to do sad puppy-dog eyes but the effort is limited because of my thick glasses. "I need your help. This will be the last time. After today's disaster I am done with men. I just want to understand why it keeps being *him*."

"The cards say what they say." She floats up and pinches my cheeks like she does every time she sees me, because some women are stately and some of us have round baby faces. "You just may not want to hear it."

I steel myself and go with one last effort. "You're not telling me all they're saying either."

Griselda smiles. "As is my prerogative."

No denial. No bait and switch. No changing the conversation. The woman is up to something—always—and has absolutely zero shame about the subterfuge.

I let my head fall back in near defeat before pulling it together again to say in as menacing a way as a woman with no magic, no power, no nothing to back it up can, "Griselda."

The older woman just lifts a glittery silver eyebrow and shrugs a single shoulder, rolling it back as if she was doing double duty to both dismiss my annoyance and get in a little extra stretch work.

Why are the women in my family so maddening? Okay, fine. Griselda is a fourth or fifth cousin once removed or something, but she *is* my godmother, which in the Witchingdom means she *is* family. She has been a near-daily loving— if prickly—presence in my life since the day I was born. According to family legend, she arrived one minute before I did, stayed three to examine my aura, and left a minute later after giving my mother *the look*. That's when they knew I wasn't going to be like the other Sherwoods.

The reminder, along with my still-fresh kiss-me-Gil humiliation, propels me forward into the house and straight into the heart of the home—the kitchen.

Ninety-seven percent of all witchery work happens in the kitchen, as it is the best place to feed the stomach, feed the heart, and feed the soul, all of which are needed for magic to take place. As my mother always says, if you don't heal yourself, you can't heal the world.

Griselda has a cast-iron pot of piney-smelling green brew sending up copious amounts of white steam on the stovetop.

"Harvest spell?" I ask.

"Nah," she says, totally unbothered by me barging into her house. "Soaking my socks."

That I don't believe at all, but I know better than to press Griselda about something she doesn't want to talk about. The woman is a vault. Literally. That is her witching level designation and why she makes such a great living as the woman Wrightsville's witches turn to with their heartbreaks and secrets.

I cross over the flagstone design in the floor and walk to her kitchen table in the middle of the room under the candlestick chandelier. Yes, it's real candlesticks. When Griselda is really cooking up a spell, it is best to stick close to the walls to avoid the dripping hot wax. Believe me, it's a lesson you only need to learn once.

"Gonna read them yourself, eh?" Griselda asks as she nimbly crosses the room, avoiding every crack in the stone floor.

"You did teach me how it's done." Every magical theory lesson I've ever gotten has been with her. Mentor, godmother, scourge of my dating life, that's Griselda.

"There's more to it than just book learning," she says. "It's an art, a craft, a—"

"Magical gift, I know. I'm aware. Just let me try." I blink back the tears that are becoming a little too common today. Stupid PMS—now *that* someone needs to come up with a spell to fix. "Please."

Griselda lets out a little huff of a sigh and grumbles something under her breath, but she takes out the jewel-colored tarot deck from the carved olive-wood box on top of her kitchen table. "All right then, go ahead."

The oversized cards buzz in my hands the second I touch them, almost like a little hello from a realm that is beyond me. It has always been like this with magical things for me. It's like looking through the Galdr Magical Shop window and seeing all of the wands, jewelry, and staffs, knowing they are more than just wood, metal, and beads, but I can't ever access any of that. If I press my hands to the window, they'd say hello with a soft vibration that starts at my fingertips and goes through my body in a slow wave, but that's it, the rest is beyond my outré abilities. It is like having sex but not having an orgasm—it feels good, but it isn't the same whoosh of pleasure that blows your back out.

"Thank you," I say as I sit down at the table and start shuffling.

I don't have to think of my question, it's right there at the front of my mind as I deal the cards, laying them out in the order Griselda taught me. A sharp sizzle travels up my arm as I turn over the first card. The fool. Thanks universe, I appreciate the reminder. Of course, in this case that means new beginnings. With Gil? Yeah, I don't think so.

That is followed by the eight of swords, the knight of cups, and the ace of swords. Okay, I understand so far. The cards tell me a story about feeling limited (hello, a little on the nose there), being romantic and following one's heart to the extent of even having an actual knight in shining armor (a woman has to have a dream), as well as a sudden opportunity and clarity (please, yes, I'd really like to know the whole point of nonmagical me in a magical world).

Hesitating before touching the final card in the spread, I glance up at Griselda. She's stirring her "soaking socks," which are probably a potion to cure a bunion, if my memory of her favorite spell book and knowledge of her many foot complaints aren't off. She's not looking at me, but her shoulders are tense and she's gripping the wooden spoon white-knuckle tight. Whatever the last card shows is the key to all of this. It has to be. Why else would the town's second most badass witch (yeah, Mom is very much number one, not that I would ever say so to Griselda) be so nervous?

I flip the last card and my stomach drops at the sight of a highly decorative globe. The world card doesn't just mean completion and the celebration of life with the Sherwoods. It also represents the family's most powerful member. It's my sister Leona's signature card. Mine? Well, since the universe has such a shit sense of humor, it is the magician (action and the power to manifest, my ass). That's neither here nor there, though, because seeing the world card, *my sister's card*, while asking about why Gil keeps showing up in my life means only one thing.

"He's going to marry Leona?"

"Is that what the cards say?" Griselda asks, her tone neutral. "That's not what they've ever told me."

I hold up the world card, silently asking for an explanation.

Griselda doesn't say anything, she just goes back to stirring her socks, leaving me to process her words, which she's obviously not going to explain further, while putting the deck back in order.

Leona and Gil?

Gil and Leona?

That is not a pairing I'd ever expect even if he wasn't a total ass. Fine, he is amazingly hot with that broad-shouldered-brooding-intellectual thing he has going, but he isn't Leona's type. She goes for the extroverted wild guys with a roster almost as long as hers. Smarmy know-it-alls with sinewy forearms and an ass that looks good even in khakis? Yeah, not her kind of guy.

Or do I have it all wrong? I look at the card with the gilded globe on it one last time before adding it to the deck. What have I missed?

"The cards see more than our eyes can," Griselda says before lifting the spoon and tasting the broth.

Please, universe, don't let her actually be soaking socks in that cauldron.

Whether the pot has tube socks or tube steak, gross as one option may be, doesn't matter as much as the cards though. Griselda has to be right. The cards *have* to be seeing something that my outré self can't when they look at a total prick like Gil Connolly—otherwise my poor sister is screwed, or I screwed up the reading like I do everything else.

All I know is that, per usual, I have more questions than answers.

Chapter Four

Gil...

It's not easy to make a covert call from this deep in Sherwood territory, but the Council isn't the type of organization to accept "it's damn near impossible" as an answer, which is why I am fiddling with a cell phone SIM card like an outré who can't summon a simple telepathy spell.

Ancient, secretive, and beholden to no witch, the Council was established at the same time as the Declaration of Independence. By the time the Bill of Rights had been added to the Constitution, the Council was well established as the secret, fourth branch of government. Congress makes the laws, the executive branch enforces them, the judicial branch interprets them, and the Council are the secret and silent enforcers when things fall through the cracks.

They are the last people I want to work for, but here I am with six months left on my contract and my parents' lives hanging in the balance.

Finally, the tiny SIM card slides into place. I have no idea why the Council insisted on nonmagical communication, but the Council does what the Council wants to do. My theory is that it's gotta be some kind of humbling mind fuck to keep everyone in their place, but it doesn't matter. It is what it is, I just have to toe the line, which is giving me the twitches a little more each day.

I sent my initial report to my handler, Cassius, last night after a deep dive in my research texts. He fired back a message to make contact today and not to document anything else. I got it. The Sherwoods are a powerful enough family that they know the Council exists. In addition, the Sherwoods have eyes everywhere—even in the Council. Not surprisingly, the Council watches everyone too—especially people like me, who they've pulled out of exile and blackmailed into cooperating. You don't end up at the top of Witchingdom's food chain without learning how to navigate the big bad.

My handler answers on the first ring. "Are you sure?" Cassius asks without preamble.

"The power was off the scales," I say, stepping back farther into the shadows of the trees that line the cobblestone streets near my rental, which the Council has surely bugged. "I've never felt anything like it."

And it's still there, a little sizzle of awareness that snaps and crackles whenever I think of Tilda, which is every other second since the almost-kiss at the coffee shop. Stepping back from her was one of the hardest things I've ever done. Even now, I can feel my connection to her—it has nothing to do with my magic, but I can't deny the extra sizzle of awareness.

I couldn't sleep last night because every time I closed my eyes, all I saw was her, that sweet, juicy pink mouth of hers begging to be kissed, wanting more that she couldn't say out loud.

That's how it works with duíl magic. Once a connection is made between two magical beings, it remains until the desire is fulfilled, and with that comes a certain amount of control. Contrary to popular belief, duíl magic can't be used to make people do something, it can't manufacture a want that isn't there already, and it can't get people to act against their own wishes. However, what it can do is focus the desire, add a healthy dash of hope to it, and make those affected get a better sense of their own personal power. That is exactly why the Council banished my entire family into exile, sending us to the edge of the powerless zone known as The Beyond.

"And you better not feel it again if you don't want to end up in exile," Cassius says, his snarling tone leaving no doubt that he wouldn't do a damn thing to act on my behalf. When it comes to the Council, everyone is on their own. "You know the rules. Use duíl magic and you go back to that shithole I plucked you out of. I'm sure your parents will love that since it'll mean they're never leaving either."

It takes everything I have not to give in to the urge to whip up a spell that will let me reach through the phone and cold-cock Cassius. The asshole has been threatening me for three years since I convinced him I could do the work for the Council that others couldn't or wouldn't. However, dragging my parents into it was something else. The prick had promised: three years and they'd get out of The Beyond, where magic doesn't work. It's every witch's nightmare and the Council's domain to rule over.

"So what's your plan?" Cassius asks.

"I need irrefutable proof. The Council will never believe just a theory, especially not from me and most assuredly not about the Sherwoods committing a massive magical felony." There is no way Tilda doesn't know what she really is. The level of magic it would take to keep it under wraps would be off the charts. There's no way the Council wouldn't have noticed that much of a peak on the mystical seismograph reports. "I have to find a way to get close to her."

"Well, do it soon," Cassius says. "I've managed to get a review of your parents' case on the docket in a month, but the odds are against them being brought back from exile unless you're able to do something extraordinary to show the Council you're a more valuable resource than a duíl agitator."

The Council is not a fan of duíl magic—or anything that is different than the status quo as they define it. Being able to link into someone's desires, sexual or otherwise, gives people ideas about change, and *that* is a little too close to rebellion for the organization with a core mission to force conformity. If the Council knew the real depth of my involvement with the Resistance and its work to expose the Council and counteract its moves, I wouldn't be doing whatever it takes to get my parents out of exile because all of us would be dead.

"I've been proving that for the past year," I shoot back, unable to keep the annoyance out of my tone and gaining the attention of Griselda as she walks by with her pet squirrel on a leash.

"Would you rather be back there?"

I force a smile and wave at Tilda's godmother as if shit wasn't about to blow up in this town. "No."

"Then stop whining and find a way to get the evidence you need," Cassius says. "The clock is ticking and there's no snooze button."

As if I had ever thought there was. There are no second chances for exiles.

Chapter Five

Tilda . . .

*B*arkley is gonna be the death of me.

Other witches have normal pets. My sister Beatrix has a rooster with an attitude and house privileges who loves to sneak into my room and cock-a-doodle-doo me into having a heart attack.

"Bea," I holler, my heart racing as I yank a towel from the hook because my shampoo is burning a hole in my eye. "Come get this demon spawn!"

Even if I could see with both eyes right now, the bathroom is full of steam hiding the vain bird's location. That leaves me dripping wet on the amethyst polka-dot bathmat watching out with my one good eye, my hand palm forward, fingers spread like I'm about to lay down the mother of all curses. The sharp click-clack of Barkley's claws on the tile floor has me girding my naked loins for attack. If this is how I die, slipping on a wet floor while running naked from an evil rooster, I am going to haunt my sister for the rest of her natural life.

Then, with an audible pop and the scent of eucalyptus, all of the steam disappears, revealing Bea with her signature honey-colored hair falling in loose finger waves down to her shoulders, eyepatch, and wild rose lipstick.

"There you are, Barkley baby, I've been looking everywhere for you." She picks up the rooster, cuddling it as if it wasn't all sharp claws, a razor-like spur, and a beak made for attempted blindings. "Are you bothering grumpy Matilda again?"

"I'm not grumpy," I grumble as I wrap my towel around me, tucking the ends above my boobs with my usual hope that this time my tiny boobs will hold it in place.

Spoiler alert: They will not. They never do. However, unlike my sister Juniper, I can sleep on my stomach and pop out to the store without a bra, so there is that.

"Then why are you yelling?" Bea asks between whispering sweet nothings to Barkley.

"Because I was in the middle of a shower"—a very special moment in the shower involving the last man I should be thinking about when utilizing the handheld showerhead at the most toe-curling angle, but I'm not gonna tell my sister that—"when Barkley the Barbarian rushed in flapping his wings and charging toward the shower stall door and scared the ever-loving crap out of me."

"Barkley, we've talked about this. Tilda is a friend, not food." She nuzzles the stupid bird—did I mention we don't even have chickens, just Barkley?—and then looks back up at me. "Your face is flush. What were you up to in the shower?"

"None of your business." Nope. I'm close to all of my sisters, but I'm not about to tell her that I have developed the very bad habit of picturing Gil Connolly while touching myself.

It has gotten bad. I can't go more than a few hours without thinking about him. Sure, he's an asshole and destined for my sister, but I can't stop myself from slipping my fingers beneath the elastic of my panties for some smarmy, know-it-all jerk relief. It's like some secret part of me I don't even want to acknowledge—fine, that I most definitely wish didn't exist—has been unleashed.

He has to have pulled some shit on me at the coffee shop yesterday. If it was a spell, I would know, because the magic detectors would have gone off the moment I walked into the house. It has to be an old-fashioned, nonmagical *head* fucking that has left me constantly thinking about *real* fucking. I'd made it twenty-eight years on this earth with a healthy sex drive, but all of a sudden I am craving and obsessed. I kinda like it. Fine. I really like it and the wild feeling that came with it, one that whispered I had more power than I realized.

Yeah right.

Bea snorts. "Like I believe that. You can lie to Juniper, but I always know." She hopped up and sat on the bathroom counter. "Tell me everything."

"There's nothing to tell." There is *so much to tell*, but no one I could tell.

Bea sticks out her tongue at me. "You're no fun."

I wrinkle my nose and make a snarly face at Barkley. "I wonder why?"

Bea adjusted the black patch over her right eye. "Deep down he loves you."

Gil? Ha! Not even close to being likely. I'm about to tell her exactly that when I realize she was talking about the rooster, not the jerk of the world destined to be with my sister and who won't get out of my head.

"Would love to murder me," I say, hoping against hope that my sister who notices everything missed the fact that I hesitated a few beats too long there.

"By the way, Mom wants to see you in her office."

A groan of pure misery rises up from the depths of my soul and escapes before I can stop it. "It's about the coffee shop, isn't it."

She shrugs and slips down from the counter still holding tight to Barkley. "Maybe."

"Bea."

Beg? Me? Hell yes, I can't walk into my mom's office without knowing the damage.

"Fine. Yes." Bea gives me a supportive smile but—thankfully, since she has Barkley, who is giving me the rooster version of the stink eye—stays on her side of the bathroom. "I overheard her and Dad talking, but I'm sure it's just that they're worried about you."

Yeah, worried I'll fail them again.

Fifteen minutes later I've navigated the nonmagical links set up for me and only me to get from one part of the house to the other. Why would anyone need magic to go from one room to another? Because the Sherwoods are not just old magic, we are also old-school and in the dark days, keeping everyone connected could mean the difference between survival and a long, slow, torturous death at the hands of a bunch of narrow-minded, reactionary jerks who go by the not-too-lame-to-be-creepy-at-all-sounding moniker of the Council. Say it with me, *oooooooooooooohhhhhhhhhh, scary*. Thank God they were defunct now.

While from the outside our house looks like a big, rambling, purple Victorian with an indigo roof, sitting in the middle of a grove of cherry trees on top of the highest hill in the Charmstone neighborhood, it is so much more. In one sense, the house is one physical building, but as soon as you walk inside, the space transforms via magic into separate homes for myself, my parents, and each of my four sisters. Yes, there are five of us—it's the Sherwood lucky number. Everyone else in the family can negotiate the magical byways connecting one house to the other, including cousins, aunts, uncles, grandparents, and anyone else with the Sherwood DNA because all of the Sherwood houses are connected.

I, however, have to follow the nonmagical links, just like Barkley.

Yes. I'm on the same magical level as a rooster.

That should explain a lot about the state of my self-esteem.

I stop in front of Mom's closed office door and take a second to pull myself together. It's just my mom. I can do this. I raise my hand to knock, and the door opens before my knuckles hit the wood.

My dad takes up most of the open doorway, his broad shoulders spanning it from one side to the other and his bald head nearly hitting the top of it. I don't know if he can sense the anxiety making my gut twist or if it's just my dad being his normal sweet self, but he takes one look at me and pulls me in for a bear hug—literally. Dad is half bear shifter and likes to say it shows everywhere but his hairline.

"Hey, pudding," he whispers before dropping a kiss on the top of my head. "Mom's almost done with a work call."

"Work" in this case means heading up the Committee, which advises the president and helps with some of the behind-the-scenes work to get all of the different factions in the Witchingdom to come together. Factions all have a base family, but then there are others who join—sorta like the mob. But with magic. And less discovering of TVs that happen to fall off a truck. Each of the factions work together—or against each other—according to age-old alliances and feuds.

Dad and I cross to the sitting area, where afternoon tea is already waiting. While I pour the elderberry tea for all of us, he adds a dollop of my favorite clotted cream to a scone on a plate that looks minuscule in his large hands and passes it to me before loading his own plate with a mountain of assorted tea sandwiches.

My mom sits at her desk, a pleasant smile on her face, but

her hands are clasped together so tight on her lap that I'm surprised the wand she's holding doesn't snap. She's facing a two-foot-high astral projection of Hazel Dray, one of the representatives of the Stinger faction. They are still stuck back in the 1700s and would have all of us wearing pointy hats and buckles on our shoes if they got their way.

"Hazel," Mom says in the tone that promises she is exactly thirty-five seconds away from I've-had-enough fireworks, "we've discussed this before. The Beyond is not there for those with witching ways you don't agree with. It is for hardened criminals who are a danger to the entire Witchingdom."

The brittle-looking woman with the lemon-puckered mouth harrumphs. "Well, if we don't get a hold on all of these witches that want to change everything, then our entire way of life will be lost, and that *is* a danger to Witchingdom. I don't like it."

"So you've made clear." Mom sighs. "The answer is still—and will always be as long as I am on the Committee—no."

"This isn't over," Hazel says, her tone as sour as old vinegar.

Dad and I exchange raised eyebrows. No one threatens Mom. She's not just kind of a badass, she is one of the biggest badasses in the entire Witchingdom. She's headed the Committee for ten years and has been known to quiet a bridge troll with only a glance.

"Actually, it is. Goodbye, Hazel." Mom waves her hand and severs the connection before the other woman can continue her complaints. "Please tell me you've got gin to put in my tea, because I need it after that."

I add a splash to her tea as she makes her way over to the sitting area.

"Matilda, darling." She gives me a kiss on the cheek before taking her cup and saucer, then sitting down in the chair next to Dad. "How are you holding up?"

Ouch.

The disappointment or disapproval I could take; I am used to it. The pity, though, is like sandpaper against a soap bubble.

"We saw the video," Dad says and then eats two sandwiches in one bite.

"Tate." Mom lays her hand on Dad's thigh. "We discussed how we would approach this."

Great. Yesterday rose to the level of a pre-sit-down discussion. That is never good.

"It's okay." I offer up a self-deprecating chuckle that sounds pretty close to genuine. "I saw it too."

It is now everywhere on social media because that's the way things go. Forget Mom's mid-spell funny face post being the most viral Sherwood content ever. It's now me wound up in the sticky arms of the dragon's blood tree, pressed against Gil and looking up at him with total let-me-love-you goo-goo eyes.

"Is everything okay?" Mom asks.

"Just a freak interaction with a dragon's blood tree." One that left me hot, bothered, and desperate for answers.

My parents exchange a look. I know that look. It's the where-did-we-go-wrong look.

"As long as you're okay." Mom sets down her tea and glues me to the spot with her this-is-important look. "We just want to make sure you're happy."

"I am." Well, mostly. I mean, my libido has definitely gone haywire, but I can deal with that as soon as I figure out how to get Barkley to leave me alone long enough for some special privacy time.

Mom and Dad stand up as one unit, so in sync with each other that I swear they know what the other is going to say before they even open their mouth.

"Then come give us a hug," Dad says, throwing open his arms.

My parents envelop me in a tight if somewhat awkward group hug. It settles something in me, and for as long as the hug lasts, it feels like everything just might be okay.

"We love you," Mom says.

And the thing is, I know she means it. It would be so much easier to be an outré if my family were awful about it. The truth is that they aren't. Are they a little too involved and do they treat me as if I'm about to either trip over my own two feet or cause a mini disaster at every turn? Yeah. But in their defense, I haven't exactly spent the past twenty-eight years of my life proving them wrong—just ask me about the incident with the chicken and the eggs and why we only have Barkley now. Better yet, don't ask (but I promise no chickens or eggs were harmed in the explosion).

That, however, is all about to change.

No more dragon's blood trees.

No more humiliations caught on video.

No more obnoxious hot guys named Gil Connolly.

But to make that happen, I have to figure out what is going on with the cards that has Griselda setting us up on date after date and why every time I'm around him I want to throttle and kiss him or maybe kiss him and then throttle him or maybe both at the same time. I don't know! All I know is that I need to ensure it never happens again. That means I need to track down the smarmy jerk himself and get some answers.

Chapter Six

Gil . . .

"*Y*ou!" Tilda strides into the Hocus and Hops Pub like a woman on a mission to eviscerate a very unfortunate soul.

I am definitely that soul, but I am too distracted by the way she's marching so forcefully that her red hair is flying around her like flames. It's a neat illusion, subtle enough to go unnoticed unless someone is really paying attention and enchanting enough to make it so I can't look away from her—not that that would be wise at the moment. A person doesn't last long in the lawless Beyond without developing keen defensive skills.

"Looking for me?" I take a sip of pumpkin beer, drinking her in and the way the tip of her impressive nose practically twitches with annoyance. "I'm flattered."

Without noticing—or at least making a good show of not noticing—the looks she's getting from the handful of customers sitting on the velvet love seats near the bar and the guy pretending to look at the arcane magic books on the shelf closest to my table, Tilda stops next to me. She puts her hands on her hips, the move drawing my attention to the strip of skin visible beneath the hem of her cropped hoodie.

I shouldn't notice.

I definitely shouldn't look.

I'm doing both anyway.

"What did you pull yesterday?" she asks, her chin tilted at a self-righteous angle.

After spending hours last night researching my theory, followed by many sleepless hours trying not to think about Tilda or the dimple in her left cheek or the way her ass looked when she angry-walked away from me or the way she'd felt in my arms or that kiss that hadn't happened, I am groggy, easily annoyed, and not in the mood for her to gaslight me.

"Not a thing," I say, putting enough obnoxious know-it-all superiority in my tone to end this conversation now. "That was you and you well know it."

"All I was doing was trying to get away from you, and the next thing I know I'm in your arms."

I smirk up at her, dialing the asshole up to twenty. "Begging me to kiss you, as I remember."

Something hot and needy flashes in her eyes so strongly that even her thick glasses can't hide it.

This is a stupid game to play with someone like her—not

just a Sherwood but *that* kind of Sherwood—but I can't help it. Watching her reveal all the passion and intensity beneath her awkward, melts-into-the-background exterior is addicting. There is so much more to Tilda than anyone else gets to see, and I want to see it all.

For work purposes, right?

Absolutely. One hundred percent.

Am I answering myself? Fuck. This is what being around Tilda is doing to me.

Also, why does she smell so good? And that twisty thing she does with her hair, wrapping it around her finger while she sends me death glares, is fascinating.

She takes the seat across from me at the tiny wrought iron table and uses her middle finger to push up her big round glasses. "I. Did. Not. Beg."

"I was there." I shrug and take another sip of my beer. "I heard what I heard."

She squishes up her face. It's fucking adorable and somehow hot at the same time. There is definitely something wrong with me. I sniff the beer but don't catch the scent of any magical additions.

"You enchanted the dragon's blood tree to trip me so everyone would see," Tilda says, her voice quiet but firm.

"Project much?" I shoot back, grasping my teacup with both hands so I won't give in to the urge to reach across the table and touch her. "That was all you."

Her short, sharp "HA!" draws the attention of secret Resistance agent Vance the unicorn at the next table over, who glares at us and then gets back to painting his nails above the finger tattoos that when he makes a fist with each hand spell out "piss off." That attitude from the customers is what made Hocus and Hops the perfect place to actually unwind and plan my next move away from the hidden eyes and tucked-away ears of the Council at the little house I rented a few blocks from Griselda's.

Tilda sinks down in her seat a few inches, looking around at the handful of other witches in the pub. No doubt after yesterday she is checking to see if anyone is recording her. The videos from yesterday were all over WitchyGram. My face couldn't be seen in any of them, but that didn't matter to anyone. The real appeal was seeing a Sherwood—really this particular Sherwood—be embarrassed. No one would dare to try that with anyone else from her family, but as an outré, Tilda is vulnerable.

That's why the Council picked her as its target in its never-ending effort to hurt the Sherwoods and, by extension, the ability of the Committee to keep the Council Witching-dom's dirty little secret. According to my handler, Cassius, Tilda is seen as a weakness if she is truly an outré. They figured if they applied enough pressure to her, she'd act as their useful idiot in helping to get information about the Committee's next moves so they could be stopped. Then, the Council would be free. No more working in the shadows be-cause everyone thought they'd been disbanded eons ago. No more plausible deniability for those who utilize their ser-vices to gain power. No more loosening of the rules and regulations that define what a witch can be and where they belong in the Witchingdom.

Any sane witch would hate the Council. I sure as hell do, but for me there is no escaping them. If they are revealed as a real secret agency and not just an urban legend, there will be no stopping them.

"What happened yesterday was all me?" Tilda scoffs and leans forward before saying in a near whisper, "Everyone knows I'm an outré."

That isn't even a little true and she knows it.

"That's not what you are," I say, dropping my own voice as I lean forward so that our faces are close enough we could almost kiss. "That's what you want them to *think* you are."

We sit there staring at each other, the air around us crackling. Tendrils of my power surge forward, responding to her nearness, being drawn closer and closer to the surface with every heartbeat. *What do you want*, it calls out to her. Whatever it is, in that moment, I want to give it to her.

This is what she does to me. This is exactly why she is so dangerous. It's like nitro for my magic.

Tilda reaches out, a confused look crossing her face as if she's not sure why she's doing it either, her fingertips barely grazing my forearm, but it's enough. Magic blasts through me, seeking a way out, and it takes all of the control I have to keep it in check.

"What I want," Tilda says, her eyes going hazy as she plugs into my power, "is to be a real witch, one with powers, who isn't a stain on my family's name." She rolls her neck and lets out a soft moan. "Someone who isn't whispered about." She glides her fingers down to my wrist, biting down on her lip. "Someone who actually has a purpose in this life." Her eyes flutter shut. "Someone who isn't failing at the one job she could get doing online branding for her family to raise their likability scores because she made a complete eejit of herself, which ended up on every side of WitchyGram, *even Goblin WitchyGram*, and has reminded everyone of her family's shame." She sighs, the sound full of bittersweet yearning. "That's what I want."

She stops abruptly, her cheeks staining bright red and her chin trembling. Then she yanks her hand away from me and looks down at her fingers as if she doesn't understand what just happened.

I'm shocked into complete silence.

Either Tilda is the best actress in the entire world or she has no clue what she really is.

Flexing her fingers as if she doesn't understand why they're buzzing, she looks up at me, confusion wrinkling her forehead. Then, before I can reach out to stop her, she hurries out of the pub, not even glancing at the people gawking at her rushed exit.

Ignoring every one of my instincts screaming at me to go after her, I force myself to stay in my seat and calmly drink my beer. There's no need to process what just happened. I already know the answer.

No one is that good at pretending.

Tilda Sherwood has no idea she's a spellbinder.

It shouldn't, but this changes everything.

Chapter Seven

Tilda . . .

The Alchemist's Bookshop and Tea Emporium, like every good bookstore that has ever existed, is home to the book nerds, the weirdos, the mistrustful, the lost souls, the misunderstood, the curious, and the introverts looking for a quiet place to people for a very limited time. I fit in perfectly. That's why it is no surprise that it's where I get most of my work done—and exactly where my two best friends know to find me a few days later when they want answers about what is going on in my life.

Too bad I don't have any.

"You are so full of it, Tilda," Birdie says as she shoots our third magical misfit musketeer a can-you-believe-this eye roll. "Eli and I know you better than just about anyone. There is no way that he didn't spell you."

The kiss.

It's all everyone except for my mom and Griselda has wanted to talk to me about. The video of Gil and I flying around the coffee shop just beyond the reach of the dragon's blood tree limbs has gone viral. My sisters cornered me in my room last night and my dad brought it up this morning at breakfast. Then, on my walk to the bookstore, absolutely no one was the least bit shy about staring to see what ridiculous magical mishap would happen around me next.

And now here were my besties, Birdie and Eli, using their morning teatime break from their corporate jobs to track me down at my usual spot on the deep green couch in the stacks, tucked between divination manuals and dusty tomes dedicated to the life stories of minor witches from the local area. They bracket me on the couch, making sure I can't go anywhere with one of them on each side and the coffee table loaded down with my food tray and laptop directly in front of me.

"I mean, yeah, there was a spell," I say, trying to find something to say to move the conversation away from the incident—yes, that's what I'm calling it in my head. "He did send both of us up in the air."

Birdie's double-raised-eyebrow look of uh-huh-whatever is all I need to see to know she isn't having it. Well, it was worth a try.

"Matilda Grace Sherwood," she says, managing to almost

sound like my mom calling me out on the carpet, "I'm talking about the 'kiss me' part."

Humiliation, my old friend, there you are making my cheeks match the bright red of my hair. Awesome. "Ugh. He's the worst. I don't know what happened."

"But you don't like him," Eli says as he snags one of my mini pear tarts and pops it into his mouth in one bite.

"I don't."

Can't stop thinking about him isn't the same as liking him. I won't go into the whole constantly having inappropriate thoughts about him and the kiss that almost was but thank the fates was not actually. No one needs to know about that. I wish I didn't know about that.

"You've called him a know-it-all jerk face more times than I can count," Birdie says, "and I'm an accountant."

"I'm aware." She even looks like an accountant today, with her puffed-sleeved white blouse buttoned up to her neck, glasses, and curly hair tied into a severe bun on top of her head. "You do my taxes."

"We really need to work on your deductions." Birdie curves her body, blocking out the rest of the customers in the bookstore, and drops her voice as if she's imparting state secrets. "You know you can put down your mileage since you can't magic yourself to where you need to go."

"You two are getting lost in the ten-forty woods here." Eli leans past me and snags the last of my mini tarts from the tray on the coffee table. "What was the deal with that kiss?"

"Number one, I didn't kiss him," I say, sending up every

prayer to the universe I can think of that would delete that viral moment in the coffee shop from the Internet forever. "I don't know what happened, but there wasn't a spell. He didn't chant, use his wand, or do anything else after he saved us from crashing into the bakery case."

"Must be fate," Birdie says.

"What, for me to make a fool of myself at every possible opportunity? Oh yeah, that definitely tracks." I glance down at my phone on the coffee table and the four billion notifications popping up on my screen as everyone and their witch cousin tags the Sherwood family social media accounts in the videos of me begging Gil to kiss me. "Look, I gotta get back to work. See you at the next meeting?"

"Sure," Eli says as he gives Birdie *the look* so she gets up too. "Don't forget, you're helping us out at the fundraiser in the park this weekend."

"I've written it into my calendar in hot pink," I say. "I'll be there."

I can tell Birdie wants to say more, but Eli nudges her forward and out the bookshop's door, which leaves me alone in my corner of the shop to sniff the wondrous smell of leather-bound books, fresh ink, and the apple-scented magic of falling into a story. Okay, fine. It isn't really magic, but it's as close as I ever get to experiencing a little of the shazam, and I'm not going to downplay it—which reminds me I promised Effie I'd pick her up a copy of *Bibbidi-Bobbidi-Boo and You: A Meditation on Magic*.

I pack up my stuff, figuring I'll grab the book and finish up my workday at home on the back veranda overlooking the herb garden my great-grandmother started as a kid. It's a bit ragged in places and wild in others—especially in comparison to the rigid formality of my mom's garden—but it is where I feel most at home. Plants cross over from one plot to another, yew trees stand among the California gold poppies and evening primrose, and there are wildflowers everywhere, growing untended in whatever direction the sun takes them. There are no mistakes there, no errors, no bad luck. Instead, everything all comes together, working stronger as a unit than apart. Family legend has it that Grandmother Hecate started the garden after a vision of the future and enchanted it so that it would be ready when needed.

Well, truth be told, I need it now.

I sling my crossbody bag over my shoulders and head deeper into the stacks for Effie's book. I make it almost all the way there when the air shifts, and I know before I hear him that Gil is behind me. Ignoring—or trying my best to ignore—the champagne fizz of anticipation in my belly, I turn around and face my nemesis. He has honest-to-the-fates suede patches on the elbows of his blazer. That should make him look old and stuffy and out of touch. Instead, it—along with the collared shirt under a dark blue sweater and jeans—just makes him look fuckable. It isn't fair. Assholes should have asshole looks, not give off vibes that are a mix between the hot hero from *The Mummy* and Indiana Jones in all of his whip-wielding glory.

I'm not gonna tell you I took a second to imagine Gil in

old-timey-treasure-hunter wear with the hat and whip, but I won't say I didn't. It's not nice to lie to friends, and by this point, that's totally what we are. Agreed? Good.

*I*magine running into you here," Gil says, managing to look smug and sexy at the same time.

"We're the only two regulars," I shoot back. "You see me every time you're here."

He just grins at that.

Ugh.

This man.

It's so absolutely unfair that someone that smarmy can be so annoyingly attractive.

"So we need to talk about your abilities."

"Nope." I start down toward the far end of the stacks toward where my sister's book is going to be shelved. "I don't feel like being mocked by you right now or ever. Just leave me alone."

Am I running? Metaphorically, yes.

And not fast enough, it seems, because he sticks with me, his long legs making easy work of the shorter steps I take.

"You can't just pretend something isn't going on when we both know it is," he says, sounding know-it-all logical in that way only a stuffed shirt can. "I know it doesn't seem like it, but you can tell me the truth."

I pull to a stop, doing my best not to notice that the warm, woodsy way he smells mixes in perfectly with the worn leather of the books and the lingering hint of a buttery salt-iness that has me craving a bucket of popcorn. "And you're in my way. If you'll excuse me, I have to go get a book."

Being around Gil messes with my head. Has me thinking about stupid things like bingeing entire seasons of my favorite show with him while we're both curled up under a blanket. That isn't going to happen. Even if I messed up the tarot card reading—and let's face it, the chances of that are pretty high—he wouldn't be the kind of guy for me even if he didn't look at me like he is now, as if I'm on a slide under a microscope. Still, he moves aside and I slip past, getting one last sniff in because I'm just a glutton for punishment.

I walk down to the end of the shelf that starts the BIB section and start scanning for *Bibbidi*, craning my neck and angling my chin higher and higher as my gaze climbs the stacks all the way to the top.

"Crap," I grumble.

Gil ambles over to where I am as if following me around at the bookshop is the most natural thing in the world for him to do. "Need some help?"

"No, I can do it myself." All I have to do is go sweet-talk the owner and known curmudgeon Vance into letting me borrow the ladder he keeps in the root cellar.

I can't keep the grimace off my face, because the last time I had to do that, Vance banished me from the shop for a week for annoying him. What I wouldn't give for a little levitation magic right about now. Instead, I pull my cell out of my messenger bag and call the bookshop's main line. Vance answers with a grunt on the seventh ring, which for him is fast. The unicorn shifter is about as friendly as a goblin with a hangover and would rather stab his eye out with his silver horn than willingly interact with his customers.

"Vance, hey there! It's Tilda." I put a lot of smile in my voice hoping I'm catching him at a good time. "I can't reach one of the books."

He lets out a who-gives-a-fuck snort. "Guess you don't really need it, then."

"You know," I say, trying to channel my inner Izzy Sherwood that has to be inside me somewhere, right? "That's not exactly what someone would call great customer service."

"So go write a shitty Yelp review. I'm in the middle of a chapter." He hangs up and, I'm assuming, goes back to reading his book.

I pocket my phone and look up—way up—to the shelf closest to the ceiling and the copy of *Bibbidi-Bobbidi-Boo and You: A Meditation on Magic* that Effie needs. I could skip it, tell her I forgot or something, but she'd realize why I'd failed to bring it home as soon as she saw its location. She'd get it and give me a sympathetic hug and that look that all but screams "poor baby," and I am so damn tired of being the object of my family's pity and everyone else's scorn.

"Sure you don't want that help?" Gil asks.

I am going to regret this, but it isn't like I could avoid seeing the smug jerk for the rest of my life if I tried really hard.

"Can you please help me get the book?" I ask, keeping my focus on the leather-bound volume and not the walking dirty-professor fantasy standing next to me.

"Of course," he says.

But instead of using a spell to bring the book to me, he wraps his arm around me and floats the two of us upward. I would love to report that I am cool as the proverbial cucumber the entire time, but we don't lie to each other. It's like an electric sizzle goes through my entire body and I can feel him everywhere. His solid, muscular chest pressed against my back. The soft blow of his breath against my ear. The protective brace of his arm around my waist that makes it impossible to even imagine he could or would drop me. All of that is bad enough, but then there's an extra blast of something that shoots us higher, like a water balloon out of a slingshot. Gil's grip tightens and he mumbles something under his breath that slows our ascent. My heart is going a million miles an hour when we stop, floating in the air a few inches too far from the book I need to grab.

Gil holds us there for a minute, then leans in close, his voice so quiet there's no way anyone else can hear, and says, "They never told you, did they? You have to let your mom know that she can't hide the truth about your powers forever."

It is like he's dumped an entire cauldron full of water over me, extinguishing all of the *zing, zap, zoom* rushing through me only a second ago.

"Too late. Everyone already knows I have no power," I

say, as if his words out of left field didn't hit like a slap in the dark. "Can you just float closer to the shelf now so I can grab my book?"

He shakes his head and sighs. "Whatever you say."

On the next breath, the book is within reach and I grab it. Then, we are sinking downward and that sizzle is back, the scent of movie theater popcorn so clear in my nose that I'm starting to wonder if I'm having some kind of stroke or something. Then the world bobbles around us as we dip forward and back, twirling this way and that way in the air. Something jerks us apart, sending the book flying outward, and my terrified squeak escapes before I can stop it.

Gil calls out a steadying spell and grabs me and pulls me close as we float face-to-face at a slow pace, my arms wrapped around his neck and my pulse racing, but not because we almost went splat on the bookstore's floor.

"I've got you," he says, his lips so close to mine that from some angles it has to look like we're kissing.

Don't judge, but if he did kiss me right now at this moment, I'd be all in.

But then my feet touch the floor, and he lets me go. For a second, it feels like I'm going to face-plant without his support, but then the rest of the bookshop starts to come into focus. Vance is looking up from his book, and a handful of witches with their cell phones aimed right at us are at the end of the aisle.

My stomach sinks as I clamp my teeth together tight to distract myself from the way my nose itches—a sure sign that embarrassed tears are on their way. *Great*. I did it again. Keeping my head down, I quick-walk past the witches and toward the bookshop's door.

"Hey, Tilda," Gil calls out. "You forgot your book."

I turn and he sends my sister's book through the air to me.

"Oh, Gil, you're so funny," one of the witches says with a giggle.

And to think he could have just magically sent the book flying to me in the first place. Had he wanted to embarrass me? Did he not realize that I was more than capable of doing that on my own?

I snag the book out of the ether and clutch it to my chest, shooting a questioning look to Vance. The unicorn shifter nods in an unspoken acknowledgment that he'll put the book on the family tab, and I head out the door, my chin high, if more than a little wobbly.

Chapter Eight

Gil . . .

*T*here is only one way to get the answers I need about Tilda, and it involves a raccoon I grabbed out of a trash can in the park, a bag of gummy worms, and a bottle of peanut butter whiskey.

Griselda swings open her front door after the second rap and before I can hit it a third time in a quick three-tap knock. Today her long white hair is pulled back into two ponytails shot through with bright purple that matches her Nirvana shirt. She's finished off her outfit with black Doc Martens, cutoff jean shorts that look like they've had a run-in with a tree mulcher, a flannel tied around her waist, and a newly acquired watercolor wrist tattoo of a parakeet flipping the bird with its middle feather.

"Finally," Griselda says, letting out a sigh of relief. "I'm starving."

I pull the squirmy creature wearing a polka-dot bow tie back from her grasp. "Are you going to eat the raccoon?"

She rolls her eyes and swipes the bag from the corner store. "No, the gummy worms."

After fishing out the worms from the bag, she hands the sack back to me, turns around, and heads toward her kitchen. I don't have a choice but to follow with the bag, a wriggling raccoon I hope like hell has had its rabies shots, and a ton of questions. We make it back to Griselda's kitchen, which also acts as her tarot reading space and is where she dries most of the herbs she uses in her potions.

It's also the place where we came to an agreement. As one of the Resistance's top agents, Griselda has the power to smuggle my parents out of The Beyond. All I had to do was share what insider knowledge I have about the Council after working with them for the past three years. Saying yes to that was the easiest decision I ever made. I don't give a fuck about the Council, the Resistance, or their shadow war. Let them fight it out. I just want to make sure my parents are safe and to go somewhere neither side can find us.

She'd also helped me come up with the "dating" plan to conduct my research about Tilda's powers, saying the cards pointed to it being beneficial for both of us. What the hell Tilda was getting out of it I had no idea, but it saved me several months' worth of working myself into her life so I could run the tests.

Of course, that all changed the minute I realized what Tilda really was, which is why I am at Griselda's house with a raccoon, candy, and alcohol.

At five feet on a good day, the sprite wanders through the large space with its huge windows without even having to consider all of the drying plants hanging from the rafters. At six feet four, it's a different story for me. I have to dodge bunches of American pokeweed, wild celery, belladonna, and wolfsbane while the raccoon tries to steal the bag with the bottle from me.

I hold the bag out of the raccoon's five-fingered grasp. "What about the whiskey?"

"That's for Newt," she says, taking the animal that is now chittering away happily out of my arms.

"You give an animal whiskey?" That seems both wrong and completely in character for a three-hundred-year-old sprite going through a grunge phase.

"Actually, it's Newt Sager from Ye Ol' Wand Shoppe." She sets the raccoon—Newt—on her stone floor. "He has a standing appointment to get turned into a trash panda, go do some digging in other folks' garbage for a few hours, and then enjoy a little nip before I change him back." I must be making a face, because she glares at me. "Don't judge. Everyone has their quirks."

Griselda definitely has more than her fair share of them.

She tickles Newt under his furry chin. "So why don't you tell me what's so dang important that it couldn't wait."

I look from her to the raccoon—fine, Newt—who is doing

that blissed-out oh-you've-got-the-spot-right-there head cock with his beady little eyes closed while tapping his right foot against the floor. Definitely animal. Sorta. Kinda. Fuck. I need a damn guidebook for this.

"Can we talk in front of him?" I ask.

"You mean can he understand you in raccoon form?" Griselda shakes her head and squats down next to the raccoon, who immediately flops onto his back to give her full access to his belly. "He's all raccoon."

"But then why the whiskey?"

"Because raccoon Newt has a taste for it while witch Newt is a teetotaler."

She starts petting Newt's stomach and I'm afraid to even look down, because the sounds the raccoon is making are walking right up to the line of weird but acceptable and weird and not acceptable. There's a good chance Newt is not just into the transformation for dumpster diving and whiskey— but I'm not going to delve any deeper into that outside of my nightmares.

"Next time you see him in the shop, don't tell him about the whiskey," she says. "He'd make me cut off raccoon Newt and you deserve to be happy, don't you, you wittle wuv muffin."

I'm trying to align my vision of Griselda as one of the leaders of the Resistance undermining the Council so they can't do to others what they did to my family with the woman who just called a transformed shopkeeper "wittle wuv muffin" and is getting him drunk. Yeah. That is not gonna happen.

So, I open the bottle of peanut butter whiskey, pour a

shot, and set it down on the floor next to the raccoon, who scrambles away from Griselda, grabs the glass, and settles in on the window seat to watch the birds and imbibe.

The world is a crazy fucking place.

Griselda takes the bottle and adds a healthy dose to two cups of tea and hands me one. "So, since I know your parents are at this moment on their way out of The Beyond thanks to the Resistance, I don't suppose I need to make any threats or cast any spells now that you worked out what she is."

I want to scream in celebration, jump, and dance. I do none of these things, though, because I understand exactly what Griselda is telling me. My parents are on their way out of The Beyond, but that doesn't mean they aren't still in danger, that they won't get stuck in exile—on purpose or by accident.

And this is why I don't trust the Council or the Resistance. Both sides are willing to do whatever it takes to ensure their side wins. No shocker that I had to take the same stance. So I play it cool despite the fact that her not-threat is indeed a threat.

There's no need to ask what she means about what Tilda is. "A spellbinder."

"It almost gives you a shiver to say it out loud, doesn't it?" She sips her tea, watching me closely as I stand on the other side of the giant kitchen island she uses to mix her potions, call her familiar, and—from the smell of it—cook tonight's gumbo. "You understand what she's capable of?"

"Juicing up other people's spells." I keep the bored tone

in my voice because this confirmation means things aren't just bad, they are on the precipice of disaster.

The Council hates duíl magic enough to exile anyone with the gift to The Beyond. A spellbinder? Whatever they'd do, it would make exile look like a vacation.

"To put it mildly," Griselda says, her attention so intense it's as if she's working a mind-reading spell while I'm standing here drinking spiked tea, "whatever the witch's power, she increases it fivefold. The Council sees spellbinders as being against the natural order of things and believes they should be destroyed at the first flicker of their abilities. So her parents decided that the best way to protect her was to keep her ignorant."

"If she was a child, the Council would destroy her," I say, blocking out the mental image of that. "But if she's made it this far in life, they'd want her power." It would give them the opportunity to come out from the shadows, to force everyone to follow their version of what's right, and to grab the reins of power with such a grip no one could tear it away. "That would be a disaster."

Griselda nodded. "Without a doubt."

"And she has no idea." I sit down on the stools lining the cooking island, trying to wrap my brain around all of this. It's one thing to have a theory about something of this magnitude; it's another to have it confirmed.

"None." She dumps her tea into the cast-iron pot already at a rolling boil and pours a shot of whiskey for herself, shooting it back in one gulp. "Do you know how rare a spellbinder is?"

I trace the skull-and-crossbones pattern on the teacup,

needing to do something to ease the worry and guilt starting to hiss through me like steam escaping the kettle. "One every generation."

Griselda snorts. "Try one or two every three generations—out of all of Witchingdom." She pours me a shot and pushes it across the island. "Do you know what happens when one is found? Chaos. Every powerful family and the faction they control would try to get the spellbinder on their side."

"Tilda is a Sherwood." They aren't like other families, they sure as hell aren't like mine. They have power, money, connections.

"Her last name won't protect her from this," Griselda says.

That's when I see it, the nearly imperceptible flinch as she considers the what-ifs. In The Beyond, they tell stories about Griselda and the Resistance, about how they're fearless. That isn't what I'm seeing now—and that worries the shit out of me.

I toss back the teacup shot, the peanut butter flavor masking the burn I need to feel at this moment. "So you and her parents have let her spend her entire life thinking she was an outré rather than letting her make her own choice about how to handle who she is?"

Her eyes narrow at me. "We've protected her the best we can."

Now it is my turn to scoff at a bit of bullshit. "She's an adult. She should get to make her own choices."

Griselda doesn't say anything for a few seconds. She just

stares at me with that look that makes the back of my neck sweat. Then she smiles, and that's when I know I'm fucked.

"And when you were smuggled out of The Beyond," she asks, her tone as sweet as the expression on her face is not, "how did you do it?"

"That's different." It was. The Council hadn't given me a choice.

Griselda lifts a silver eyebrow. "You let your parents think you'd willingly gone to work for the Council so they wouldn't endanger themselves by voicing their objections."

"It's for their own good," I say, my voice rising enough to make raccoon Newt let out a protective growl.

"Exactly." She pours each of us another shot. "And if Tilda uses the power she has, the Council's magic spectrometers would pick it up right away. They wouldn't stop until they figured out who was making the numbers spike. Your little spikes in juice have been bad enough; if she were to amp up an intentional spell, it would only be a matter of time before the Council brought the hammer down on her."

"If she's so powerful, can't she just zap them?"

"That's not the way a spellbinder works," Griselda says. "She has to work with the right partner to do an epic-level spell. If she does it with a witch who isn't prepared to act as a kind of conduit, the spell will go pear-shaped."

"I can't keep playing double agent with Cassius." I've been walking that line since I showed up in Wrightsville and had my first meeting with Griselda. The Council is watching me. Cassius is watching me. Griselda is watching me. Tilda is the only person who isn't, and she's the one who should be. "He's suspicious. I know he is. I have to help my parents get out of there before it's too late."

"You don't have to worry," Griselda says with a happy little twirly dance in the middle of her kitchen. "Smuggling witches out of The Beyond takes time, but they're almost free and clear. I promise."

Can I believe her? I want to, but at this point everyone is lying to everyone else about nearly everything. But this is my parents. I have to be sure. "I need to talk to them."

"Soon. Right now, they're in a safe house. Give it a couple of days to move them to a place where the Council can't reach them first." Griselda takes her shot and stares at me until I do the same.

I have to weigh my odds.

The Council doesn't give two shits about my family beyond how they can be used to keep me in line. The Resistance, though, isn't like that, at least not according to the stories my mom used to tell me, but all of that could be nothing more than wishful thinking, which is why I'm going forward with both eyes open and ready for a double cross.

"Keep an eye on Tilda," she says, flicking her fingers in the air and sending the shot glasses to the sink, where the clean spell takes care of doing the dishes and putting them away in the cabinets. "Not that you aren't already, but this time pay attention more with what's between your ears than inside your pants."

Guilty as charged, but still. "Griselda."

"What?" She lets out a lusty sigh that I really did not need to have ever heard. "I was quite the player in my day. I still remember what it felt like when Eliphas did that thing with his tongue. Whew, there are some things that keep an old woman warm on a cold night."

"I could do without that mental image." I've never turned down a good research project though. Maybe Eliphas kept a journal with technique notes.

"Stop pretending you're all stuffy." Griselda rolls her eyes and yanks the flannel tied around her waist tighter as she rounds the island to do a little hovering magic that has her floating up so she looks me in the eye. "You don't fool me for a minute. I've heard what the cards say about you."

I'm hoping for the answer to be "a peaceful life in the library with no Council or Resistance agents looking over my shoulder and my parents off enjoying their lives as free people again," but one look at Griselda's face confirms that it is not going to be that. "What do the cards say?"

"That your whole life is about to change."

From his spot at the window, raccoon Newt lifts his glass in a toast.

Fuck. My. Life.

Chapter Nine

Tilda . . .

It's not every day I get summoned to go see Griselda, but here I am on her front porch with a few sprigs of fresh thyme from our family garden and exactly thirteen dried blue violet petals pressed between sheets of thin parchment per her message sent via hummingbird. I have no idea what spell she's going to be cooking in her kitchen cauldron, but it's going to smell better than her bunion soup from the other day.

Griselda opens her front door and lets out a relieved sigh. "Thank the fates, you're here." She snags the bag of goodies I brought and clutches it to her vintage Soundgarden shirt with tour dates from 1994 on it.

"Come inside."

I follow her back to the kitchen, where there's a tipsy-looking raccoon and also the hobgoblin of my nightmares sitting at the table and drinking what looks like whiskey. Okay, it's actually Gil Connolly, but that's practically the same thing—especially since he's wearing a woolly sweater that is almost the exact shade of woodsy green of a hobgoblin's hair and, you know, he's mostly evil.

He glances over at me and there's a flash of shock in his green eyes, and for a second his lips start to turn upward as my pulse skitters into overdrive and every nerve in my body becomes a tool of divination tuned in only to him. There's a whole inhale of an almost-moment when everything feels light and the soft kind of warm, like when you wrap yourself in a towel straight out of the dryer. However, by the exhale, he catches himself and the smile inverses into a scowl directed right at me. All that fuzzy heat turns into a backdraft fire of embarrassment at getting fooled again that toasts me to a burnt crisp.

Determined to ignore the asshole at the table, even if I'm still pretty curious about the raccoon, I sidle up to Griselda at the island. "Why is he here?"

"Because," she says as she stirs the thyme-scented broth starting to bubble in her cauldron, "I'm sending you two on a mission."

Gil's jaw tightens and he shoots up from his chair. I swear I can see him counting to sixty billion in his head as he strides across the flagstone floor over to us. Paying me no mind—who cares if I am ignoring him, it is so rude of him to pretend I'm not even here—he stops on the opposite side of the island from Griselda and plants his palms on the slate countertop, practically vibrating with annoyed disbelief.

"*She's* going on a mission?" he asks, his voice low as if I'm not *right here*.

"Yes," Griselda says as she adds in the blue violet petals one at a time. "I need you both to go out and gather agaric mushrooms for a spell."

That announcement makes Gil's jaw drop and my brain jerks to a stop for a second before I blurt out, "But they're poisonous."

"Bah." Griselda waves her hand dismissively. "That's highly exaggerated."

"Yeah, that whole death-cap-mushroom PR campaign they've got going with posters in every herb shop and apothecary is a real stroke of genius," Gil grumbles.

"Keeps the supply available for those who have legitimate use for it," Griselda says. "I just use them for a little nonmagical zombie powder—temporary, of course. For fifteen minutes, the witch or goblin or mean fairy is mellowed to the point of inactivity."

"Why do you need it?" I ask, racking my brain for any spell that isn't deadly that calls for one of the most poisonous ingredients that can be found in witchery.

"If I wanted you to know," my godmother says, the first bit of annoyance creeping into her tone, "I would have told you in the first place."

I know from experience that that is the end of that conversation, and yet one glance out of the corner of my eye at Gil and the way he is now looking at me with a determined snarl has my mouth going anyway. "But why do I have to go with him?"

"There's a troll." Griselda stops stirring and looks from Gil to me before leaving her cauldron—the wooden spoon continuing to stir on its own—and walking over to her supply pantry.

My stomach tightens with worry. "As in a club-you-in-the-head troll or a solve-my-riddle troll?"

"Bit of both." She comes back from the pantry and hands me a small, hot pink burlap bag that looks like it would hold a bag of whole coffee beans and not much else. "Now go and don't come back until the bag is full."

The raccoon gives us a little wave as Griselda hustles us out the front door, slamming it shut the minute we cross the threshold, leaving us alone on her porch, neither of us looking at the other as we stare out at the tree-lined street.

Awkward?

So very much.

Gil holds out a hand to me. "Shall we?"

"We can Uber." Which would alleviate the need to touch him, since being a big ol' null means I can't fly.

He scowls at me because of course he does. "This is faster."

I wish I could argue the logic, but I can't, so I swear to myself that this time I will not let whatever it is that comes over me when I'm near Gil knock me stupid. I will not beg him to kiss me. I won't wrap my arms around him. I won't take surreptitious sniffs of his cologne. Yeah. That's it. I will will it and make it so.

But life doesn't work that way, does it?

We both know it doesn't.

Which is why when I take his hand, a sizzle of awareness sets wave after wave of want through me, each one stronger than the last. It's enough to take my breath away, but then he calls out a quick flying spell and we shoot up in the air like a rocket and breathing isn't an option anymore. The wind whips my hair back and my glasses press against the bridge of my nose as we race through the sky, rushing through clouds and the crisp fall air. I won't say that I'm holding on to Gil for dear life, but I sure can't say I'm not.

"Can you slow down?"

He grimaces. "Just hold on."

I tighten my grip on his hand as the houses in Wrightsville get smaller and smaller until they are only little dots below us. The Killjoy Forest is tucked in the Blue Ridge Mountains. There aren't roads leading to it and there isn't a single map showing its location, but every witch in the area knows the perfect flight plan to get there. Or at least that's what they say.

I can't help but let out an awed sigh as I watch it unfold below us. "It's beautiful."

"You haven't been before?" Gil asks.

"It's not exactly accessible for outré." That's putting it

mildly. We aren't exactly refused entry, but without any option besides flying in, it's pretty damn hard to make it there.

"Then," he says, slowing down, "we have to make sure you really get a good look."

"You don't have t—"

But I don't even get to finish the sentence before he hooks a sharp left and sends us soaring over the trees, dipping down into meadows gone golden with explosions of autumn-blooming flowers and gliding so close to the waterfalls that I can dip my fingers into the cool mountain water rushing down into the creek below. I close my eyes and commit it all to memory—the feel of the air brushing my cheeks, the scent of the pitch pine trees, the thrill of sailing above it all in the bluest, clearest sky that belongs in a museum, and the steadying strength of Gil's hand around mine. When I open my eyes, he's watching me, a smile playing on his lips.

"Amazing, right?" he asks.

All I can do is nod, because it's almost too much, the blast of certainty that hits me at this moment, as if this is how my life starts and everything up until now has just been prelude. I can't explain it—I can't even process it—but it's there, rock-solid and confusing as hell.

He sets us down near a limestone arch that has to be more than two hundred feet tall and nearly a hundred feet across. A creek runs below it, gorgeous and blue, the water clear enough that I can spot bright neon fish swimming around the rocks that glimmer in the light.

I do a full three-sixty trying to memorize every inch of it. "It's beautiful."

For once, Mr. Know-It-All doesn't say anything, he just takes my hand again and squeezes it as we stand there taking it all in. Then the earth shakes beneath our feet and birds scatter from treetops as part of the limestone bridge breaks away from the rest and small rocks splash down into the creek. The moving mound of limestone transforms as it comes closer, the illusion of pale stone evaporating and revealing a massive twelve-foot-tall bridge troll, complete with a nose ring made from bones and a snaggletoothed smile.

"I was just thinking about how a snack would be nice about now," he says as he rubs his well-padded stomach. "What are you doing in my forest?"

The low baritone of his voice bounces around inside me and makes my teeth practically vibrate, like during a witch party when the music is blaring out of the speakers and the bass becomes a physical force. Even though I'm prepped for seeing him, the sight still sucks the breath out of my lungs.

Gil takes half a step forward, dropping my hand and drawing the troll's attention. "Picking mushrooms for Griselda."

The troll tugs on one of the three long black hairs poking out from his chin. "I'd say tell her hi from Eugene, but that won't be possible when you're in my belly."

"Only if we can't solve your riddle," I say, my voice shaking only a little compared to what my knees are doing at the moment.

"Oh, you won't." Eugene chuckles. "I've eaten well off of this one."

Gil crosses his arms over his chest and tilts his chin up in challenge. "So give it to us."

"Anxious for your death. I approve." The troll looks over his shoulder and hollers toward the forest. "Harold, start up the fire. I feel like witch kabobs." The trees shake and the loud crack of a trunk snapping in two booms a few seconds before the flash of flames shows up on top of a nearby mountain. Eugene turns back to us and grins his terrible grin. "You get one opportunity to answer the riddle, and you can't discuss the answer with each other, you just have to trust each other or not trust, as the case may be. Don't say I didn't warn you. Witch tears tend to sour the snack."

"How awful for you," Gil says, sarcasm thick in his tone.

Eugene sits down on a boulder that, compared to him, looks about as big as a footstool and rubs his hands together before offering up the riddle. "One day, a witch was boasting about how she could stay underwater for six minutes. An outré laughed and said, 'That's nothing,' and that she could easily be underwater for ten minutes without the use of any spells since she was a null. The witch said, 'Oh yeah? Prove it.' The outré did. How did she do it?"

Gil opens his mouth, but I smack my hand over it and shoot him a shut-up-already look. Trolls are a lot of things; kidders isn't one of them. Eugene said no discussing the riddle and he meant it. Gil nods and I step back, my palm tingling where it touched his lips.

I start pacing, rolling the riddle around in my head, as Gil stands stock-still, his hands clasped behind his back. The birds begin returning to the tops of the trees near our quiet spot by the creek, the only sound being the babbling of the water over the rocks half-buried in the mud at the bottom. It reminds me of the time my sisters and I went swimming and had a contest to see who could tread water the longest. They all went with a levitation spell to stay afloat but ran out of spell juice before my legs got too tired to keep going. Magic was amazing, but I'd spent my whole life figuring out other options, just like—

The answer to the riddle hits me like a punch in the nose.

I turn to Gil and level a huge smile at him. He lifts an eyebrow. I nod and try to figure out how in the world I'm going to express how certain I am of the solution. Charades has never been my game of choice. However, instead of waiting for me to do some kind of interpretive dance, Gil just nods. Now it's my turn to raise both of my eyebrows in question. He nods again.

Letting out a deep breath, I turn to Eugene, who is flossing his teeth with a tree branch that still has a few orange leaves stuck to it. "The outré poured a glass of water and held it over her head for ten minutes."

The troll growls, a low rumble that sends the animals in the forest on either side of the creek scurrying for cover. "Harold, kill the fire."

Adrenaline spiking in my veins, I sprint over to Gil and practically jump on him. He wraps his arms around me and picks me up and then swings me round and round in cele-bration. By the time we've stopped, breathless, the sound of the forest has returned, but I can barely hear it. Instead, I'm ultra-aware of Gil's arm around me, holding me tight against him, and the way everything in the world seems absolutely close to perfect at that moment in the soft light of the late afternoon.

"How did you get to that answer for the riddle?" Gil asks, lowering me down to the ground and stepping back. "I had nothing."

My heart's racing and I'm wobbly on my feet, but I manage to form words. "When you're an outré, I guess you see things from a different perspective."

"You know, Tilda Sherwood, you're pretty great."

"Is that a compliment, Gil Connolly?" Translation: Are we flirting? I mean, it definitely feels like we're flirting, but why would that happen? He hates me. I loathe him. He's a giant jerk who maybe is destined for my sister. And yet, when he looks at me with an intensity powerful enough to set that bonfire the trolls just extinguished, like he's doing right now, a whole squadron of butterflies start maneuvers in my chest.

He nods, a strange tension coming off of him in waves as he shoves his fingers through his hair, almost as if he's hoping to yank some of it out. "It is."

What in the world am I supposed to say to that? I have not a single solitary clue. That all too familiar awkward weirdness enters the chat again, blasting away the comfortable camara-derie that had been there only a moment ago. I have no idea what I did this time, but I've obviously fucked things up again, per usual.

Great. Just perfect, Matilda.

I'm grasping for something to say when a fat, hairy boar with curled tusks moseys by us and trots into the tree line.

"That's a wild pig." I grab his hand and pull him along as I follow the snuffling animal. "It'll lead us right to the mushrooms."

Saved by the pig? Hey, some days a witch has to take the wins she can even if—the fates help me—kissing the big jerk next to me sounds better.

Chapter Ten

Gil . . .

The sun is setting, turning Tilda's hair fiery shades of red and orange, when I land us in Griselda's front lawn, the fall leaves crunching under our feet.

The good news is that I'm finally able to exert more control over the power surge whenever I run a spell while touching her. The bad news is that I don't want to let go of her even though I've run out of excuses to touch her, and the unfamiliar twist of guilt has me bent up inside. I'm holding on to her hand even though I know this connection is just the connection caused by my fucked-up family magic.

It's not real.

At least that's what I'm telling myself as I stare at her hand in mine like some kind of dumbass.

"Wow," Tilda says as she straightens her glasses, which had gone cockeyed somewhere between the Killjoy Forest and Wrightsville. "That was something."

"Yeah." I force myself to let go of her hand and shove my hands in my pockets so I don't change my mind as we start walking toward Griselda's porch.

"Thank you." Cheeks pink, she holds the bag of mushrooms close to her stomach like a shield as her gaze shifts from the house to the leaves dropping from the trees to the witches walking down the lane not so covertly watching us. "I really appreciate it and—"

Tilda lets out a high-pitched squeal and jumps back as Griselda's pet squirrel leaps off the porch railing. Parsnip sails through the air, its arms extended and its squirrel-sized paisley tie flapping in the air over its tiny shoulder. Tilda dodges, but she's not quick enough. The gray squirrel lands on Tilda's right shoulder, grabs a handful of red hair, and yanks down hard enough that Tilda yelps.

"Parsnip!" Tilda hollers. "Stop!"

The squirrel pats her cheek, grabs the bag of mushrooms, and scrambles up Tilda's head while Tilda whirls around and grasps for the furry tree rat. I rush over, but before I can get there, Parsnip springs upward, bites down on the string holding the bag closed, and grabs ahold of a tree limb. Then it's swinging Tarzan-style from branch to branch until it gets to the white-painted gutter on the house. It slides down the drainpipe to the porch, offers up a middle finger to both of us, and scampers inside the house.

"Are you okay?" I ask, looking her over for scratches, not wanting but needing to make sure she is okay.

"Familiars are the absolute worst." She eyeballs me as she rubs her scalp where Parsnip pulled her hair. "You don't have one, do you?"

"No, they aren't part of my family's magical tradition." Not a lie, not the whole truth either.

"Ours either, but that didn't stop my sister from getting Barkley, the biggest asshole of a rooster you'll ever meet." She glances over my shoulder and groans. "Of course someone had to see that. My little dance with Parsnip will be everywhere before I even get home. Mom's gonna love it."

Turning around, I see the handful of witches on the other side of Griselda's front yard fence. They're giggling as they hold up their phones, no doubt ready to post the squirrel versus Sherwood video to WitchyGram as soon as Tilda goes inside. That isn't what makes my blood go cold though—Cassius is standing just beyond the coven of bitchy witches.

Fuck.

My handler has never shown up at any of my other jobs. I've only ever seen him once, but there is no mistaking him. The man is pale enough to be confused for a vampire, especially with the way he wears his straight black hair down to his shoulders as if to silently encourage the misidentification. Then again, no Council spy is what they seem to be, it's kind of the job description.

"Go inside," I say. "I'll distract them."

"Are you sure?"

I give her a curt nod, already bracing for whatever fresh hell my evening is about to turn into. My usual glare back in place, I cross the street mean mugging the witches already walking away while typing on their phones—no doubt coming up with the perfect mocking captions for their WitchyGram posts. They aren't my target though. I stop just outside Griselda's gate and wait. It doesn't take long.

"Connolly," Cassius says. "You two look cozy."

And just like that, I'm back in The Beyond, skating along the edge of disaster. I snort dismissively. "Just doing my job."

"Of course," he says, his smile cold enough to freeze the melting polar ice caps.

He laughs, a slimy, slithering sound that makes my skin crawl.

"We all break the rules every once in a while. I wouldn't report you for a little diversion," he says. "You can trust me, you know."

Said the gator to the bunny riding on its back across the river.

Mom used to tell me that story at night when tucking me under the covers on short breaks from the boarding school at The Beyond. The bunny always thought it was in control of the situation, but the gator always bounced the bunny off his back in the middle of the water far from shore. The bunny asked why, and the gator told the bunny that he knew exactly who the bunny was when he got in the water and then he ate the bunny whole, not even leaving a tuft of fur from his bunny tail in the water.

It was a good lesson for a child trying to stay alive in The Beyond and the Witchingdom in general.

"Of course I know I can trust you." I force my shoulders to lower a few inches and imitate a looseness in my body that I don't feel, especially not when my Tilda-sense starts to tingle, letting me know she's gotta be near even if I can't see her. "We're on the same side in all of this."

"Exactly." He looks past me to Griselda's front door. "Any news on your hunch? The Council is getting itchy about this whole operation."

I pivot, putting myself directly between the house and my handler, fighting to keep my usual cool and to not search for Tilda's hiding spot when it feels like there's a coked-up goblin rampaging through my veins. The Council can't find out Tilda is a spellbinder. Griselda is right, not even the Sherwood name would protect her from the Council. That's why Cassius is here checking up on me. Capturing a spellbinder wouldn't only make his career, it would make him a legend within the Council and open up paths to power unobtainable otherwise. Cassius wouldn't hesitate to do whatever it took to make that happen.

"She's just an outré." I shrug, ignoring the soft crunching of leaves off to my right that has to be Tilda because I need to sell the lie to one of the most consummate liars I've ever met—a task made all the more difficult by the flash of red hair I catch out of the corner of my eye. "There's nothing to her beyond that: no magic, no something special, not a damn thing beyond a null sheltered by her family."

"You're sure?" Cassius glares at me, obviously pissed his plans for advancement have gone up in flames.

"Without a doubt."

"Then wrap up your report." The vein in his temple pulsates and it takes everything I've got not to grin at his absolute fury at being thwarted. "The Council has another job for you." He gets right up in my face, so absolutely confident in his superiority. "Don't forget what's riding on your cooperation. I'd hate to see your parents stay in The Beyond forever."

Fury, white-hot and lethal at the bald-faced lie of the statement when there's no way Cassius doesn't know my parents are missing courses through me, and the urge to knock Cassius on his ass has me by the balls, but I can't give in to it. No matter how good it would feel in the moment, I have to play the long game, keep Tilda safe. Sure, she has her family and Griselda to watch out for her, but for some reason I can't explain, she has me too.

I really have well and good cursed myself.

"Clock's ticking, Connolly," Cassius says before snapping his fingers and disappearing into the ether.

Grinding my molars to dust, I hustle into Griselda's house and find her alone in her kitchen sharing a plate of cookies with the squirrel as they both sit at the tiny round table where she does her tarot readings.

"She's already gone," Griselda says before I can ask about Tilda. "Seems she heard someone saying something that hurt her feelings. Can't imagine who that was."

Yeah, and the elderberry tea in her cup isn't liberally spiked with absinthe.

My gut sinks. "What do I do?"

She shrugs her bony shoulders. "Depends on what you want to do."

I glance down at the tarot cards laid out in a cross pattern on the table. "Was all of this in the cards?"

"You know I can't tell you that." She shuffles the deck, making quick work of moving the cards as a purple aura grows in strength around her. "All I can say is that life is messy. Get used to it."

As if I have any other choice—especially when it comes to fucking things up with Tilda.

Chapter Eleven

Gil . . .

*T*he first thing I need to do to unravel what is going on is to find Tilda, who is avoiding her usual haunts like a troll avoids hot soapy water unless it's time for their yearly bath.

Turns out that that is easier done using the Internet than whipping up a location spell. As a Sherwood, her every move is well documented by the gossipmongers on WitchyGram, one of whom has just posted a pic of her going to a meeting in the basement of the Alchemist's Bookshop and Tea Emporium.

Hurrying out of Griselda's neighborhood, I turn onto Main Street just as a light purple protection dome that will block interlopers from gaining entry is starting to drape over the three-story shop. My shoulders relax about half an inch before they boomerang up to my ears again and a triple jolt of adrenaline shoots through my veins.

Magic works on an opposites spectrum; the dome not only protects, it also traps everyone inside. If Cassius still harbors suspicions about Tilda being the weakest Sherwood link, right now would be the perfect opportunity to cast a spell to get her to do the Council's bidding without interference from the Sherwoods—and because she doesn't know she has any power, she wouldn't have any idea she could stop them.

Fuck.

I have to get to her.

Now.

It isn't a thought so much as it is an action plan formed out of thin air and a desperation I can't explain. All I know is that it is DNA-deep, wrapped so tight around every part of me that I am running toward the shop before I realize it.

Witches jump out of the way as I sprint toward the building, tossing curses in the air after me—as if developing a raging case of poison ivy is going to slow me down when I am about to be separated from Tilda. Sprinting even faster with the help of a Hermes kicker incantation, I cover the three blocks in fifteen seconds and make it to the building just as the purple-tinted dome line is almost to the top of the first-floor windows.

A sharp right into the alley nearly goes completely concussion-worthy wrong when I almost slam into the opposite wall, but I can't slow down. No. That's not it. I *won't* slow down. I refuse.

Racing toward the stairs leading down to the Alchemist's basement back entry, I slide under the purple line seconds before it hits the ground with a hard thump that sends dirt and debris into the air. My lungs are aching as I try to catch my breath and assess the damage from sliding down the stone steps on my ass to beat the dome. I clock the third that's-gonna-leave-a-big-purple-mark bruise when I hear the ticking.

Shit.

I know that sound.

I'm up before I know it, my entire body practically vibrating with the effort to call forth another Hermes incantation so soon after the last. It hurts the way only overuse of magic can, like jagged nails gouging my brain or staying conscious while a tooth fairy gnaws on my vital organs.

I have half a breath to give to the pain though, and then I'm running again. With only ten seconds to get down the stairs, through the door, and into the meeting room before I'm shut out, I don't have time to give in to the hurt.

I make it inside the room half a breath before the last tick. The meeting room door slams shut and another *whoomph* sounds from outside the door before the scent of warm apple pie fills the air.

I'm sweating, my shirt's come untucked, and I'm breathing as hard as that time I outran a trio of trolls looking for a donation for their bone broth—but I made it, and that's all that matters.

Or at least I think so until I look up and each of the

twenty-ish people in the room are staring at me with open curiosity—except for Tilda. Judging by the look on her face as she adjusts her glasses with more disgust in such a small gesture than I'd known is possible, I'm lucky she has no clue just how powerful she really is.

After a few seconds of silent gawking, everyone turns back to the groups of people they'd been talking to before I rushed in, shooting glances my way.

Tilda marches over to me, looking every bit like a warrior witch ready to inflict brutal and significant damage. I have no doubt that she overheard what I said to Cassius, and man, is she ever pissed.

It shouldn't be hot.

It so fucking is.

That last spell definitely messed with my head, because watching her walk over to me is the hottest thing I've ever encountered. It isn't just the way her jeans-covered hips sway as she stalks over or the pouty swell in her pink bottom lip as if she just got done biting it. It isn't even the very definite curve of her tits that no oversized sweatshirt can hide. It's the woman herself, all of her, and the glimpse of who she is behind the sanitized version of herself that she shows the rest of the world. Tilda is all Sherwood—confident, demanding, powerful, smart, cunning, and so much fucking trouble that I don't know whether to fight my way out of here or kiss her.

I am so fucking screwed.

She doesn't stop until we're practically toe to toe. She smells like extra-butter popcorn, the kind at the movie theater that should come with an addiction warning, and her eyes are so blue behind her glasses that I can't help but picture her running naked through the woods.

No.

Wait.

What in the hell is wrong with me? This isn't me. At least not with Tilda Sherwood. She's too this and I'm too that and the only thing I need to be focused on right now is keeping my parents safe, keeping the Council from torturing her, and not having the wrath of the entire Sherwood clan fall on top of me when they find out—and eventually they will—what I know and who I've told.

She puts on a smile as she glances around at the other witches in the room, giving a wave here and a head nod there, but that melts away when she turns her focus back to me. "What are you doing here?" she asks, getting the words out from between clenched teeth.

My dick twitches and my fingers itch to reach out and sweep the hair that escaped her ponytail back behind her ear. All of this is weird as shit, but I can't deny it. What Witchingdom may think of as love spells are actually just lust spells focusing all that free-floating desire on one person with the theory that from there something real will happen. It's part of why witches like me with duíl magic are considered so dangerous—we supposedly can create love. We can't, but that doesn't stop the rumors and the—

Oh fuck.

That explains it. Why didn't I realize it sooner? The almost-kiss, the blast of her powering up my duíl magic, and the fact that I can't stop thinking of her since.

You feckin' eejit, Connolly. She didn't just supersize your magic. You cursed yourself with your own damn duíl powers.

Locking down all of the implications of being under a lust spell with the worst woman in all of Witchingdom that I could be magically connected to for who in the hell knows how long, I fall back under the armor of smarm that I built back in The Beyond and have worn ever since.

"Oh, Tilda." I give her nose a playful tweak because I can't stop myself. What is next? Will I pull her pigtails? "That sounds like you missed me."

"Why would I ever do that? I'm nothing, remember?" If she'd realized she could have flames shooting from the side of her face by simply touching someone doing a fire spell, she would have at that moment. "I'm only a null who doesn't matter."

Oh yeah, she definitely overheard the BS I sold to Cassius.

Okay. I knew she'd be pissed when she saw me, but her anger may be exactly what I need to clear my head until I figure out how to break my own curse. All I have to do is annoy the fuck out of Tilda and she'll take a few steps back so I can breathe and think again.

She inches closer, the move putting her feet between mine, and plants her palm on my chest above my heart. The whole world stills as every part of me focuses in on her.

I swear I can feel the air crackling around us and there's

no one—absolutely no one—in that room but us. She looks up at me, her eyes dilated and her lips parted. If I didn't know better, I'd think she wanted me to dip my head down and kiss her, reach lower and cup her ass as I lift her up so she can curl her legs around my waist.

"You need to leave," she says as she grasps my shirt, holding tight and not letting go so there is no way I am going anywhere even if I want to.

"Can't." I shrug, knowing it's gonna push all her buttons. What can I say, I am a desperate man holding on by the thinnest thread of self-control. "The dome's down."

"This is what I get for agreeing to Mom's overprotective demands." She lets out a harsh groan and tugs on my shirt, pulling me closer to her, obviously as caught up in the duíl spell as I am. "You don't belong here."

Don't I know it? But there is nowhere else I want to be unless it is in the closet on the opposite side of the room with the door closed and our clothes in a pile on the floor. My cock thickens and I'm leaning in, watching the way her tongue wets her bottom lip. Her gaze is lust hazy and she moves her hand from above my heart to the buttons lining the middle of my white button-up.

We're not gonna make it to that closet.

"Oh, Tilda," a woman interrupts, sending both of us stumbling back to the reality of where and who we are. "Who's your friend?"

Tilda looks over at the tall woman with curly hair so black it's nearly blue and a face full of freckles in the bright yellow dress and blinks as if she's never seen her before. While it is nice to know I'm not the only one with a scrambled brain right now, I can practically hear her berate herself for going blank. I reach out before I think better of it, holding her hand and giving it a gentle squeeze. We both look down in confusion, and I let go, my fingers tingling.

"Birdie," Tilda says as she flexes her fingers behind her back, "this is Gil. Gil, this is Birdie."

"Nice to meet you," Birdie says, her smile genuine.

She reaches out to shake my hand. I hold my breath as I shake her hand, but there's not a single spark, not even a sputter. The accidental spell from my duíl magic is definitely localized to one curvy redhead who is currently pretending to be completely focused on cleaning her glasses.

"Thanks for having me."

"We're always happy to have a newcomer," Birdie says.

"He's not a misfit." Tilda slides her glasses back on but still doesn't even so much as glance my way.

Birdie's dark eyes go wide as she looks from me to Tilda and back again. Yeah, I can't explain it either, but here I am grinning like a loon at a woman who is determined to show she can't stand me.

She clears her throat. "Well, allies are important too. I wish we had more of—" Whatever she was about to say next gets swallowed by a huge sneeze.

In an instant, every lightbulb in the room turns pink, then blue, then red as Birdie continues sneezing.

Dome magic is usually effective, but the chance of something going wrong is never zero. I step between Tilda and the door, ready to face down whatever malevolent force either made it through the perimeter or got in before I did. That's when I realize no one else in the room has flinched. Birdie sneezes one more time, this one big enough that it sends her thick dark hair flying around her as if she's made a decision out of nowhere to start headbanging, and all of the lights—even the ones out in the hallway—go out.

"Sorry, everyone," Birdie says, then leans close to me and whispers, "Magical allergies."

Several people swipe on their cell phone flashlights.

"I got it," a huge guy with a goofy grin who towers over everyone else in the room by a good foot and a half hollers out.

"Oh dear," Birdie says under her breath.

"Et erit ... et erit ... hold on ... I've got it ... I swear ... Et erit tenebris." All of the lights from the phones go out too. "Shit," he mumbles. "Sorry."

A familiar male voice calls out, "Et erit lux."

All of the lights flash on bright enough to make me squint.

Vance, an agent for the Resistance, the bookstore's owner, and the unicorn shifter with "piss off" tattooed onto his knuckles, stands in the doorway, his usual surly expression on his face underneath his unicorn horn that never goes away even when he is in human form, holding a tray full of tea sandwiches.

"Eli"—he points a finger at the tall guy—"you're supposed to write it down so your anxiety doesn't get the better of you. And you"—he turns to Birdie—"get Griselda to refill your allergy meds."

If either of them is offended by the unicorn shifter's orders, they don't show it.

He focuses on me. "What are you doing here?"

"That's what I'm trying to figure out," Tilda says.

Vance gives me a once-over, and before I can think of a cover story to explain my appearance, he brushes by me and starts toward the front of the room.

"I'm sure we'll figure it out soon enough," he says over his shoulder. "Welcome to the meeting of magical misfits support group. Anything said here, stays here. There's food after. Now sit down, everyone, and let's get this over with."

Everyone starts toward the seats arranged in a circle in the middle of the room as all of the pieces come together in my head. Sure, I know that nulls aren't the only witches to have issues with working magic. Sometimes it is physical, sometimes it is mental, and sometimes it is a combination. I know Witchingdom has its outcasts, but I had no idea that they'd banded together to stand with each other. My gut twists; if the Council finds out, they won't like it. They'll do what they can to end the practice. Keeping witches isolated or afraid to rock the metaphorical boat is what helps them to maintain power.

"Don't look at them like that," Tilda says, obviously taking my grimace as being for her friends, not the Council. "Yes, some of us find strength in being with others facing the same challenges. Not everyone wants to lone wolf it—except for the werewolves. They're like that sometimes. You aren't part werewolf, are you?"

"No. Just smart enough to know that people are always in it just for themselves and you can't really trust other witches." There are at least twenty people in the room. Any one of them could be a Council spy, a double agent like me. Tilda, though, is completely oblivious to the prospect. Her family may think they're protecting her, but they won't always be around to watch out for her—so when that curtain comes down, it's going to be even harder for her to stay out of the Council's clutches. "Not all of us are spoiled Sherwoods who get to take the easy way out by believing that the world is full of rainbows made out of sunshine."

She snorts in disbelief. "What a sad little world you live in."

It isn't sad, it's reality. Depending on other people is what ends up getting you tossed into The Beyond. The fact that Tilda doesn't realize that just goes to show how sheltered she is and why she needs me.

Chapter Twelve

Tilda . . .

*T*did it.

Again.

What is it about Gil that has me making a complete fool of myself in public every time I'm near him?

As soon as the dome lifted at the magical misfits meeting, I hurried out of there without even staying for the eye of newt muffins Eli had brought and hustled my way home as if goblins were nipping at my heels. I'd blown kisses to my family gathered around the cauldron in the kitchen—what, it isn't like I could help with any of the magic going on there— and sprinted up the stairs, followed the markings that lead to my section of the house, and grabbed the emergency chocolate.

Fine.

I'm a big chicken. *Bwak. Bwak.* No wonder Barkley won't leave me alone. Even now the rooster is scratching at my closed and locked bedroom door.

"Go away, Barkley," I grumble. "I'm wallowing in misery."

Flopping back on my bed, I let out a huge sigh. I cannot keep running into the guy my sister's destined to marry. Maybe. If I read the cards right. Plus there's the fact that I do something stupid almost every time I see him. Oh yeah, and the fact that he talks shit about me when I'm not around. Who needs that? Not me. I hate him. Can't stand him.

And yet, you still want to kiss him anytime he's within reach.

What in the hell is going on, Matilda Grace?

It's getting beyond awkward. Fine, scratch that, it has been awkward since the beginning because I'm me and that's pretty much my M.O.

Still, all I have to do is close my eyes and my whole body is buzzing again with that sense of something so good, so right, so fucking perfect when he looks at me that it's like . . . well . . . magic—or at least what I imagine it's like to have a spell rushing through you. And I'd almost kissed him. Again. In public.

Fates preserve me, there is no way this is going to end well. I have got to make sure to avoid him no matter what. That shouldn't be that hard.

"Yeah, completely," I mumble to myself because, yes, I've

been driven to talking to myself. "It's not like you see him every time you turn around." Just at the bookshop and tea emporium, the coffee shop, the grocery store, the magical misfits meeting, and everywhere else I seem to be, including Griselda's front porch that one time when I nearly slammed into him in my rush, which the doorknob cat loves to remind me about every other visit to my godmother. "So everywhere."

"Oh, shut up."

Great. Now I'm answering myself.

The air shimmers on the other side of my open window as the wind sweeps in the smell of salt and old books. My stomach drops as my pulse kicks into high gear, anticipation whooshing through me like an unexpected gust of wind. There is only one person I know whose magic has that scent.

"Really?" I ask the ceiling as if the wood beams are going to fess up an explanation for this latest level of hell.

Excitement and dread doing a two-step through my body, leaving me unsure if I want to jump up or throw up, I rise up to a sitting position on my bed and focus my attention on the tiny balcony outside my window. It's only big enough to hold a couple of containers full of hollyhocks, foxgloves, and moonflowers, with a single, slightly straggly lavender bush thrown in for good measure. Standing on the delicate wrought iron balcony is out of the question, but there Gil is, right between the purple foxgloves and the white moonflowers just starting to open. I take a closer look. His edges are just the slightest bit wonky, like an image of a person that's been photoshopped but the background didn't get the same level of attention to detail.

So it's not Gil on my balcony—which is good for him, because my balcony is not builder rated to hold a six-four guy who, according to my recon efforts this evening (fine, my inability not to touch him), has a whole lot of muscle underneath the sexy professor aesthetic he's got going. It's Gil's astral projection, a shadowy almost-real version of him right down to the perma-smirk that annoys me in part because I'm starting to like it.

Ugh.

What is wrong with me?

The only answer to that one being so, so much.

"You ran away," Gil says.

"I did not."

Yeah, you only skipped home at a very fast speed with your metaphorical tail tucked between your legs.

"Really?" His smirk gets smirkier. "I happen to know the eye of newt muffin is your favorite, and Eli made three whole dozen of them."

My stomach growls. I can't blame it. Eli's muffins are absolutely mouthwateringly good. I have no idea what he does when he makes them, because the fates know my version never turns out the same even if I use the same recipe, but his are all-caps DELICIOUS. However, I am not about to give into McSmirky McSmirkerson and his astral projection of broad-shouldered, slightly-mussed-haired, I-bet-if-he-turned-around-great-assed smirkdom.

"The muffins are okay." I grab one of the square throw pillows by my headboard and hold it over my still-growly stomach to muffle the sound of "Gimmie!" it's emitting.

He starts to peel the paper wrapping from around the bakery miracle. "So you don't mind if I eat this in front of you?"

"It's not like you can since you're just body walking." I surreptitiously check to make sure I'm not drooling over the projected muffin or man.

He tears off a piece of the crumbly muffin top and pops it into his mouth, closing his eyes in ecstasy the minute he does. This is torture—the kind I cannot look away from because muffin eating seems to be my kink tonight.

"I got you one as an I'm-an-asshole apology." He motions with his head over to the left. "Look over by the lavender bush."

Yeah, I'm off the bed and across the room to my window in an embarrassingly small amount of time. There it is, right where he said. I snatch the muffin in its plastic sandwich bag from the bush's spindly branches. Do I act all cool and carry it back to my desk and leave it uneaten to make a point? No. No, I do not. I stand there in front of my open window and unzip the sandwich bag, taking a deep inhale of cinnamon, vanilla, and candied newt, and then plucking it out and biting straight into the crumbly muffin top.

"Why does this feel like a bribe?" And gastronomical heaven.

Gil takes a few steps closer. "How about thinking of it as a peace offering instead? I'm sorry for what I said before."

"You didn't mean it?" Ugh. Why do I sound so damn hopeful? He is a jerk! An asshole! The worst witch ever—well, if you don't count me. I mean, at least he can cast a spell. "Then why'd you say it?"

I should be moving farther back into my room, but here I am, a bump on the log of life. It's not like he can physically touch me or throw a curse or charm on me while he's body walking, but it still seems prudent.

I, however, am very imprudent, turned on, and suckered completely by the fact that he brought me an apology muffin. You gotta watch out for the ones who come bearing pastry. Dangerous people.

He finishes his muffin, balls up the paper wrapper that had been around the bottom of it, and tosses it away into what I'm assuming is a trash can at his house. "I can't explain why I said it right now, but I had my reasons and I'll explain them all as soon as I can."

I shouldn't accept such a lame-ass excuse, but there's a ribbon of sincerity winding through his words that I feel all the way down to that bullshit meter that's never done me wrong.

"The whole mysterious thing is highly overrated." But hot, oh so damn hot. He's all broody, annoying, smirky hotness that has obliterated my otherwise impressive vocabulary.

I shouldn't forgive him. I don't forgive him. All the warmth in my belly is from the sweet, sweet carbs.

Uh-huh, sure, Matilda Grace.

Fates help me, I am so screwed in the head—but unfortunately not the body—when it comes to him.

No man should have a jaw that square and covered in what looks like the softest brown beard ever that I want to pet and have scratching against my inner thighs. And his lips? Fates alive, the things I have thought about those lips doing to me while I was in the bath angling the jets to hit just so should have turned the water to steam. Even his nose is hot—and that's something that shouldn't be allowed. Noses? Who in the hell thinks nostrils can be sexy? Apparently me when it comes to Gil Connolly. I can't look at the man without getting worked up, and even now while I'm holding a half-eaten muffin, I'm all horniness and dirty thoughts while he . . . Well, he's glaring at me and a vein in his temple is all bulgy, and his hands are closed into tight little fists at his sides. What the hell? He's the one who showed up—uninvited, mind you—at my house.

"Why are you looking at me like that?"

He all but growls at the question as the brown of his eyes darkens with an intensity that has me second-guessing the astral projection part of him not really being here.

"Like what?"

Look, I'd like to say that extra sandpaper in his tone doesn't make my core do a happy clench, but I'd be lying, and you and I are closer than that.

"Like I'm pissing you off." I step toward him to show I'm annoyed and standing up for myself, and oh-my-fates because I just can't help it, I need to be closer to him. "I'm just eating the muffin that you poofed here and you look like you want to yell at me for it."

"I don't want to yell at you," he snarls.

And there he is, the big jerk I know and lust after like a total fool.

If I could have grabbed his shirt and yanked him closer at that moment I would have. "Then what do you want?"

His gaze drops to my mouth, and it's fucking fire—not literally, thank the fates, but little sparks of want and need and gotta-have dance across my skin, and I drop the muffin. That's right. I drop bakery gold right on my floor because my whole body is buzzing with anticipation that has my belly tight and the rest of me going loose and bendy and desperate to wind myself around him.

"I said,"—I let out a shaky breath—"what do you want?"

His gaze snaps away from me as if he can't stand to look at me anymore. "Too many damn things I can't have."

"You, me, and everyone else," I snap back, my skin cold again now that he's looked away. "That's called life."

"You have no idea what you're talking about," he says.

"Oh, piss off." I take another step forward. We're so close that if it had been Gil instead of his astral projection, I'd be almost plastered against him, which isn't possible because you can't actually *touch* someone who is body walking. "You've been acting like this toward me since you showed up in town."

His attention lands back on me and the air cracks and sizzles around us. "I have my reasons."

"Yeah?" I snap back. "Well, they suck."

Heat and promise and just-fucking-kiss-me-already is whirling around us. It's almost like the coffee shop again, that floating, fizzy, electric feeling that has me looking up at Gil with my lips parted in anticipation. He can't, I can't, we can't, and yet here we are. My heart is hammering against my ribs, my nipples are so hard a cool breeze would have me halfway to orgasmic bliss, and my core aches for attention. He dips his head. I raise up on my tiptoes. Our lips brush and for one improbable second it's real, and then on the next his astral projection pops like a soap bubble, and I'm standing at my window making out with the air.

Like a fool.

Again.

Fuck. Me.

Chapter Thirteen

Tilda . . .

*O*ne night of tossing and turning later and I'm still all betwixt, bothered, and bewildered by last night and why I can't seem to get my horniness under control when it comes to Gil Connolly.

It's not that I don't have a healthy sex life between my vibrator collection and hookups that are great for orgasms but don't work for long-term relationships, but this is something different. This is more, and it's really starting to freak me the fuck out, which means it's time to do what I do best—avoid confrontation. So rather than spending any time doing a deep dive into what is wrong with me now, it's time to go to work.

I grab my phone and my social media planner book, and

head downstairs to the library, where Effie and my mom are bent over looking at an old leather-bound book, the kind with yellowed pages curling up at the corners, that's laid out in the middle of a reading table.

I plant myself by the big bay window with the blue velvet seat built into it and plaster on an encouraging smile. "Who's social media ready?"

Mom shoots me a withering look. The woman would rather be a null like me than willingly participate in one of the family WitchyGram posts. That's why she ends up being featured in candids only and that's how things like the viral pic of her making weird faces mid-spell happen. Not that I'm going to tell my mom that. I like being alive.

Effie looks up from the book. "I'll be your victim, Tillie."

"Excellent." Not the nickname part—I am very much not a Tillie—but the willing victim part. "All I need to do is get some video and still shots of whatever you're doing, and that'll be it."

"Well then"—Mom pats her blond topknot, no doubt making sure that not even a single strand of hair will dare to defy her wishes—"I'll leave you to it."

With a dramatic sweep of her wide, white linen skirt, she strides out of the room before Effie can rope her into participating, which is pretty much the only way Mom ends up on the family WitchyGram account. Effie and I hold it together until Mom is out of the library, then the second my sister waves her hands to close the double doors, we both break out in a giggle fit. We can't help it. Mom's hatred (according to me) or fear (according to Effie) of social media always cracks us up—either way, the result is her avoiding it as much as possible and micromanaging me, the family failure, about what I post.

"The dialect in this book is almost as ridiculous as Mom's reaction to being on the WitchyGram feed," Effie says once we get our breath back.

"What's the book?" I take a peek at the oversized pages complete with intricate drawings of plants and herbs bordering the text.

"Some old book Dad found at Aunt Agatha's house."

This was the usual answer when it came to a new-to-us old spell book that found its way into our library. Aunt Agatha lives up near the arctic circle among the reindeer and a free love commune of craft-obsessed elves. Even traveling by magical map would take a solid week, but thanks to the Sherwood house spell, each Sherwood across the globe is connected through the magical strings binding one far-flung home to the other. Rumor is that this connection is what kept the Sherwoods safe in dangerous times by allowing our familial magic to mix and strengthen each other when needed. Now it's mostly used to cut down on commuting time for family visits.

"Okay, let's use it," I say, taking in how the light coming from the stained glass windows between the floor-to-ceiling bookshelves that line the walls is bathing Effie in a soft pink glow. "You read as if you're spell casting."

She shoots me a disbelieving look. "Without the family cauldron?"

Yes, everyone knows that only the most powerful witches can perform magic without a cauldron, but it isn't like there is anyone out there who still thinks social media is real. "Everyone knows socials are staged."

"Juniper hasn't fully translated it yet." She glanced down at the book, gnawing on her bottom lip. "What if it's a curse?"

That was the boogeyman myth parents told their little witches to make sure they didn't practice magic before they were licensed, that this spell just might be the curse that hurts your family. It was as big a tall tale as the story that Santa is a gift-giving alien instead of a mushroom-smoking nudist with a serious addiction to Oreos.

"Curses, the serious scary kind, aren't any more real than the Council," I say. "Anyway, unless you've become Mom-level powerful overnight, it's not like you have enough juice to cast a serious spell on your own, that's why you guys work the circle for the big magic."

Effie nods in agreement as I climb up on top of the table to start at an angle above my sister. The hesitant expression on her cherubic face disappears as my logic sinks in, and she gives me a jaunty wink before starting to read.

"Maxime qui diligitis," Effie says as I shoot video. "Haud custodiant"—she exhales a breath, cocking her head to the side, obviously working out the archaic pronunciations—"ut ex illis nocere se defendat, et ad gelu et transit usque ad periculum." She looks up at me and mugs for the camera, making a perfectly adorable can-you-believe-this face. "Tempus esse casum vocabis eos et glacies." She starts twisting her curly hair around one finger, a sure sign that she's gone into super concentration mode. "Tempus quis sustin—no. Tempus quis cusstane—no, that's not it either."

I squat down, putting my elbows on my knees to act as a witch tripod as I get Effie in profile. "What kind of Latin is that?"

"That stilted kind. There's no romance, no lush texture, no sweep you up in the magic and whirl you around until you feel like you're flying. There's just . . ." She lets out a huff of breath that sends all of her curls swirling around her head.

Her hair comes to rest at weird angles that look a little like horns. Because I've learned my lesson from *the face incident* with Mom, I reach out to smooth an errant ringlet back into place.

My fingertips brush the shell of Effie's ear as I tuck the curl behind it just as she says, "Tempus quis sustinebit."

There's an audible pop, like a champagne cork. Then, Effie's eyes go wide as she looks at me in shock and confusion. The sharp, citrusy, fresh-lemon-zest smell of Effie's magic mixed in with buttered popcorn fills the air.

"What did you do?" Effie asks.

I don't have time to answer even if I knew what is happening, because a boom of thunder in the library shakes the books off the shelves and knocks the family portraits hanging above the stained glass windows askew.

"Tillie," Effie says, pressing her fingers to her cheeks, "I feel so cold. I'm—"

She doesn't finish the thought—she can't. Ice crystals start to form on her eyelashes. Her lips turn blue. Her already pale skin goes even whiter.

She blinks once, twice, and then on the third time, a thin layer of ice appears over her skin.

Then another.

And another.

And more, one right after the other, faster than I can breathe, faster than my frightened heart can beat, faster than I can even react until finally Effie is frozen in place, encased in a sheet of ice that looks like it was poured over her, catching her mid-question.

Panic and horror grab me by the throat. "Effie!"

I grab the ice surrounding her, trying to break it apart with my bare hands. I scream for help as I attack the ice, beating it, pulling at the corners, tearing at the thin but un-breakable layer of ice covering her from the top of her curly hair to the tips of her hot pink painted toenails. My hands are frigid, my fingertips starting to turn blue and my nails broken, by the time the initial terror recedes enough for me to realize I can't strong-arm my way in to save Effie.

"Mom!" I try to scream, but it comes out as a whimper. "Mom."

I run through the house, doing my best to scream her name. Catching a glimpse of Mom's signature blond topknot, I veer into the kitchen, trip over something in the doorway, and land with a hard thunk on the floor. When I look back to see what in the world knocked me off my feet, my stomach sinks to the earth's core. Barkley is in the middle of the doorway, frozen just like Effie. Even though I know what I'm going to see, I force myself to stand up and look around the room. Mom and Dad are by the cauldron, peeking into its depths, little smiles frozen on both their faces. Bea, Juniper, and Leona are at the table, ice covering them from top to bottom, in the middle of a tarot reading.

"Mom," I beg, still hoping against hope that she can hear me, that this isn't real, that I haven't just done this to my family.

She doesn't answer.

She can't.

No one can.

"What in the hell have I done?"

But there's no one who can answer the question.

Usually we only do magic in the kitchen by the family cauldron as it bubbles and hisses. We each have designated spots, even me, who does nothing to help. I stay over in the corner with Barkley while the rest of my family forms a circle around the cauldron, standing in order of oldest to youngest and holding hands. The power of touch amplifies spells and eases the energy suck of performing magic by dividing it among each member of the circle.

I gasp at the realization and collapse onto the hard stone floor.

All magic is two-sided, and it's only the skill of the circle's members that controls which path it takes—to heal or to harm. I've obviously fucked it all up by being a null and touching Effie in mid-incantation. As a circle of two, I would have had as much control over the spell as my sister—if I'd been magic. As a null, I'd glitched the spell, which really had been a curse—just like I am. So the curse in the book and the curse of being without magic combined and two wrongs made one disaster.

This is my fault and I can't fix it—but I know how to fix it.

I sprint across town to Griselda's house. By the time I'm reaching for her cat door knocker, I can barely breathe and sweat is rolling down my back. The second my fingers touch the cat's tail, the door swings open and the scent nearly overwhelms me. Lemon zest and buttered popcorn.

"Griselda?" I holler as I rush inside, praying to the fates to show a bit of mercy by having my godmother at home.

She is—frozen solid as she hands a shot to a raccoon wearing a bow tie, his tiny little black paw barely touching her hand as he accepts the glass. That smidge of connection must have been enough to freeze him along with Griselda even though he isn't family.

This isn't just bad.

This is the worst thing that could ever happen.

I'm not just a null. I'm the null that froze her entire family, and if I can't find someone to help me reverse the spell, they'll be like that forever.

But the thing is, there's no one left to help, and I can't do a damn thing.

Chapter Fourteen

Gil . . .

Twenty-four hours and no Tilda.

She didn't show up at the Alchemist's Bookshop and Tea Emporium, where she normally spends a few hours on a velvet love seat checking social media and crafting posts. Earlier today, instead of finding her tucked in the corner of the love seat by the window with her glasses having slid nearly down to the tip of her nose and a cup of elderberry tea within easy reach, I found Vance fluffing pillows and grumbling about lazy fucking witches who can't pick up after themselves.

Next, I'd checked Salem's Bakery and Coffee Shoppe, the site of our last date. She wasn't savoring an eye of newt muffin or doubling up on her espresso. In fact, I'd swear the leaves of the dragon's blood tree had perked up when I'd walked in as if it had been hoping she was behind me. However, when the door shut with no Tilda, the tree's leaves dropped back down and its limbs went slack with what I could only assume was dejected disappointment.

It's close to sunset when I turn toward the town square, a desperate worry scratching at the back of my neck.

I am out of options if she isn't at the annual Magical Misfits Bake Sale to Raise Awareness for Nonmagical Beings, or MMBSTRAFNB—whoever was in charge of that name really needs professional help. I will have to make an in-person appearance at the Sherwood compound, which is exactly the kind of thing that would tempt even the nicest asshole on the Council to turn my balls into moldy raisins.

Literally.

The bake sale is set up around the large yellow gazebo. There are a dozen six-foot tables loaded down with magical treats for the nonmagical, figwort pie to protect against the evil eye, blackberry-leaf tarts to conjure up some wealth, saffron bread to boost fertility, and poppyseed cookies to help with insomnia or, if eaten a few dozen at a time, about ten minutes' worth of invisibility. I spot Eli in the middle of the gazebo, which is probably the only place where he can stand inside the structure without hitting his head on the rafters. Next to him, surrounded by a crowd of witches, twelve gnomes elbowing each other for better position, a few leprechauns, and a trio of fairies flitting around her dark curls, is Birdie. Inspecting the crowd inside the gazebo and outside of it, I search for a mop of red hair and listen for Tilda's signature hiccupy laugh but come up empty.

Weaving my way through the crowd lined up to buy Eli's muffins—he has got to have elves in his family tree somewhere, because my mouth is watering already at just the thought of them—I make my way to Tilda's friends.

I cut in front of a pair of gnomes to get ahead of Birdie. "Where is she?"

"Well, hello to you too, handsome," she says, holding up an individually wrapped baked treat. "Wanna muffin? Five bucks for a good cause."

Birdie might seem all flighty and sweet, but there is more than a little ghost pepper I-will-fuck-you-up-son in her eyes. I grab my wallet and pass over a fiver.

"So where is she?" I ask as I unwrap the muffin.

"Oh, that money was only for the muffin. If you want information,"—she picks up a pickle jar with a hole punched into the top and shakes the dollar coins in it—"you gotta donate to the cause."

"I thought you'd been busted for being a pickpocket as a kid, not extortion."

Birdie doesn't look the least bit embarrassed about her former criminal activities. She just shrugs and says, "What can I say, I've expanded my horizons."

This is when I should walk away.

What the hell do I really care about Tilda Sherwood? It isn't my job to watch out for her. My actual employment contract outlines my duties and they include spying on her, not looking out for her. I'm just supposed to be finishing up my report that will convince Cassius and the Council that she's just a null with no access. She means nothing to me.

And yet, here I am putting ten bucks into the stupid pickle jar and doing my best to ignore the that's-what-I-thought look of triumph on Birdie's face.

"I have no idea where she is." She hugs the glass jar tight to her chest as Eli joins us. "Honestly, I was kind of hoping she was with you stuck in a cabin with only one bed because the roads were washed out."

"And he has to chop wood in a Henley," Eli says, rubbing the enormous slab of concrete he called a hand across her upper back in that easy way people do when they are used to comforting each other. "Wait, no, shirtless—while she watches from the window."

"You two read too many romance novels." Or smoke too many dandelion pipes, but I wasn't going to judge about that.

Birdie lifts one shoulder and rolls it back in a dismissive gesture. "Which is why we're happy."

"And also why we refuse to give in to the ridiculous societal expectations of being who Witchingdom wants us to be instead of who we are." Eli raises his fist, knocking his knuckles against the gazebo's rafters and wincing, but covering it by continuing, "Fly the freak flag."

Birdie nods. "Proudly like in a parade."

All of that is a lot to process, and my brain, quite frankly, doesn't know what bit to go with first, so I pivot back to why I'm here in the first place.

"Tilda," I practically shout her name. "Neither of you know where she is?"

"You're serious." Birdie gulps and starts fidgeting with the pickle jar lid. "You don't know where she is either?"

My frustration peaks. Have I been talking in troll? It takes everything I have and my left eyelid is definitely twitching, but I manage to get out an answer without casting a begone annoyance spell on either of them. "No."

Birdie and Eli exchange a look that says a million and a half things in 2.3 seconds.

"We need to find her," Birdie says as Eli hustles over to another person at the table and tells them that they've gotta blast.

"I'm coming with you," my mouth says even as my brain is telling me I've done more than enough for someone who shouldn't—doesn't—mean anything to me.

Yeah, keep saying the words that sure don't seem to mean what you think they do.

Shoving that know-it-all inner asshole of mine into the corner, I get into the back seat of Eli's land yacht of an ancient model car. The door's shut and I'm buckled in before either of them can say anything about it. Eli makes eye contact in his rearview mirror and opens his mouth, but I intensify my snarl. He shrugs and starts the engine. Birdie peppers me with questions that I only half listen to and barely answer on the drive to the Sherwood compound.

The Sherwood house sits on the highest hill in the exclusive Charmstone neighborhood. It's a rich shade of blue that's nearly purple with black shutters and a gray stone path inscribed with runes to eviscerate those who mean to do the inhabitants harm. Like most witches' houses, it's small on the outside, looking as if it has barely enough space for a galley kitchen, a small living room, one bedroom that might have a double bed and a dresser if there's space, and a single bathroom without a tub. In reality, as soon as a person crosses the threshold into a witch's home, it is always the size the owner wants with as many rooms as they want and with the layout they want.

Being magical does have its benefits.

I'd made my appearance in a body walk the other night but had never put a foot across the property line. Standing on the sidewalk on the public side of the black picket fence lining the front yard, I hesitate. Unease creeps up my spine with all the delicacy of a rhinoceros in the middle of a roid rage meltdown doing an Irish step dance routine in six-inch heels.

"Change your mind?" Birdie asks.

"No." Because it isn't like I'm using my brain right now. This is all gut feeling, intuition, and the fuckery that is the spell I cast on myself using my family's magic.

"Then let's go," Eli says, heading toward the house with his unique loping gait. "It's not like Tilda to flip on silent mode."

This is true. Even during our dates, when she was doing her best to glare a hole into my chest right where my heart is, she talked—about the latest social media trends, the fact that her nickname for me is Mr. Tall, Dark, and Dickly (that one made me laugh, which I'd had to cover with a coughing fit), or her absolute unfettered and nearly orgasmic love of eye of newt muffins. Something is wrong. Tilda is in trouble and she needs help, I can feel it all the way down to the second joint in my big toe, the one that flares and itches before a big storm or looming disaster.

I take a last look at the warning etched in Latin onto the first flat gray stone. It translates roughly to "here there be dragons." If it's metaphorical then the entire Witchingdom has misjudged Izzy Sherwood's unspoken promise to bring down the full strength of her power on anyone who fucks with her family.

This is when a normal witch, a smart witch, a witch who hasn't cursed himself with old-school desire magic, would walk away.

Of course that means I stride forward, bracing for an incoming blast of fire shooting upward aimed straight at my nuts.

The possibility of future children doesn't go up in flames before I reach the front porch, and I let out a sigh of relief. Birdie is already clanging the iron dragon door knocker's top and bottom jaws together. We all wait as a melodic roar sounds on the other side of the door.

Then we wait some more.

And some more.

"I don't like this," Eli says.

Birdie whacks the dragon's mouth together again. "That makes two of us."

I would have added "Three of us," but that's when the door opens.

Tilda looks like shit. Her nose is red. Her eyes are puffy. Her skin has a bloodless pallor that immediately has me concerned she's run into vampires. I've never wanted to murder someone more than I want to strip the skin off of whoever or whatever made her feel as bad as she obviously does.

"Who?" The single word comes out as a snarl.

"Who what?" she sniffles.

My hands are curled into fists and I'm already prepping to snap, crackle, pop my way into the home of whoever is about to have the worst day of their life. "Who did whatever is wrong?"

She lets out a wail and drops her face into her hands. "Me. I did it. I froze my entire family—even Griselda and Barkley."

Clamping down on the six hundred and forty-one questions that pop immediately to mind, I give Birdie and Eli a strong shove into the house as I look around to make sure no one is within earshot. I don't spot anyone, but that doesn't mean anything.

The trees have ears in the Witchingdom.

Literally.

They'd know immediately that they didn't just have a juicy bit of gossip to sell to the highest bidder. No. This isn't idle talk or rumors. This is information that will change everything.

Nature abhors a power vacuum and witches love to fill them.

If the Sherwoods were displaced from their place in Witchingdom's hierarchy, another faction run by a powerful family—or, more likely, the Council—would fill it, and then anyone who didn't subscribe to their very narrow version of what is acceptable would end up in The Beyond or worse, and those who were already in exile would never get out. A memory comes to mind of my parents in the magicless void trying to heat a drafty cabin on the tundra and forage for whatever creature they could trap with their bare hands. Icy panic squeezes my chest. Griselda told me that they were out of exile, hidden in a safe house, but I know better than to trust anyone. She could have lied. Or she could have been telling the truth and I'll never find out the safe house's location if she stays frozen.

Whatever has happened, whatever spell Tilda tapped into and juiced up to freeze her family, we have to fix it before anyone finds out what happened.

If we are lucky, we'll have a week. Realistically, we have two days. Tops.

I shut the door behind me, wave the locks closed, and then turn to Tilda, who is crumpled on the couch, a silver pillow clutched against her chest like a shield—as if that would help against the impending doom we are up against.

"Tell me everything."

Chapter Fifteen

Tilda . . .

$\mathcal{S}$o, I've spent the past day reaching out to anyone with even a smidge of Sherwood DNA. Everyone—every single one of them—is frozen."

By the time I'm done explaining to everyone how my being a null glitched Effie's spell so badly, I'm out of breath, out of tears, and out of Kleenex. Birdie is next to me on the couch, holding my hand and murmuring soft words of encouragement as she sneezes her way through a spell to conjure a new pack of tissues, which I gladly accept. Eli is sitting on the coffee table in front of me, his hulking frame making even the magically constructed piece of furniture groan under his weight. His eyes are damp with unshed tears; the man may look like the runt of a litter of giants, but he's as soft and squishy inside as a warm gummy bear in August. Meanwhile, Gil is a little cloud of doom leaning against the door frame with his arms crossed and a scowl on his face.

Birdie lets out a gasp of understanding. "The connector spell in your house that acts as a magical link to everyone in your family."

"Exactly," I say with a nod.

"So where's the book?" Gil asks as he looks around the living room.

My eyes get all watery again and my chin trembles. "Frozen in Effie's hands."

"So we unfreeze her." Eli bounds up from the coffee table, rubbing his hands together. "We can use a ventus calidus spell."

"Plus a little portum tutum sprinkled on top." Birdie gets up and yanks me from the couch. "Come on, time's a-wasting."

We rush into the library—well, Eli, Birdie, and I sprint out of the living room, down the hall, and into the room where it all happened; Gil (I still have no idea why he's here) moseys in behind us when Eli is in his third attempt to get the warm winds and a dash of safe harbor spell right. Gut churning and my lip starting to ache where I'm nervously chewing on it, I'm in the corner with my hands shoved in my jeans pockets because the last thing in the world I want is to accidentally touch anyone in mid-spell.

"Ventus kalidose porti talun," Eli says with a wave of his hands, his nose crinkling up, no doubt because he realizes the words have gotten jumbled in his head.

Not surprisingly, nothing happens.

He shoves his big fingers through his shaggy hair and lets out a sigh that ends with his shoulders drooping. "Maybe if I wrote it down and read it. I know that lessens spell potency, but—"

"Here, let me," Birdie says as she clasps her hands together in front of her belly like an opera singer about to go into a power aria. "Ventus"—her nose twitches—"calidu-uh-uh—" The sneeze explodes out of her like a projectile, then another and another. She holds up a hand. "I can do this." She sneezes again. "Just give me a minute."

"Ventus calidus, portum tutum." Gil's voice booms in the room.

For half a heartbeat there's nothing, and then all I can smell is the ocean as a steamy breeze stirs the tips of my hair. It builds in strength and heat until my hair is flying around my head like the papers on the desk are around Effie, whirling and turning and dancing on that hot, humid, salty air.

At the same time, something, somehow is tugging me, pulling at my shirt, coaxing me to take a step and another and another until I'm pressed against Gil, molded to him. His hand comes down, curling around my waist, holding me close. An electric sizzle fills the air and suddenly the soft island wind in the middle of our family library becomes a hurricane. Lightning flashes. Thunder crashes. Books go flying off the shelves and slam into the furniture.

It isn't just warm anymore. It's so humid it's hard to breathe. The heat blazes like an invisible fire and I'm immediately drenched in sweat and gasping for relief. Another hot gust blasts through the room, and the three-foot-high framed oil painting of Azmerelda Sherwood goes sailing through the air. I barely have time to register that it's coming straight for me when Gil shoves me away from him and I tumble to the floor under the large oak desk.

"Consummavi," Gil roars against the deadly wind whipping through the room.

And just like that, the gale and overwhelming heat are gone, leaving only the smell of buttery popcorn and salt behind.

Eli, Birdie, and I look as bad as we each obviously feel. Gil seems to be his usual snarly self with the addition of humidity-caused curls in his brown hair. Effie, however, is as frozen as she ever was, standing behind the desk, the book in her hands, and her eyes wide with fear. There isn't even a drop of melted ice around her toes.

It's all I can do not to fall onto the floor—again—and cry—again—knowing that I've really fucked things up—again.

"What was that?" Birdie asks as she tries to finger comb the rat's nest of knots her hair has turned into thanks to whatever the fuck that was.

Gil cuts an are-you-going-to-tell-them glance at me as if I've got a fucking clue.

When he realizes I've got nothing, he lets out a string of not-even-a-little-bit-muffled swear words that would have made Griselda blush, then he looks at the rest of us and lets out a resigned sigh. "We're gonna need a bigger spell."

"Scintillam ignis?" Birdie asks.

Gil shakes his head.

"Ignis tempestas?"

He waves off the ideas of a spark spell or a firestorm. "We need a novis spell."

Eli, Birdie, and I break out in giggles. Is that appropriate at a time like this? Absolutely not, but when you've broken your entire world so completely that there aren't even any pieces left to pick up, your brain gets a little goofy. All that fear and panic and dread have to go somewhere, and instead of uncontrollable weeping this time, it's a giggle fit that has me snorting like a goose by the end. The whole idea of a novis spell, when no one has been able to find a spell that actually does what it promises, is just that fucking funny.

There have been about a dozen documented instances of witches trying to cast novis spells, but what actually happens is disaster. People end up with extra ears or dogs start talking or suddenly there's an eclipse or a natural disaster. They really are all talk and no magic—at least not the successful kind.

"Yeah," I manage to get out between chuckles, "and if reverse magic actually worked, then that would be a plausible solution."

Gil glares again but with more annoyance. Who knew the man had any left in the tank?

"It does work, and there is a spell to reverse a curse," he all but growls. "The Liber Umbrarum has a novis spell."

Birdie, Eli, and I are rolling on the ground now. I'm laughing so hard my sides ache. I can't catch my breath. I've got tears streaming down my face and they're actually not from being a mix of sad and mad at the same time. Oh. My. Fates. Who knew that Mr. Tall, Dark, and Dickly had it in him to be so funny.

Gil, however, isn't laughing. He's not even smirking.

The man is serious.

My sister Juniper is the family expert on rare and under-utilized magic. She's always sworn there is more out there than we realize. Spells and monsters and fabulous adventures just waiting to be had. Of course, she also cheats at Scrabble and organizes her lipsticks according to name instead of shade, so one does have to take her words with a smidge of doubt.

But if she is right, then there is a way out of this.

For the first time since I touched Effie, I have the smallest ember of hope glowing. "And you just happen to have a copy of the unbelievably rare Book of Shadows in your back pocket?"

Gil shakes his head. "But I know where one is, and we just have to go get it."

"We?" My brain does that whole jolting-to-a-stop thing.

We? I check his pupils for dilation and his nose for pink splotches, the telltale signs of someone who's hit the dandelion pipe hard. I glance over at Eli and Birdie, who are wearing matching skeptical expressions.

He lifts his chin and looks down his prominent nose at us. "You can't do this without me."

I open my mouth to argue and then reality rears its pain-in-the-ass head.

Ugh.

I hate that he's right, but he is. I'm a null, Birdie's allergic to her own magic, and Eli gets his spell-casting wires crossed somewhere between his brain and his mouth. But Gil? I can feel the magic practically vibrating around him. The air shimmers when he moves, and I can't help but hold my breath in anticipation of something different, new, unlike the magic of anyone else I know. I have no clue what kind of inherited power runs through his family, but it's gotta be extraordinary considering the fact that even as an outré I can feel it.

Still, I can't drag my friends into my mess.

Turning to face the two people who were my first magical misfit friends, I take their hands in mine. "I can't ask any of you to do this, to take these risks." Because there were always risks when dealing with a spell book like the Book of Shadows. "I can't—"

"Shut up," Birdie interrupts, pulling me in for a hug. "We're in."

"Exactly," Eli says as he curls his arms around both of us. "We magical misfits gotta stick together."

Fuck.

And now I'm crying again, only this time because I realize I'm not alone in this. In a world where so many witches seem to relish the chance to tell me how apart from everyone else I am, how isolated my being an outré makes me, I know they're full of shit. Eli and Birdie prove that.

"Thanks, you guys," I say, my words muffled because Eli doesn't realize his own strength and has me tucked so close against him that my nose is too squashed to take in oxygen.

"You want in on the group hug?" Eli asks over my head.

I can picture Gil's mortified expression without even having to try.

"Absolutely not," he says, because of course he does.

It's like the man comes from a place where witches don't bond by the power of touch—a reminder that even though he came with Eli and Birdie that Gil is most definitely not a magical misfit. That brings me back to the first thought I had when I opened my front door earlier and found him on my porch. "Why are you even here?"

The expression on his face goes from summer thunderstorm to tsunami at sea. "I have my reasons, but they aren't important—getting ahold of that book is though."

I look over at my sister and my stomach twists itself into a triple knot.

Whatever it takes, I'm going to fix this, Effie. I promise.

"So where do we have to go to get it?" I ask.

"The Svensen family is dedicating a new wing of the Marie Laveau Museum at a gala and exhibiting several priceless items from their private collection, one of which is The Liber Umbrarum. The gala is in two days and will take place under the tightest security imaginable."

"So we're gonna ask the Svensens—the Sherwoods' biggest rival in all of Witchingdom—if we can just borrow their old, rare, and priceless spell book to unfreeze my entire family?"

Yeah, that seemed about as likely to happen as me being one of the most powerful witches to have ever witched.

"No," Gil says with a predatory grin that says Mr. By-the-Book-Know-It-All actually likes breaking a few rules and sends shivers through my whole body. "We're gonna steal it from them."

Chapter Sixteen

Gil . . .

*E*veryone is staring at me. Not in the oh-that's-an-interesting-idea way, but in the how-many-times-did-he-hit-his-head way. Okay, Tilda might have a dash of didn't-think-you-had-it-in-you too, but I shouldn't focus on that. We have a plan to develop, a book to steal, and the entirety of Witchingdom to save.

Not an exaggeration.

But where the ideas should be in my head, there is Tilda.

Tilda, who froze her entire family without even realizing how she'd done it.

Tilda, who is herding us all into the kitchen because that's where the most important witch business takes place.

Tilda, who is now standing still as a statue in front of her frozen mom, her eyes going all watery, and the upturned tip of her nose turning red.

I'm heading across the stone floor to her before I realize it—to do what, I have no fucking idea—when Birdie whips an oversized purple dish towel off the oven handle and drapes it over Izzy Sherwood's head.

I jolt to a stop halfway across the room and involuntarily brace for the magical matriarch's wrath to come crashing down on us—and I'm not the only one.

Tilda's eyes have gone round and she has a hand pressed to her open mouth. Eli takes a protective step in front of Birdie, who is sucking in great gasps of breath as if she can't believe she did that.

"Well," she says, nervously winding a large clump of curly hair around a finger as she peeks around Eli at the now-covered head of the most feared woman in town, "if we can't see her, then we can't be scared of her, right?"

If only Birdie knew how many invisible things are out there that can hurt her. Plots, plans, schemes, and spells woven and built in kitchens like this but belonging to the Council. Once you know how to spot the telltale signs of their shadowy interference, you start to see them everywhere: the barely-there scent of charcoal and honey left wafting in the air after a secret spell, or the people left behind who have only a soft-focus memory of what happened, almost like a dream that feels so real when they first wake up but they can barely remember ten minutes later.

Tilda takes a step back from her mom. "Is that like when a dog sticks its head under the bed and acts as if the rest of the world doesn't exist anymore?"

"Pretty much," Eli says, still mostly blocking Birdie from Izzy Sherwood's direct line of sight—if she didn't have a dish towel over her head.

Tilda chews her bottom lip and rubs her palms up and down her arms. She's doing that cute thing where she squishes up her nose and cocks her head to the side as if she's trying to get a look at an intangible idea from all angles. She did it at the beginning of our second date, when she was trying to work out if I was supposed to be there or if she really did just have the shittiest luck. Her gaze skitters over to me and whatever she sees on my face has her cheeks turning pink.

She turns back toward her ice-encased mom. "Sorry, but we're gonna go with it," Tilda says, her voice barely louder than a whisper. "I promise, no social media pics, Mom."

I swear Mama Sherwood's fingers twitch just the tiniest bit at that.

It sets my Council alert siren off too. I know my place is dirty with the Council's bewitched listening devices disguised as candlesticks or mantle clocks or other household items. It would make sense that they'd do the same thing with the Sherwood house if they could. The house is thick with protective runes, but those lost potency when Izzy Sherwood stopped being able to act as a power generator. To put it simply, all of the runes are running on emergency power reserves and those will tap out within the next forty-eight hours. We don't have time to waste.

"We need to form a circle," I say, walking toward the cauldron hanging in the large, brick, cooking fireplace that fits between the stainless steel Sub-Zero fridge and the restaurant-quality commercial stove.

Tilda blinks back some tears pooling on the edges of her eyelids as she turns her back on her mom and levels a hard look my way. "Why?"

"We need a protective dome," I say, each word coming out cramped and terse.

Did I use my no-shit-Sherlock tone? Yeah. Did it replace the fuck-my-mom's-frozen look on Tilda's face with a rush of annoyed fire that has her straightening her spine and looking like she's thinking about whacking me upside the head with the cast-iron skillet on the stove? Pretty much.

Gotta love it when a plan comes together.

She plants her hands on her hips and glares at me. "Aren't you being a little paranoid?"

I don't mean to snort in disbelief, but it just comes out. Is this woman for real? "Does your family have enemies?"

Her gaze flicks to the ground before she brings it back to me, her defiance wavering. "A few."

I raise an eyebrow.

"Fine." She sighs. "There are people on the Committee who would love to see Mom kicked off."

"And if they found out she was frozen?"

Tilda's jaw is tight and she looks like she can't decide if she wants to defrost the frozen rooster to come peck my eyes out or stubbornly refuse to admit I'm right, but in the end, she lets out a huff of ugh-do-I-really-have-to-agree-with-this-asshole and says, "They'd definitely use that to their advantage."

I shrug. There's really only one logical solution here. "So a dome."

Eli and Birdie hold hands and reach out their free hands toward me. Physical touch isn't just an extra for witches working strong magic, it's a must. Tilda, however, keeps her hands at her sides and her shoulders drop. The urge to reach out, tangle my fingers with hers, pull her tight against me, and feel her relax against my side is nearly overwhelming—but I can't. What happened in the library is proof that the power she has is so untrained and so deep that she can't guide it. Not yet.

I take Birdie's and Eli's hands as Tilda wraps her arms around her middle and stares down at the stone floor. Around the three of us, the air starts to scent as our magic perks up. My salt mixes with the fragrance of honey and warm cinnamon sugar as the spell begins to vibrate through me—a hint, then an idea, then a thought, then the words to form the incantation.

"Protegat nos in praesidium."

A line of bright white magic comes down from the wood beams in the ceiling, reaching outward and encompassing the width of the entire house before lowering in a protective shell over it that lands with a soft thud.

"Okay, what now?" Birdie asks me as she takes a step

closer to Eli, the curls at the top of her head not even reaching the man's chin.

"Now we figure out how to avoid detection from a squad of half-rabid guard gargoyles, disarm a security system designed by the queen's coven leader, and disappear with a book the size of a Monopoly board all while the elite of Witchingdom watch each other for any hint of something worth gossiping about."

The corners of Tilda's lips curl up into a grin. "Oh, so just a little light thievery?"

"Exactly," I say, matching her is-that-all expression. "You'll be our ticket in since you know the family."

Her blue eyes widen behind her big round glasses. "They hate us."

"True, but they'll love being able to rub the Sherwood noses in the fact that they own a piece of greatness your mom can never get her hands on." It is the way of Witchingdom—every witch for themselves, always trying to one-up each other, and loyalty to none.

"Buuuuuuuuut," Birdie says, dragging out the word as she looks around at what is admittedly a pretty ragtag group, "our magical skills are a little lacking."

Eli scoffs. "That's putting it mildly."

She jabs him in the side with a sharp elbow. "I'm trying not to be an asshole here, Eli."

"I know I'm a null, Birdie." Tilda offers up a self-deprecating chuckle that makes me wonder how often she does that. "It's okay to say I won't be any help."

I crack my knuckles, already seeing an operational plan come together in my head. "That's where you couldn't be more wrong."

Tilda doesn't say anything. She just snorts in disbelief.

"Well, since no one will be able to access their magic while in the museum," I remind everyone, going into snooty-professor mode, "the fact that all three of you know how to function without it will be our greatest advantage."

Tilda lets out a gasp. "So you're saying being an outré will be good for once?"

"What I'm saying is that each of you have a unique set of skills that will be needed to pull off this heist, and the first thing that needs to happen is you need to get us invites to that exhibit."

I keep my mouth shut about the other four hundred and sixty-eight things we have to make happen to pull this heist off. The most difficult of which is to get a pain-in-the-ass unicorn to join in—unless, of course, I count the fact that I can't stop thinking about Tilda in ways that have absolutely nothing to do with this mission. But I am not counting that. And neither should you.

Agree?

Good.

Chapter Seventeen

Tilda . . .

*G*il keeps watching me—not like in a creepy way, but in an I-really-want-to-know-what-you're-thinking way. I wanna say that I don't like it, but you and I both know that would be a lie. Usually most people do everything they can to avoid making direct eye contact, let alone actually wonder what might be happening in my head because, really, what can an outré add to the conversation?

Nope.

Stop.

I am not going to sink into the stew of all that negativity right now. I can't when I'm about to make a call that could save my family or at least get the ball rolling on making that happen. Oh toad warts, there is no way this is going to go well.

The Svensens and the Sherwoods have been enemies since both of our families made it to these shores—us in Virginia and the Svensens in Massachusetts, specifically Salem. Since the 1600s, it has been nothing but distrust, disgruntlement, and dislike between what are really the two most powerful families in the Witchingdom. In other words, barely concealed loathing and feuding. Those who were on these shores before our families were the smart ones; they'd taken one look at us arriving on our ships, negotiated a land sale in their favor for a narrow strip along the East Coast, and lived in prosperity and peace spread out across the rest of the continent without having to deal on the daily with any of our bullshit.

Now here I am almost five hundred years later going through my mom's contact lists to find a phone number for Erik Svensen, my best hope at getting four tickets to the exhibition. Family rumor has it that he and Leona had a thing back when they were both at university, but my sister won't even hint at what it was. Hate fucking? Star-crossed lovers? Unrequited romance full of hot glances and secret kisses in the library stacks? Leona won't say, but whatever it was, she still blushes every time his name gets mentioned. It doesn't take a level twenty witch to know she still has a thing for him.

Gil stops in the doorway of my mom's office off the kitchen, and my pulse kicks into gear like a jackrabbit being chased by a werelion. It's not just that he practically fills up the whole doorway with his broad shoulders, or the way my fingers itch to brush back the lock of dark hair that hangs down in front of his forehead, or even the way his thick muscular thighs look in his not-a-lie ironed jeans (really, do you know how hard it is to look hot in ironed jeans????) that has me ready to fan myself. I know lust, she and I are very good friends. This isn't just wanting to yank someone into the nearest closet and go to town though. There's more to this. It's like a dark red velvet ribbon that winds around us, and if I pull, it's going to unravel and I'm not sure what will be left of me.

Overdramatic?

Me?

My whole family is frozen because of my fuckery, I think I'm allowed to have a bit of a breakdown here—and that's what this is, not some superpowered attraction to the guy my sister is destined to marry.

"Find it?" Gil asks.

I pluck the card labeled Svensen from my mom's ancient Rolodex. "Yeah."

When I don't move—because I am having thoughts, people, bad thoughts that you do not need to know about because I do not need witnesses to the lewd depravity in my head all centered around the absolutely worst man ever, who keeps starring in my own personal never-ending fantasies—Gil steps into the room and crosses over to Mom's massive oak desk. He looks me up and down, not in a judgy or a creepy way, but as if he just needs to reassure himself that I'm okay.

That shouldn't make me feel just a smidge better.

It does anyway.

Fuck me, I am so screwed.

"Are you gonna call?" he asks when he stops on the opposite side of the desk.

I just stare at the three-by-five card with Mom's distinctive swirly handwriting, because looking at him is not an option with all these thoughts in my head wondering how dexterous he is with his fingers. "Yeah."

He picks up the cell phone off Mom's desk and holds it out. "That usually means tapping the screen."

"I do know how to use a phone," I grumble as I take the phone, moving very carefully so as not to touch his fingers.

"Which works in our favor."

He punctuates the declaration with a smile that has just enough let's-take-the-bastards-down in it to make my heart skitter from one side of my chest to the other. Fine. It doesn't literally do that, but whatever is going on with me whenever I'm around him sure makes it feel like it could, the undisputed facts of witch anatomy be damned. And does that make me bat my eyelashes and do some sexy pout thing?

Hello. Have we met?

Of course not!

"Why's that?" I ask, clutching the phone tight as I adjust my posture to make sure the giant-ass chip on my shoulder is still there where it belongs. "Because they'll automatically assume I'm a loser?"

Don't give me that look. We all have unhealthy defense

mechanisms. What are you going to do, come for my raw cookie dough habit next?

"No." He rounds the desk, coming to a stop next to me, close enough that every nerve in my body tunes into him like he's the one available radio station on an entire spectrum of static. "Because they'll underestimate you, just like everyone else does. Let them. They'll never see you coming."

The chip doesn't just fall off. It evaporates—poof—like magic.

See? That's what I'm talking about. How dare he say that and then how dare my body react like I just might be able to take off and fly up to Massachusetts?

That way lies disappointment, Tilda. Don't forget it.

Grimacing, I dial the number, my finger striking the screen harder than necessary, but it is better than jabbing it into his really defined bicep. The guy is a researcher, a nerd, an academic. What in the world is he doing with a thirst-trap body? It isn't fair. Also not right? His forearms. I don't mean to look, but my eyes have to focus on something while the phone rings and rings in my ear. So here I am trying not to drool over Gil's arm-porn forearms, visible because he's rolled up the long sleeves of his button-up, and all I can think about is how his corded muscles would flex as he worked his fingers in me—and that is not what I am supposed to be even kinda sorta maybe thinking about.

That's it. I am definitely having some sort of break.

"Hello?" A man on the other end of the phone answers. "Hello?" he says again when I don't respond because my brain is trying desperately to stop my mouth from saying anything stupid to Gil. "Heeeeelllllllooooooo, is anyone there? Bobby, is this you? You know you're a little shithead. I had to fight off the goats to answer this damn thing."

"Um . . ." *Come on, Tilda. Engage!* "I was looking for Erik Svensen?"

"Fuck me." The man on the other end lets out a deep groan. "You're not Bobby."

"I don't even know who Bobby is." Really what I know about the entire Svensen family could fit on the back of this Rolodex card. Long-standing rivals of the Sherwoods. Rich as all get-out. Stuck-up. Deadly good-looking right down to the herd of goats they keep as familiars. Don't ask me how goats could be considered handsome, I don't know, I'm only reporting what I've heard.

"Bobby is the neighborhood unicorn," the man says.

And that makes total sense. "We have one of those."

"Total prick most of the time?"

"I wouldn't quite put it that way," I say, even though everyone else in town would describe Vance as exactly that—including the unicorn himself. "But he can be really grumpy."

"Okay, so now that I know you're not Bobby, who is this and how did you get this number?"

"It's in my family's contact list." I really should have planned out what I was going to say instead of getting distracted by Gil. "I'm Tilda Sherwood."

He lets out a low whistle. "That's not what I was expecting."

"Are you Erik?"

"Nah, I'm Cyfrin Svensen—but everyone calls me Cy," he says, managing to make it sound like absolutely no one calls him that but he *really* wishes they would.

"Okay, Cy." Flatter, who me? Hey, when you don't have magic to fall back on, you learn to adjust. "I'm calling for a favor."

"What's that?"

Deep breath in, deep breath out. "I need four tickets to the exhibition this weekend."

"Yeah right." Cy lets out a cackle of a laugh. "Good luck with that."

Next to me, Gil lets out a series of low, mumbled curses of the fuck-me variety rather than the turn-him-into-a-toad kind.

"It's only a couple of tickets," I say, trying not to let my desperation seep into my voice. "Please."

Something in my tone must give him pause because he lets out a harsh groan. "I'll see what I can do, but it's probably a no."

"I appreciate any help." My shoulders go down a smidge with relief that it wasn't a straight up no. "I'll owe you one."

"Yeah?" Cy asks. "Can you get your hands on any juniper berries? There's been some kind of run on them up here."

Gil flinches next to me, then his whole body goes stiff.

That's weird. Juniper berries are low-level protection spell ingredients. Usually they're so easy to find, grocers give them away for free in thank-you goodie bags. "I'll look around and bring what I can find."

"You bring the berries and I can guarantee the tickets, no questions asked."

A shiver of unease zips up my spine, then I look over at Gil and he looks like he just ate a bowl full of glass. Whatever is going on up there, it can't be good, and now we're heading straight for even more trouble.

Because a frozen family isn't enough.

Nor is having all kinds of dirty thoughts about the guy you can't stand who is destined for your sister.

That's it. Wherever the unsubscribe button is for all of this BS, I need to find it.

"Berries for tickets. You got it," I say, sounding a lot more confident than I feel. "See you then."

Cy hangs up without a goodbye. Gil shifts and his arm brushes mine, sending a sizzling spark of oh-yes-we-like straight to my clit.

Fuck. Me.

Yep. Definitely need to unsubscribe. Like yesterday.

Lucky for me, Birdie and Eli pick that moment to stroll in bearing honey cookies and mini fruit tarts. Sugar is exactly what I need. We are all munching away, sitting on the throw pillows on the floor by the ginormous bay window looking out on the massive herb garden on the south side of the house, when Birdie pulls her knees up to her chest and lets out a shaky sigh.

"I'm not sure we can carry this off," she says, looking a little lost as her gaze bounces from one of us to another. "What if we mess it all up?"

I take one of the pillows and hug it close to my belly as if the square of fluff-filled velvet can protect me from my own mistakes. "You mean what if we go all magical misfit on this like I already did?"

"It wasn't your fault," Eli says, but he doesn't look at me.

I doubt he can after saying a whopper that big.

"We all know that's not true." I squeeze the pillow tighter to smother the panic starting to wind up into a tornado in my stomach. "I'm scared of messing things up. Again."

Gil looks over at me from his spot by the unlit fireplace, his hard gaze sending a shiver dancing across my skin as if someone just opened up the front door during the middle of a snowstorm. He doesn't blink or break eye contact, and it takes every little bit of confidence I have left to not glance away as his gaze intensifies.

"I have a plan," he says, his tone so sure it borders on cocky.

"You sound very sure."

"That's because there are no alternative outcomes." He picks up a bundle of sage off the mantle, bringing it to his nose, and taking a deep inhale before putting it back. "There's more at stake than just your family. All of Witchingdom is at risk."

"From me?" Ouch. Like I'm not already feeling shitty enough as it is.

He shakes his head. "From the Council."

A near-hysterical laugh escapes before I can stop it and keeps going until my stomach hurts and I'm wiping away tears from my cheeks. Look, it's been a rough few days and I'm more than a little slaphappy at this point, and the mention of Witchingdom's boogeyman pretty much sends me over the edge.

"Gil," I say once I can suck in a breath and get the giggle fit under control, "I am not in the mood for scary kids' stories right now."

"This is no story." He crosses his arms over his wide chest, and something about the way his stance changes is reflected in the haunted look that turns his eyes dark and hazy as if he's seeing a nightmare he knows isn't a dream. "The Council is real and your mother is one of their most powerful foes. If they find out she's out of commission, they'll see it as an opportunity to take over that they can't pass up."

"Fine, I'll play along," I say, trying to make my tone light even though a frigid blast of dread has me rubbing the outsides of my arms to ward off a sudden, intense chill. "Let's say the Council is 'real,'"—I put the word in air quotes—"how do you know their plans?"

Life snaps back into his eyes as his gaze lands on me, and his body stiffens as if he's expecting a blow. "Because I work for them."

Just when I thought it couldn't get worse.

Chapter Eighteen

Gil . . .

$\mathcal{N}$othing like a real wand-drop kinda moment to make the entire room go quiet. Of course, that isn't going to last.

"What the fuck, Gil!" Eli says, breaking the silence as he takes a step forward, doing his best to look intimidating, but I've faced down much scarier people on a daily basis for more than a decade.

Birdie sinks back against Eli and sighs. "We are so screwed."

Tilda, though, doesn't flinch or shrink back or get angry. Instead, she cocks her head, pushes her round glasses up her nose, and gives me a slow, assessing once-over. "Who *are* you?"

"Exactly who I said." Sorta.

She lifts an eyebrow and shakes her head. "But that's not the whole story."

Of course she would see that. Like me, she's had to live off her wits. "Not even close, but it's a long story and we don't have time for this."

Tilda reaches out, her hand brushing against my arm, setting off warm waves of awareness through me. It is more than desire, more than attraction, it is like finally walking through your front door after a long day, or that first deep inhale of your favorite meal when you're starving, or the first taste of mulled wine when the sun begins to set on Samhain. The tension in my shoulders loosens, I let out a deep breath, and my entire body just sort of unwinds.

"Make time," she says.

There is no saying no to her. Sure, Eli and Birdie are just as curious, but I'm not about to open up for them. This is all for Tilda. Fuck me. I have to figure out a way to dial back the duíl curse I put on both of us or it won't be long until I forget completely that I want our magical bond broken.

"My family has been in Saint Augustine since it was founded in the 1500s—and my mother's side was there even earlier than that—and for that entire time we've been hiding our core magic. We are duíl."

Birdie lets out a gasp and presses her hand to her heart, and out of the corner of my eye I watch Eli put an arm around her waist and tuck her against him. My focus, though, stays on Tilda, watching for any sign of fear or censure, bracing myself for either or both or worse. Instead, all I see is curiosity.

"That's rare magic," she says.

"And hunted." That's why we moved so often growing up. We never lived in the same town for more than a year or two and never in a city where we were likely to attract the attention of the Council. Of course, we were on borrowed time and we all knew it. "When I was fifteen, the Council came for us in the middle of the night. We spent a month going through tribunal judgment before being exiled. I got sent to a boarding school that was more of a reeducation center." Cold. Clinical. Controlling. It hadn't taken me long to learn that no one could be trusted, not when spilling secrets meant getting a rare lukewarm shower or an extra helping at lunch. "My parents spent those years learning how to survive on the tundra in The Beyond. By the time we were reunited, they were living off the occasional wild hare, turnips, and undersized potatoes, with just enough food donation boxes dropped by drones to keep them from dying but not thriving." The point had never been to kill us, only to break us and make us pliant to their demands. "And when the Council came to me with an opportunity to move my family from the tundra to the warmer coastal district, I did what needed to be done."

"For your family," Tilda says, understanding softening her gaze. When I nod, she asks, "Where are they now?"

I clamp down on my emotions, shove my fears into a box

in my mind just like I'd learned in The Beyond, but they leak out anyway and my voice shakes as I answer. "I don't know."

Tilda makes a sympathetic groan and wraps her arms around me, her cheek resting against my chest above my heart. Everything stops for a moment, and the salty scent of my magic mixes with the buttery smell of warm movie theater popcorn and fills the air around us. She looks up at me, a divot of confusion between her eyes as if she's not sure why she's comforting me. This is the exact moment when I should tell her everything and explain how I cursed us both without meaning to and that I'll fix it as soon as we unfreeze her family and find my parents.

But that's when she squeezes me a little tighter in a hug, and it's like standing by the fire after walking in from the cold and finding a hearty rabbit stew simmering in the cook pot hanging above the flames—as if even only for an evening, everything is going to be okay.

"The Council has them?" she asks.

"I don't think so," I say. "Griselda said the Resistance got them out, but I don't have any more than that."

"And now she's frozen." Tilda swallows hard and steps back. "I'm so sorry."

"We're gonna fix it." There isn't another choice. "And this is how."

Making sure there's at least three inches between Tilda and myself, I summon up my magic.

"Ostende," I say as I wave my hand at the fireplace. The kindling sparks and catches fire, revealing a copy of a museum in the flames. Tiny Degases line the walls, along with a wall-sized oil painting of Washington crossing the Delaware on his Continental Army–issued broom made from birch twigs and a hazelwood handle emblazoned with the army's seal. In the middle of the room, set in a glass case high above the average height of a witch is The Liber Umbrarum.

"There it is," I say, using the iron fireplace poker to point at the book. "That glass was enchanted to be unbreakable prior to its installation at the museum. It's seven and a half feet off the ground and accessible to one person at a time for viewing via a narrow, enclosed staircase that locks at the top and bottom so that whoever is viewing the book has to be let in and out by a guard who unlocks the door with an optic scan. There will be more than one hundred úlfheðnar guards placed strategically through the museum and on the grounds. Oh yeah, and there will be a protection dome so no one can summon any spells."

Eli strides over to the flames and swipes his hand through them, scattering the magical blueprints before turning to stare at me, disbelief etched into his face. "Stealing The Liber Umbrarum is impossible."

"True," I say, sending a know-it-all smirk the big witch's way just to make him glare all the harder. "But only if you don't have a witch with giant relatives in the family tree so he stands over seven feet high with a three-foot reach." I turn to Birdie, who has a police file on her an inch thick, which Cassius slipped to me as part of the background report for my mission. "Or a witch who spent ten years as a pickpocket before becoming an accountant." Turning from Birdie's shocked expression, I look at Tilda and force myself to shove my hands in my pants pockets so I won't reach out to touch her. "Or one of the most distracting women in all of Witchingdom."

She scoffs and rolls her eyes. "Is that your way of saying that everyone stares to see what I'll mess up next?"

"Yes," I say, because what's the point in fluffing it up? "And we're going to use that to save your family."

"Both of our families." She slips her hand into mine, looking at our joined hands as if she can't quite believe she did that either.

"Exactly," I say through gritted teeth, because that's all that's keeping me from completely coming clean and spilling my secret that I cursed her into wanting me.

While telling her the truth seems like the most urgent thing in the world, I know I can't. This isn't the kind of world where people trust each other. In Witchingdom, there are alliances, not friendships. To pull this heist off, Tilda has to trust me, and the duíl makes that possible. She could hate me for it later. Now, I need her to look at me like she is at this moment, as if I am capable of planning this heist, as if I'm worthy of her.

So I do the only thing I can. I pull my hand from hers, glare at the trio of faces aimed my way, and stalk out of the room to go walk the grounds until I can look at Tilda without wanting to believe that the thing building between us is real.

Two hours later, I have myself under control and have

just stopped outside the library and am wedging a foot into the slightly open door so I can walk through with the tray laden down with elderberry tea and lemon coconut macaroons when Tilda's voice stops me dead in my tracks.

"I'm telling you," Tilda says, her voice an urgent whisper, "we can trust him."

I edge closer to the door while using a quick quiet spell to silence my steps.

"He works for the Council," Birdie says. "Which I still can't believe is real, by the way."

"I get that," Tilda says without hesitation. "Validate a thousand times. Buuuuuuut he's here, he's helping us, and he is giving it to us straight."

"Do you really think so?" Eli asks.

"I do," Tilda says.

I can picture her without any aid of a magic seeing incantation. She's twisting her red hair around her pointer finger while gnawing on her bottom lip and looking at her friends with those big eyes of hers made even bigger because of the thickness of her glasses. Guilt plucks at me. Letting her go to bat for me when I'm holding back the truth about the curse and what her powers really are is a shitty thing to do, and yet here I am. It's for the greater good. My family. Her family. All of Witchingdom.

Yeah, and it still sucks hairy werewolf balls on a full moon.

"And if he's not?" Birdie asks, her voice soft. "There's a lot riding on all of this. It could be a trap. The only way a spell can be reversed is with the help of the person who called it. You. And if you're out of the way, then your family stays frozen and any threat they offer disappears."

"That only counts if you aren't an outré. Let the Council grab me, as long as you all have The Liber Umbrarum then you can bring everyone back. My mom will save me once she defrosts." Tilda lets out a self-deprecating chuckle that doesn't hide the nerves. "I mean, she'll be pissed enough at me that I may not want her to defrost, but she won't leave me with the Council. If nothing else, she won't want the bad PR of a Council prisoner as a daughter."

I'm white-knuckling the tray, guilt rising like bile burning the back of my tongue, when my Council phone vibrates in my front pocket.

"Shit," I mutter under my breath as I back away from the door and hustle back to the kitchen, where I leave the tray on the island before answering the call.

"What's going on with the Sherwoods?" Cassius barks out the second I swipe answer.

"They're not up to much of anything." My heartbeat is erratic, but the words I'd planned for the call I'd known was coming sooner or later are calm and a little surly per usual. "As far as I know, they're all at the house." Not a lie. Not the whole truth, but not anything that will set off the falsehood detector on the phone.

"Well, something is going on. No one has heard from them in more than a day."

"I'll see what I can find out." Again. Not a lie. Just not all of what I know now.

"Do that. The Council is getting antsy to make their move against Izzy Sherwood," my handler says. "You need to find out what's going on or you and your family can look forward to an eternity freezing your ass off in The Beyond."

I'm clenching my teeth hard—cracking a molar isn't out of the realm of possibilities—but I still manage to get out, "I said I'll look into it."

"Good, because you can't afford to fuck up now. The Council is watching your every move."

Which is exactly what I'm counting on, because then they aren't watching Tilda.

Chapter Nineteen

Tilda . . .

*P*acking to go steal the most valuable spell book in all of Witchingdom isn't like throwing shit in a bag for a girl's weekend at the beach. For one, I wasn't offering up my eternal services as a rooster babysitter to my sister so she'd magically make my travel-sized bottle of SPF four billion into a never-ending supply of sunscreen. For the other, I had to figure out how to sweet-talk my way into bulk orders of juniper berries without Orwell at the alchemists' club telling everyone I was up to something—or more likely that my family was, and then everyone would be trying to get in touch with my mom to see what was wrong.

The solution, obviously, is to run a contest on Witchy-

Gram—but that doesn't mean I'm not getting some questionable looks from Eli, Birdie, and Gil as we all sit on the brick patio looking out on Mom's herb garden under the midnight full moon. Eli is walking through the garden checking out all of the plants my mom has nurtured into an organic who's who of witchery herbs. Birdie is pouring tea for everyone in between rescheduling her tax-prep appointments so she can take off work for the heist. And Gil? He's just standing under the patio's awning, his arms crossed, and his usual surly expression on his face.

I don't get it. The man either looks at me like he hates me or wants to kiss me or both, and it's got me more bubbly inside than a cauldron on a night when there's a full blue moon. His gaze catches mine and my internal meter goes from "he's a self-righteous jerk even if he's helping" to "fates alive, how do I get him naked" in 0.3 seconds. It's awkward but manageable—unless we're touching. Then it's like all the attraction short-circuiting my brain gets a shot of nitro— horny, gotta-touch, please-kiss-me nitro.

Even now, without us touching, my cheeks are flushed and my pulse is hammering as I jerk my attention back to the table and the matter at hand.

Yeah, you know, saving your family.

Priorities, Tilda. Priorities.

Birdie pours me a cup of elderberry tea from the porcelain teapot shaped like a black cat. "Are you sure this will work?"

"When it comes to how to get people to react on social

media?" I take a sip of the tart, earthy tea and pause for a second to savor it before answering. "It is my job and I am good at it. I can't do magic, but I'm pretty great at getting things to go viral."

"So what's the plan?" Eli asks as he inspects the purple coneflower growing along the edges of the patio, the lavender flowers and purply-brown spiky centers, which my mom would dry out and crumble into the cauldron to increase the power of her spells.

I set down my cup and take out my version of a magic wand—my cell phone. "Well, we can't exactly buy up all the juniper berries in Wrightsville to take up with us in exchange for the tickets."

"Yeah." Birdie nods her head. "That would definitely get people talking and wondering and headed over here to talk to your mom."

"So we make it a viral challenge to build a statue from juniper berries that they magic onto our front yard by midnight." My fingers fly across the virtual keyboard as I craft the perfect copy to get everyone talking. "The most fabulous statue as decided by a panel of judges who just happen to be sitting at this table wins." Text perfected, I aim my phone at the tall, blue juniper trees flanking the path from the patio to the moon circle at the far end of the garden. "We get all of the juniper from the entries, and the winner gets to spend the next full moon herb harvest in my mom's herb garden gathering what they need for the next lunar cycle."

A little photo manipulation of the nonmagical variety,

and I have a graphic, a message, and a winning plan just waiting for me to hit post to set it in motion.

"This garden is legendary." Jaw agape, Birdie glances around at the pokeweed, several varieties of vervains (all varieties of which weaken vampires), and nightshades that aid in flying and act as a poison, as well as silverweeds, garden parsley, wolfsbane, and smallage, which is key to preventing cramps while flying long distances. Then she turns to me, a huge grin on her face. "That's brilliant."

I mean, I'm not going to say it is, but yeah, for once, it feels really good to contribute instead of just watching from the sidelines.

"Hard agree," Gil says, his voice all grumbly.

Pleasure floods my system at the praise, and I accidentally hit post before I get a chance to give my text a second read. By the time I finish giving it a quick read to see if I need to delete, fix, and repost, Gil's disappeared inside, which is for the best. He's the king of mixed messages, and I have a whole family to defrost, so the less I think about him the better.

Of course, he is all I think about for the rest of the night alone in my bedroom. I mean, sure, I have dream after dream about the heist, but he's there for each one. In one, Gil and I are dancing across the ballroom to cause a diversion just like a scene out of *Dimond Eight* when a band of badass witches steals a priceless tiara during an art museum heist. In another, we're hiding out in a hotel hallway when the bad guys come by and we have to pretend to drunkenly make out so they pass us by. Then there is the dream that definitely is not part of a heist movie, because there is no way anyone would green-light a movie where the plot centered around bluffing our way into an orgy and . . . Let's just say I woke up out of breath but amazingly refreshed and relaxed after that one.

Still, a bad witch's work is never done, so I hustle on down to the kitchen before anyone else wakes up to start the first kettle of the day. I'm standing there in my sleep shorts and a tank top that's seen better days, filling up the kettle at the sink when I look out the window and see our front lawn is thick with statues made from juniper berries. There are brooms, witches around cauldrons, dragons curled around eggs made of juniper berries that have been enchanted to glow, pointed hats the size of large dogs, and more.

"It worked," I say to the empty room.

"Of course it did," Gil says.

I let out a yelp of surprise and jump back, adrenaline shooting through me like fireworks, sending unheated water sloshing over the top of the open kettle and onto the stone floor. I don't have to tell you where I land. Yes. Exactly in the right spot to send my feet one way and my ass another.

"Tutum." He calls out the spell for sending someone to safety, and on the intake of breath I'm hovering above the floor before I can land on it, and on the exhale I'm flying through the air straight toward Gil.

It's not something I can control, and I doubt it's what he is expecting, because Mr. Always Cool, Calm, and Collected's eyes go wide and he has just enough time to brace himself before I'm plastered around his body, hanging on for dear life before I glitch out the spell any more and we end up in Timbuktu. The scent of salty butter wraps itself around me as his arms close, holding me against him so I don't fall on my ass. It's all I can do to keep the few pre-tea working synapses of my brain functioning as I look down into his face. His five-o'clock shadow is there even at six in the morning. I want to touch it to see what it feels like under my palm—but that's not all I want.

In truth, I want so much that it turns me soft and pliant against him as my nipples pebble. Our faces are so close, our lips nearly touching. I swear I can feel his heart beat in time with mine as desire swirls through me, sharpening every nerve until all I can feel is Gil. His gaze drops to my mouth and then back up as he shoots me a look practically on fire with intensity and all I want to do is burn.

My eyes start to flutter shut and his body stiffens beneath me.

Realization hits along with an unrelenting wave of humiliation.

Fuck. Way to get lost in your own head there, Tilda.

"I'm sorry," I mumble, wishing I had any magical ability just so I could poof myself into another room.

His large hand cups the back of my head as he dips his head lower. "I'm not."

And then he's kissing me for real, and I forget about everything else except for the fact that Gil Connolly is a fan-fucking-tastic kisser. Hot and demanding, he kisses me like a man who has been waiting his entire life for just this moment. I tighten my legs around his waist, settling my core against his hard length. The gray sweatpants he's wearing don't offer a thick barrier, but it's still too much. I shouldn't rock against him. I do anyway, because fates preserve us, it's not just his hands that are big and I can't seem to help myself.

He breaks the kiss and lets out a groan of frustration before moving his hands to my waist and taking a step back so that I slide down his front and then am standing on my own.

He shoves his fingers through his hair and glares at the floor as if it has wronged him mightily. "That shouldn't have happened."

Ouch. That stings, but I do my best to make a jaded chuckle, which sounds more like a squawk, and say, "Weirdness of the moment and—"

"No," he interrupts. "The last place the magic should have sent you is to me."

Then, without another word, he stalks out of the kitchen and back down the hall toward the library, where he slept on an overstuffed couch in front of the fireplace.

And that's when my brain finally translates the activation word of his spell—"safe." I'm not magic, but even I know that the thread of magic running through the universe that witches tap into is always true. Magic doesn't lie. It doesn't falter. It is never wrong.

And the magic powering Gil's spell to send me to safety pushed me right into his arms. Literally.

A shiver works its way through me, because the fates help me, safe is exactly what I feel when I'm with the last man in Witchingdom I should want.

At least things couldn't get worse.

Chapter Twenty

Gil...

$\mathcal{T}$hat kiss was a mistake.

A mistake I can't stop thinking about.

Not during the awkward breakfast where Tilda wouldn't make eye contact with me while Birdie and Eli kept looking between us and then having a silent conversation with each other as if they knew exactly what had happened.

Not at the briefing in the library, where we got our plan together for heading out tomorrow at dawn, when I kept forgetting the name of The Liber Umbrarum, which is necessary to melt her parents and undo this duíl magic we unleashed at the coffee shop.

Not as we walked the winding paths through the Sherwood herb garden, which has everything a witch could ever want and more than a few varieties of spell-casting ingredients that most of the Witchingdom thinks are extinct.

I wish I could chalk it all up to my duíl magic, but I can't. That only acts on desires that already exist. I can't use it to make her want to kiss me like she needs me to be whole. I can't use it to give her that soft, satisfied look she had after I broke the kiss. I can't use it to make her want me the way I want her every second of the day.

The smart move is for me to keep as much space between us as possible because I'm not the kind of guy who goes where this is leading. I don't do commitments. I'm loyal only to myself and my family. Love takes something I don't have— the heart of a sucker.

And that's what I keep telling myself while Tilda and I are in her mother's garden gathering herbs for the trip while Eli and Birdie are moving all the statues to the backyard so they can strip them of the juniper berries without the whole town knowing what they're doing.

The last thing I need is more alone time with Tilda— especially when she's wearing the kind of flowy skirt that hits just above her knees and has me thinking every dirty thought imaginable about what I'd do if she'd only let me slide my hand under the hem and up her thick thighs to tease that clit of hers until she was lost to the pleasure of it, and then I'd dip my head underneath her skirt, spread her thighs wide, and feast on her sweet center until she came all over my face.

The duíl magic has gone rogue. It's not enough that I want

her more than I've ever wanted anyone else. Now it's not a case of *wanting* to be near her, it's *needing* to be near her.

She clips some unopened deep pink flowers off the clove tree, puts them in an enchanted cheesecloth bag for fast drying, and then drops that into the oversized wicker basket I'm carrying around to collect all of the herbs.

"What are we doing gathering herbs for spells?" she asks as I ignore the way the sun turns some strands of her hair golden as if spun by princesses locked in towers. "I thought magic wasn't going to work in the exhibit."

Gripping the basket tighter so I won't reach out and touch her, pull her closer, kiss her again and again, I grind out each word of my answer. "It won't work inside the museum during the gala, but everywhere else is fair game."

She stops in front of a bunch of potted snapdragons and starts to expertly clip the blooms, careful not to lose any of the pollen that is crucial for a protection spell, and drops them into another enchanted bag. "So what's wrong with speaking spells as opposed to the old-fashioned cauldron-brewed spells we're collecting for?"

"That's not going to hold up against Council magic." So little actually did. Our best hope is getting all of this done before they realize I've gone rogue, but the chances of that are slim. "We'll need to go all in if they find us."

Tilda nods and lets out a shaky breath before looking at me with a determined gleam in her eyes. "So what's left on the list?"

I glance down at the list we came up with earlier. "Comfrey and catnip."

"Travel protection and attracting luck," she says. "We're gonna need those in bulk. Well, we're in luck, because my dad is a borderline herb hoarder."

"Everyone likes to keep a stash." Witches may test the fates, but they never want to leave anything up to chance.

She throws back her head and laughs. "Oh no, it's more than— Here, it'll be easier just to show you my dad's den."

We walk out of the garden proper to the moon circle, which is inlaid with light opals that form the shape of a dragon.

A family's moon circle is always a powerful centering place for their magic, and the Sherwoods' is no different. Even with almost the entire family being frozen, a shiver works its way through me, raising the hair on the back of my neck as I take my first step onto it. Is it the power of the Sherwoods? The extra burst of magical energy that always comes with being near a spellbinder like Tilda? Either option is possible. Not that it matters. My job here is to follow Tilda, and that's exactly what I do, making sure to avoid stepping on the milky-white opals. The fragments of color inside each one are catching the light as we cross and making the dragon look like its scales are shimmering in the early-morning sun.

Once on the other side, we stop in front of a small witch's den. Some people have gone modern with glass walls and stainless steel. The Sherwoods have kept it traditional with witch hazel branches for the shed's walls and a thatched roof made from long straw. It looks like it belongs in a fairy tale out in a tangle of woods where the trees are so dense you just know the whole place is haunted. There are a pair of dragon's blood trees bracketing the door, which is intricately carved to look like a dragon with its mouth open. I swear, the closer we get, the more I can feel my skin heating up as if I'm stepping closer to a bonfire.

There's magic here, and every instinct in my body is yelling at me to step the fuck back and get away from here as fast as I can. It starts to push against me, sharp little points of agony poking against my skin as the Sherwood protection spell tries to edge me back from the den. It knows I don't belong here, not a nobody from The Beyond like me.

"Gil?" Tilda asks, cocking her head in concern and reaching out for me. "Are you—"

She doesn't get to *okay* before her fingers touch my arm and the magic snaps around us, pushing us together and then sending us careening toward the closed door of the witch's den. I twist so I'm between the door and Tilda to lessen the impact for her of us being smashed against the wood. But right at the last moment, the door whooshes open and we are carried inside, where we land with a thud on the slate floor.

In the next heartbeat, I'm rolling up into a sitting position, holding on to Tilda so that she's on my lap facing me, her bare legs falling on either side of my hips as I skim my palms over her, checking for damage. "Are you okay?"

"We didn't land on *me*." She cups my face in her hands, stilling me with the softness of her touch. "How are *you*?"

She inches closer on my lap, the move settling her panty-covered pussy against my cock as it pushes against my jeans. And in the sliver of a moment between one heartbeat and the next, everything changes. My hands are on her ass, pulling her hard against me. She responds by tightening her legs around me and rocking her hips just enough to make me forget who we are, what's at stake, and why this is a very bad idea.

Tilda Sherwood is a spellbinder from the most powerful family in all of Witchingdom. I'm a shifty double agent from The Beyond and I've been lying to her since the day we met. First about not getting Griselda to set us up. Then about being one of the Council's agents. And now about her being a spellbinder. All I do is lie.

When she finds out the truth, she's going to hate me even more than I hate myself for what I have to do right now.

Moving my hands so I'm clamping down on her hips, I lift her up and off me. The sight of her skirt falling back into place, floating down like a curtain to block my view of her, is like taking a knife to the kidney.

I stand up and take a few steps back from her, clasping my hands behind my back to keep from reaching for her because I'm holding on to my sense of control so tightly that I'm afraid I'll break it myself. "We can't."

"So you keep saying." She stands up and straightens her glasses, her gaze locked on the floor as if she couldn't force herself to look at me even if she wanted to.

It is better this way. No one in Witchingdom should be trusted, least of all me.

I'm halfway to the door to get out of this place and away from Tilda before I forget who we are to each other again when a bright, crackling, light blue glow appears around the door frame. It zips around the frame and lights up the doorknob like a neon sign hanging in a bar window for a few seconds before it turns off with a snap.

Tilda jumps up and sprints over to the door, turning the knob and yanking. "It's not moving." She turns to me, her eyes huge and round behind her glasses. "What did I mess up now?"

Realization slaps me across the face. "It wasn't you."

The pieces come into place in a heartbeat. The protective push I felt from the Sherwood magic. The snap of my duíl magic hitting back at it. Using magic is like fucking with the universe. You have one thing, you want another, so you cast a spell. You need something but don't have it, you cast a spell. You want to protect someone you love, you cast a spell. The thing is, though, that sometimes the universe fucks with you back. The magic zipping through the ozone and wafting on the wind decides it wants something too. Add to that the iron ribbon of hereditary magic that connects everyone in the same family together (like my duíl magic) that, because it thinks it knows better, occasionally takes hold of that magic for its own ends without a single witch in control and it takes on a life of its own, shoving us in one direction or another.

Locking us in here is a test, an experiment, a spell cooked up by my duíl family magic in an act of supernatural match-making to force us together and see what comes of it. This is the last fucking thing I need right now when I can barely resist Tilda as it is. "We're not going anywhere. We can't."

"Can't you just whip up a quick unlock spell?" she asks.

I scan the Sherwood witch's den. It's on the large side, with room for several dozen dried herb stations, a canning area to store the herbs until needed, and even a greenhouse section for the herbs that are too delicate for outdoor growth, but it is still the size of a large walk-in closet. And if I keep looking and noting each terracotta pot, stainless steel gardening tool, and purple watering can, then I can pretend I'm not in here with Tilda. "No."

She marches over to me, looking like she is ready to do battle, demanding my full attention. "Why?"

Something inside me snaps, splitting like an old twig under a werewolf's paw. All of that frustrated need and want and can't have explodes inside me.

"Fine. You want to know everything? Well, buckle up." It takes everything I have not to reach out and grab her, pull her close, and kiss her until both of us are desperate for more. Blood pounds in my ears as adrenaline and lust rush through me, shrinking the world down to just us. And she wanted to know why I couldn't stop the spell? "Because that day with the dragon's blood tree? Something happened with you and with me and with my family magic. I didn't mean to, but I cursed myself and now I can't stop thinking about you, wanting you, obsessing over how hot you look when your glasses go crooked and what it would be like to touch you." How I manage to censor myself so I don't confess to becoming a walking hard-on whenever she is around I have no fucking clue. "Even worse, the duíl magic can't force a desire into being that doesn't already exist, which means I've wanted you since the first time I saw you. Something in you connected with some part of me, and that has fucked up all of my plans. I don't do relationships or commitment or looking out for anyone but myself—only a fool would look at you and see anything but a person who makes a witch want to be that person."

"And all of that is a curse?" she asks, a dangerous look in her eye that has my thickening cock pushing against my zipper.

"Fuck no." I step closer to her. I can't help it. The need to fuck her and keep her safe has wound me up to the point where I have no clue if I'm coming or going. All I know is that Tilda Sherwood has cast a spell on me without even fucking trying and I'm not sure it will ever be broken. "I want you. I can't stop wanting you. And now it's reached a point where the magic is taking over and I don't even care because you are everything I want. That blast of magic shoving us in here? The door? It's all duíl magic making a point. It wants to complete the spell to give us each what we desire."

I'm breathing hard by the time I'm done and there's a raw edge to the atmosphere inside the witch's den as if anything could happen.

Tilda stands just out of reach, her eyes round and her pretty pink lips forming an O of surprise, of anticipation, of excitement? I don't have a fucking clue, because I'm a man about to jump happily into the abyss as long as it's with her.

She closes the short distance between us, her hand coming to rest on my chest above my fast-beating heart. "But with duíl magic, the witch just has to get what they desire and then they're fine, the spell is complete." She pauses, looks up at me, and moves her palm lower so her fingertips are resting against my stomach. "Right?"

"Supposedly." The word comes out as a whisper that barely registers above the fuck-yeah from every part of me desperate to touch her that I very definitely cannot listen to. "But you don't have to worry. I'll figure something out." My palms are sweaty and my heartbeat erratic; I scan the area, looking for some way—any way—out of here. "We can get out. Somehow. There have to be tools in here we can use to break out." I grab a metal spade from the shelf to my right. "You holler for help. I'll use this to hack my way through the wood or—"

Tilda stops me with a kiss, her soft lips teasing mine.

I'm not a great man; really, I'm not even a good one with all of the lies I'm juggling, but for a second it feels like I could be—and there is nothing more dangerous in the world than that.

Chapter Twenty-One

Tilda . . .

$\mathcal{I}$ should be pissed about the fact that Gil thinks wanting me is a curse. I should be straight up irate and plotting his nonmagical comeuppance. I am neither. I am trying to figure out how to get him naked without ending this kiss because I'm not sure I can or will ever want to.

I'm grasping his shirt with both hands because I'm afraid if I don't that I'll slide right off the face of the earth and float right out into space. No, that doesn't make logical sense to me either, but what does when it comes to Gil Connolly? I shouldn't trust him, but I do. I shouldn't feel safe when I'm with him, but the spell this morning correctly sent me to him. There's something here in the push and pull between us, a soft chenille thread that winds around us both, bringing us closer and closer until we're bound to each other.

That's why I don't want this kiss to end, why I open up beneath him, deepen it. It's why I wrap my arms around him, entwining my fingers in his dark hair. It's why I tilt my chin upward as he moves his lips down my throat and revel in the feel of the hard bristles of his beard scraping just so against my sensitive neck.

Every part of me is tuned into only him. The press of his fingers on the small of my back at that spot where the hem of my sweater meets the top of my skirt. The push of his hard cock against me, so close and yet so damn far because of the layers of clothing between us. I slide my fingers down and start to tug his shirt upward when he breaks contact and steps backward. The shock of missing him hits immediately, like having a door slammed in my face.

"Tilda," he says, managing to make my name sound like a plea and a prayer as he backs all the way up to the stone workbench in the middle of the room. "I want you, fuck do I want you." His whole body is strung tight with an all too obvious tension, his eyes are dark with a wild lust, and his movements are jerky as he shoves his fingers through his hair. "But the spell is the only reason why you'd act on wanting me—otherwise you'd keep your distance. You'd know better than to be with someone like me. I can't—"

"And what about what I want?" I interrupt, striding over to him, the air between us crackling with awareness. "Does that factor into things at all?"

"It's different for you. I'm not the kind of guy you should want." He lets out a shaky sigh as he grips the edge of the workbench behind him as if it was the only thing keeping him from reaching out toward me. "We can—"

"And what about for you?" I put my hands on the workbench on either side of him; there's several inches of empty space between us, but it might as well be nonexistent. Being this close to him has me on edge, craving what I shouldn't want but I can't stop needing. It might be the duíl magic bringing all of this from my subconscious to the forefront—it probably is—but at this moment, I don't care. All I know is that every part of me is desperate for him to touch me, to kiss me, to let me feel every part of him. "Is it just the magic for you?"

"I don't know." His knuckles are white with the effort not to give in to the enchanted air swirling around us. "There have to be other ways to satisfy the duíl magic that don't put you in such an awkward position, if we take a second to think and—"

"Is that what you want?" I cup his face, tilting it down so he has to look at me, so I can see the naked want in his eyes. "Is that what you *really* want? And if this"—I drop a hand to his chest above his fast-beating heart—"is only this strong because of the duíl magic, then maybe we should give it what it wants. No harm. No foul. Only magic giving us what we both need."

He lets out a ragged breath that goes to show he's fighting this attraction. "And after that?"

"We'll figure it out." I can't think about that. I can barely think as it is being this close to him. "Have a little faith in your fellow witch. You just might like it—almost as much as you like kissing me."

"Kissing you only makes me want more," he says, his voice that low and rumbly pitch that makes my core clench.

I rise up to my tiptoes. "Then more seems like the best option."

He lets go of the workbench, his hands going to my waist, setting off a chain reaction of sensations that make it feel like I'm flying—maybe I am, I could care less because Gil is kissing me and it's more than I can take, but I can't get enough of it. The next thing I know, I'm sitting on the edge of the workbench and Gil's standing between my spread legs. His hands are on my knees and then my thighs as he kisses me like a man who can't get enough and doesn't think he ever will. It's different than our kiss in the kitchen. Hotter. More demanding. Walking that fine line between I'm-gonna-die-if-you-stop and all-of-this-pleasure-is-gonna-kill-me-dead.

His thumbs come to rest at that spot on my inner thighs that's as close as he can get to the damp center of my panties without actually touching them. My whole body is buzzing with anticipation and I am barely holding it together because I swear I can see potted herbs and my dad's set of growing crystals floating around us inside the witch's den.

"Tilda," Gil says, his voice strained. "Can I touch you?"

"Yes."

"Just say the word and I'll stop."

"If you do, I'm gonna hit you with that garden spade you were gonna try to chop your way out of here with." He nudges the center of my panties aside, sending my whole body into oh-my-fucking-yes alert and frying every thought in my head, but my mouth keeps going. "I mean, I wouldn't really hit you. Consent goes both ways, and if you—"

"Tilda," he says, whispering my name in a tone I can't even describe beyond reverentially horny.

Is that a thing? Because that is exactly how he sounds at that moment when he flips the front of my skirt upward. It doesn't matter, because all I can muster at this point is a soft, "Yeah?"

He looks down at my dimpled thighs—the ones that make chafing cream a necessity in the summer—and pink panties with the white daisies on them as if he's been waiting his entire life to see something so gorgeous. "I'm gonna eat you out now."

I swear I have something witty to say back, but then his mouth is on me, working my slick folds and swollen clit like a virtuoso. Seriously. There is not a sex toy in my nightstand drawer that can do the thing he is doing with his tongue, the pulsing, circling, teasing thing that has me gasping for breath and seeing neon lights exploding on the edge of my vision. Then his thumb joins in, tracing my opening with the kind of sadistic patience that has me babbling words I don't even know the meaning of beyond begging him not to stop. Thank the fates he doesn't. He just feasts on me, licking and sucking, tormenting me with his thumb in the best possible way.

I'm balancing on my forearms, my head hanging back, my mouth open as I make moans of pleasure I didn't realize were possible. Yet he continues, moving his hands so he's cradling my ass, holding me up to his mouth as if there is anywhere I am going to go at this moment—not with the way he is making me want to bask in the electric fire of his touch. There are snaps and crackles in the distance that should probably worry me, but I can't be bothered. Everything feels too good, too powerful, too overwhelmingly amazing to pay attention to anything beyond Gil's face buried between my legs.

I'm on the brink of orgasm, all of the sensations building in my core until I can't take it anymore and my climax hits me, bowing my spine as the world turns bright purples and blues and I swear that if I could keep my eyes open against the wave after wave of pleasure, I just know I would see the colors twining to form a shade of violet indigo I've never seen before.

Still breathing hard, I force my eyes open to see Gil there, standing between my legs, his mouth wet, his gaze dark, and a delicious shiver goes through me because I know whatever is coming next is going to shake my world.

Then my dad's witch's den literally starts shaking as a rainbow-colored light illuminates the magic-locked door. The power makes the walls shake, and the door frame squeaks under the pressure. Gil turns and moves so he's between me and whatever is about to come through that door.

Yeah, he's not gonna be heading off whatever is about to

come through there alone. I grab the garden spade—hey, it's better than nothing—and go to stand beside him just as the door flies open. Whatever—whoever—I'm expecting, it sure isn't Vance wearing a worn black T-shirt that says "Sorry I'm late, I didn't want to be here."

I let out a relieved breath. Vance is a pain in the ass, but he's not the boogeyman. Beside me, though, Gil is still tense, primed and ready to throw down with the unicorn shifter. Before he can do that, though, I take a half step so I'm in front of him.

"We got literal fireworks going on out here above the den," Vance grumbles. "What in the hell are you two up to?" He looks from me to Gil and back again. "On second thought, don't tell me. I don't wanna fuckin' know. But if you're done— and even if you're not—we need you inside. This whole plan of yours just went straight to shit."

He stomps off back to the house, his unicorn horn sparkling in the setting sun's rays.

If I had it in me at this moment to be embarrassed, I would be mortified. However, the level of satisfaction floating through my bloodstream pretty much eliminates any feeling but blissed-out contentment.

Gil wraps his arm around my waist from behind and pulls me back against him while we both stand in the open doorway trying to catch our breath. There's no missing the hard length of him pressed against my ass. With my orgasm still making me feel all floaty and loose limbed, the duíl spell should be over for me now that I've satisfied my desire, but I'm already hungry for more.

Starving.

Famished.

Ravenous.

"So I guess we'll have to finish this later?" I ask, trying my best not to showcase the fact that I am still dick drunk and possibly... probably... fine, very much still wanting him as much as I did before he curled my toes so tight I lost half a shoe size.

He dips his head down, kisses that sensitive spot behind my ear, and says with a low growl, "Tilda, you and I both know this is far from over."

Chapter Twenty-Two

Gil . . .

*B*ack in the library, I can't keep my eyes off of Tilda. She's practically glowing as she moves around the room, her fingers flying across the keyboard of her phone as she posts old photos of her mom and sisters around the family cauldron to WitchyGram to keep suspicions at bay about where they are. Eli and Birdie keep sneaking peeks at her as they pack the last of the juniper berries into enchanted wooden boxes as big as large suitcases that will walk themselves to the train station for our trip to Salem. Meanwhile, Vance stands by the fireplace glaring at me as if the fact that I'm breathing offends him.

The unicorn shifter cracks his tattooed knuckles and

then crosses his massive arms across his chest. "The Council is on to you."

It is expected, but I had been hoping there was more time.

"How?" I ask, not that it matters, but curiosity and all that.

Vance snorts and shoots me a withering look. "Ever since the Council started to really make moves to take over Witchingdom, Cassius and I have been battling back and forth. He's about as trustworthy as a leprechaun with a pot of gold to hide, and that man probably has you spell bugged six ways to Sunday."

Tilda walks across the room and sits down next to me on the love seat across from the huge fireplace, her hand resting on my thigh like it's the most natural thing in the world. "But we're under a protective dome."

"And that's probably what sent him scurrying to the Council like the plague-carrying rat he is." Vance's gaze drops to Tilda's hand and his snarl increases by ten degrees. "So it's a damn good thing I'm going to escort you on my train to Salem to get The Liber Umbrarum and unfreeze the entire Sherwood family—minus our Tilda here—before the Council figures out what's happened and makes its move to take over."

"The train?" Birdie asks. "But aren't those for carrying goods only? No witches use them."

Vance's face is transformed by a smug grin. "Good thing you're traveling with a shifter then, because it's the last form of transportation anyone from the Council will be monitoring."

It all makes sense, and that's what sets off the warning bells in my head. "Why should we trust you?"

"Because with Griselda frozen, I'm the only Resistance contact you've got who can help. Also, there's this." He tosses a ring on the coffee table.

One look at the silver and sapphire engagement ring that has been in my family for generations, and I can taste bile on the back of my tongue. My mom never took it off. Not when she did spell work, not when she foraged for items to bargain with in The Beyond, and not when she could have traded it for a few loaves of bread out on the tundra.

"They're okay. They're in a safe house on Tybee Island. She sent this and said to tell you Kiehl says hello."

The breath I've been holding comes out in a whoosh.

Kiehl has been our code for all's well since we got banished to The Beyond, one that only my parents and I know about.

"So we're really doing this?" Birdie asks as Eli wraps his arms around her and tucks her close against his side.

"Yeah." Tilda nods, her answer firm even though her hands are shaking as she picks up a cup of tea from the ornate silver tray on the coffee table and takes a sip. "We're really doing this."

The library goes silent beyond the crackling of the logs in the fireplace. Tilda looks up at me, her eyes wide behind her round glasses, and something roars to life inside me that doesn't feel anything like the dull magic. This isn't about what I want, it's all about Tilda.

"Then let's not fuck it up," Vance says, shooting back something from the flask with the words "fuck being polite" engraved on it that he always carries with him. "We leave in thirty. I grabbed the agaric mushroom powder you two gathered for Griselda and took care of her with a spell to keep folks away from her house so no one discovers her doing her icy pop impression. You two"—he points at Tilda and me—"take care of the rest of your family while the three of us load everything we need into the train."

Twenty minutes later, I'm using a dolly to wheel the frozen matriarch of the Sherwood clan, who still has the towel draped over her head, to the witch's den, which is without a doubt one of the most bizarre things I've ever done, and I've eaten cold cod's-oil pizza on purpose. Of course, turning around and seeing the parade of bedraggled magical misfits and a surly unicorn shifter just adds to the outlandish effect. Eli walks into the den behind me with a Sherwood sister under each arm. Vance carries Tilda's dad and her oldest sister through the door next. Birdie follows with Leona, apologizing the entire walk across the opal dragon guarding the den. Then there is Tilda, apologizing to a frozen rooster named Barkley as she hefts the overweight fowl, who manages to look unhinged, confused, and pissed off all at the same time.

Tilda looks around the now-crowded witch's den as she chews her bottom lip, concern forming a deep V between her eyes. "You think they'll be safe?"

Without thinking first about who is watching or why I am doing it, I reach out and take her hand and give it a reassuring squeeze. "Between the protective dome and the dragon magic guarding the witch's den, they'll be safe."

Tilda leans into me, resting her head against my shoulder. "Thank you for helping me. I know the spell isn't making you do this, and with your parents safe now, you could just walk away." She smiles up at me as if she knows me better than I know myself. "Hell, you could take The Liber Umbrarum once we get it and sell it for more than enough money to live out the rest of your life in luxury on a private island somewhere warm."

"Maybe that's my real plan." I make it sound like I'm kidding, but the smart part of me probably isn't.

Forget probably, it would have for sure been my plan before Tilda. Steal the book, sell it, get my parents somewhere neither the Council nor the Resistance can get them, somewhere they can be free from all of this bullshit. It is a no-brainer—or at least it would have been.

"Nah," she says with a shake of her head. "For all you try to hide it, you're really a softie underneath it all." She looks up at me, her gaze direct and sure. "You forget as an outré I have to utilize my skills of observation and instincts to ferret out what most witches get from using their magic." She lowers her voice so only I can hear her. "I see you, Gil Connolly. I mean, you're good at hiding it, which is why you were such a jerk to me in the beginning, but I see the real you with the soft gooey center."

"You see what you want to see." It's the truth, and yet I can't deny that I wish Tilda *could* be right.

Maybe in another life I could be that guy, but not in this one.

Tilda rolls her eyes and shakes her head at me before heading back to the house. I'm about to follow her, not because of the duíl magic, but because there's nowhere else that feels as right as being with her when Vance grabs me by the shirt and yanks me back a step.

"Sooner or later she's gonna find out that she's a spellbinder—yeah, Griselda told me years ago—and that you knew the whole time. She's gonna be rightly mad," Vance says, his tone hard with warning. "The clock's ticking for you."

Yeah, like I need to be told that. My clock is always ticking—that's the thing about being from the wrong side of exile, you are always looking over your shoulder to see what direction disaster is about to come from next.

The damn time bomb just waiting to go off is ticking so loud in my ear I can still hear it an hour later over the sound of the train as we rush down the tracks heading north toward Salem.

The train is a small one, but there's plenty of room for us. Behind the engineer's car, ruled over by a goblin with a taste for excessive speed, is a lounge car filled with couches, a continental buffet, and all of us gathered around a magicked map of the museum as everyone memorizes the entrances and exits just in case the book heist goes sideways. Behind that car is one filled with four sleeping berths, each with a huge window for all the sightseeing we won't be doing any of.

Tilda is holding court, outlining her plan for the heist. I may have come up with the idea, but she figured out the logistics, the timing, and everything else.

"I'm the one they're expecting, so I'll be the one they see. Well, Gil and I will be." She looks over at me and smiles. "We'll be good little guests during the party, dancing and drinking and drawing the attention of everyone there. That will give Eli and Birdie dressed in servers' uniforms plenty of freedom to dose the guards by the book's case with a puff of the temporary zombie powder I swiped from Griselda's house. The book weighs fifty pounds, so you'll swap the book for the block of agate. You'll have about half a heartbeat after lifting the book to make that happen before the nonmagical sensors go off, so whatever you do, don't hesitate. After that, you'll head out the back to the train. Vance, that's where you'll be making sure we can get out of Dodge as soon as we have the book. Gil and I will stay as long as we can to divert attention away from Eli and Birdie and then we'll head back to the train. Then it's back to Wrightsville and defrosting my family."

It really is a sight to see. She has a calm confidence that is the sexiest thing ever.

"So we each have a handle on our jobs?" Tilda asks, looking at each witch, who nods. "Then, after we get back home, use the book to fix the spell I glitched all over, I'll return the book to the museum, and take care of whatever repercussions there may be so you all don't have to worry about it."

Of course she'd think about how to best protect her friends.

If I didn't realize how special she is already, that would have pushed me over the edge. I don't know whether to shake her or wrap her up in a Bubble Wrap spell to keep her safe.

The urge to tell Tilda that she's a spellbinder is getting stronger with every minute I spend with her, but I know Griselda was right. Telling her the truth only puts her in more danger unless she has the right witch around her. That's not going to be Eli or Birdie with their well-meaning but fucked-up magic skills. Vance isn't even a witch. It sure as hell can't be me. My own parents couldn't depend on me to keep them safe. I tried, but it was Griselda who actually got them out of The Beyond, not me. It has to be a Sherwood who delivers the news that will change everything for Tilda, and after that she won't need my help, won't need me.

That's how it should be.

Still, I can't help but try to warn her before she learns the hard way like I had to.

"The Witchingdom is all about transactional relationships." No one knows that better than I do. It's why I've spent my entire adult life playing both sides of every situation. "All that matters is what you can do for me and how I can benefit from helping you."

"You're full of shit," Tilda says with an eye roll. "If you weren't you wouldn't be here."

I don't have an answer to that. How can I, because what feels like the truth at this moment is just a lie I'm telling myself. No matter how much the duíl magic makes me want to think so, the world hasn't changed just because of Tilda.

But maybe I have.

Fuck. I'm losing it. I have to get the fuck out of here, but beyond jumping from the moving train, there is only one place I can escape to. I mumble my good-nights, ignoring the hurt on Tilda's face and the censure on everyone else's, and get the hell out of there before I do something stupid.

The truth of it is that everything has changed because of Tilda and the duíl spell isn't ever going to be completed because I'll never stop wanting her. I know it all the way down to the marrow of my bones.

I am fucked and there's nothing I can do about it.

I'm halfway through two fingers of whiskey, watching the moonlight hit the whitecaps on the Atlantic as the train click-clacks its way up the coast when there's a knock at my door. No doubt it's Vance to give me a gruff reminder of what's at stake here—as if I'm not aware.

But it's not the unicorn shifter on the other side of my door. It's Tilda.

Her lips are upturned in a shy smile, and she's holding two eye of newt muffins. "Can I come in?"

Chapter Twenty-Three

Tilda . . .

I may have made a mistake just showing up at Gil's room. He's got that growly set to his mouth that is definitely a warning, but my body interprets it only as an invitation. Yeah, I know I'm a horny mess when it comes to Gil Connolly, but there's not much I can do about that—even if there wasn't the duíl spell, which, come on, I think we can both see there is more to all of the damn-he's-so-hot than that. The truth is, I'm pretty sure I'm falling for him, which is probably not the smartest move on my part, but feelings aren't exactly something even the most powerful witch can control—let alone a null like me.

So here I am, a dork of an outré, standing outside the door

of the guy I have a crush on willing him to say "come on in" so we can finish what was started in my dad's witch's den.

Gil's gaze flickers to the muffins and back to me. "I'm not good company."

"When are you usually?" Falling into old patterns of insulting the guy I like? Guilty.

One side of his mouth kicks up. "Feeling feisty, huh?"

"Try nervous as hell." Okay, that was probably more truthful than necessary, but it just popped out.

He takes a drink of his whiskey. "About the heist?"

"About being on this side of your door hoping you'll let me in." I hold up one of the muffins. "I brought a bribe to improve my odds."

"This is the last place you should be tonight." His grip on his glass tightens and the vein in his temple bulges. "When it comes to being near you, I can't be trusted."

"That is exactly what I'm counting on." I walk in, adding a little extra sway to my hips—fake it until you're confident, right? "You know, it just might be time you admit to yourself that you aren't nearly the jerk you try and make everyone—including yourself—believe. If you were, you wouldn't be here."

"You don't think I'm playing the long con?" he asks as he shuts the door and leans against it, crossing his arms.

"No." I hand him his muffin. He doesn't look like he believes me, but he takes the muffin anyway, the brief contact of our fingers sending a shiver of anticipation up my spine. "Now eat. Eye of newt muffins make everything better."

We settle down on the love seat that converts to a bed, not that I'm thinking about that—I'm totally thinking about that—and we eat the muffins in silence. I'm horrified to tell you that he doesn't just eat the top of the muffin first and then devour the rest of it like a normal witch, but instead unwraps the paper cup from around the bottom and then eats from the underside up, closing his eyes with ecstasy. Yes, this is exactly when my brain flashes back to him between my legs in the den. Suddenly the train is a good ten degrees warmer than it was on my last inhale, and I'm having to shift my position in an effort to ease the needy ache in my core. Who knew watching someone eat could be such a turn-on?

And if you ask me about it later, I'll totally deny it, but yes, I pivot on the love seat so I'm mostly facing him and taking in all the details of his face, from his thick eyelashes, which are just long enough to make me jealous; to the random strands of red hair in his otherwise brown eyebrows; to the small scar right above his top lip mostly covered by his short, clipped beard.

He finishes the last bite of muffin while mine sits forgotten in my hand. He glances down at it, then back up at me, a kind softness in his eyes as he pats my knee. "You came up with a good plan for the heist."

My brain blanks the moment he touches me.

Heist?

"It's smart to use the fact that everyone watches your every move already as the perfect distraction to stealing The

Liber Umbrarum," he says. "You don't have anything to worry about."

Stealing?

Worry?

Gil cocks his head and shoots a questioning look my way that is the absolute most adorable thing I've ever seen.

Liber Umbrarum?

He reaches over and straightens my glasses, his fingers brushing my temples and sending shock waves of lust straight to my clit. Fuck. What is going to become an erogenous zone next? My chin? My nipples pebble against the lace of my bra, offering themselves up as tribute.

Damn, Matilda! Get your brain together!

Frazzled and driven to the edge of sanity with lust, I set my barely touched muffin down on the table at the end of the love seat and clasp my hands together to keep from reaching out and grabbing him. "Do you think we're gonna pull this off?"

"Honestly?" He grins at me. "Yeah, I do."

What I wouldn't give to be that confident. There are a million things that can go wrong—and that's even without my inability to think of anything but Gil Connolly naked when I'm in the same room as him. "Why?"

He leans forward and puts his hand down next to my thigh, not touching me, but close enough that I can feel the zing of awareness. "Because when you're involved, I don't see how anything can go wrong."

"Is that the duíl spell talking or the muffins?" And why is my voice so high and squeaky all of a sudden?

He brings his hand up and cups my chin, brushing the pad of his thumb over my bottom lip. "Just the truth."

Yep. There's a lot I can take. I have been mocked to my face and online. I have spent my life as the family disappointment. I have resigned myself to the fact that humanizing my family via social media, hanging out with my magical misfit buddies, and having one-sided fights with Barkley the rooster from hell is pretty much as good as my life is ever going to get—and that's okay.

It's a fine life.

But sitting here with Gil as the train rushes up the East Coast on the way to an event where we're going to try to steal the unstealable, it feels different. In that breath of space between now and the next moment, I would swear on The Liber Umbrarum that there could be more, that I could be more, that this something between Gil and I could be more.

I've never wanted that more desperately in my entire life.

So I take it, embrace the possibilities, and kiss him.

Best. Decision. Ever.

The love seat, his tiny cabin, the passenger car, the entire train, the rest of the world all disappear as Gil kisses me back. Things go from hot to sizzling as he cups my face and tilts my head, slips his tongue into my mouth, and deepens the kiss. He's not touching anything below my face and yet every single part of me feels him; my breasts grow heavy and my nipples harden into tight, sensitive peaks while an electric sense of want buzzes through me and sets loose a wave of desire that takes my breath away. I could drown in this man and I'd go under happily. Everything is full of promise, and the anticipation of what's coming next is so palpable I can feel it in every cell of my body, exactly how the books describe a potent spell. That doesn't make any sense for a null like me to experience, but Mom always said that love is a magic so powerful it gives nonbelievers faith, makes the impossible probable, and inspires hope in the most dire of circumstances.

Love is dangerous, powerful, and as scary as facing down a goblin with a grudge and, until this moment, I have never understood the books where the main character said they were willing to risk everything for a chance at it.

Now I do.

I'm still trying to process that revelation when Gil breaks the kiss. There's something fierce in his eyes, as if he's not sure he can control what's happening either. As the hero in my favorite holiday movie says, welcome to the party, pal.

"Tilda," he says, an edge to his tone, "there's something you don't know."

This man and his need to overexplain the duíl spell. Fates love him, but this is more than just the spell and we both know it. I start on the buttons to his shirt, revealing a little bit more of his broad, muscular chest with each slip through the buttonhole. "Tell me about it later."

He covers my hand, stopping my progress in stripping him naked. "Are you sure?"

"Never more sure about anything in my life." Until I said the words, I hadn't been, but now? One hundred percent.

Gil must see it, because he lets go of my hands and moves his to my sweater, tugging it free from my pants as his mouth crashes down on mine. This kiss is different. It's hard, demanding, and full of a million possibilities. Then his lips go from kissing me stupid to my neck, hitting every single one of the responsive areas. The soft moan of pleasure filling the room is mine, and in another life I'll be embarrassed about that, but right now it just feels too good.

Then his fingers are on the bare skin of my stomach, sliding upward at the kind of slow pace that thrills as much as it tortures. It's like a wave of sensations that starts on the slice of skin above my waistband, moves upward to the who-knew-it-was-an-erogenous zone around my belly button, and progresses up to the spot just below my bra, that has me holding my breath in anticipation.

He kisses that spot where my neck meets my shoulder— you know, the one that makes your brain melt into a puddle of all the horny feels—and looks up at me. "We stop whenever you want."

"Do you want to stop?" Please, please, please say no.

His jaw tightens as he watches me, desire making his eyes dark. "It doesn't matter."

He shrugs as if it's no big deal, but we both know better.

"Actually, it does." I stroke my fingers featherlight across his squared jaw and the muscle twitches, as he seems to be nearly grinding his molars to dust. "This involves both of us."

"Tilda, you're the very last witch I should want, and I'm definitely the worst witch for you to want back." Tension wafts off of him while he looks at me as if I'm the answer to every question he's ever had. "But I can't stop needing to touch you and thinking about you. I wake up in the mornings thinking about you and go to sleep wondering what's going to happen with you tomorrow." He pauses, taking in a deep breath before continuing, his voice barely above a resigned whisper. "If I could stop wanting you, I would for your sake—but I can't. Matilda Grace Sherwood,"—he says my name with such a fierce possessiveness that my heart catches—"I'll never stop wanting you."

I have no idea what to say to that. My brain is a total blank and filled to the brim with words at the same time, the contradiction making the absolute most sense to me of anything at this moment. So I answer the only way I can, lifting my sweater up and over my head before letting it drop to the floor and then reaching behind myself to unhook my bra. The lacy dark emerald material joins my sweater as Gil watches, a barely contained wild look in his eyes.

I open my mouth, but nothing comes out still.

"Yes?" he asks.

I nod.

He lets out a half groan, half growl and the last thread of his control snaps right along with mine and I fall back against the love seat's arm, my hands scrambling to undo my jeans as he tears off his clothes—not literally, but whew, he is not messing around. The man is fucking magnificent and I can't help but take a long, slow look from his broad shoulders to his hard chest to the dick of my dreams that has my mouth watering and a million and six ideas for exactly how I want to touch, suck, and lick it rushing through my head.

Before I can pick just one of them though, he winks at me, mutters a spell I don't catch, and then we're naked, intertwined together on the love seat he manages to magic into a bed while kissing me as if we're meant for each other and always have been.

Chapter Twenty-Four

Gil . . .

I'm fucking cursed and I'm too fucking happy to fucking care, because Tilda Sherwood is mine, at least for tonight.

Tomorrow I'll tell her everything—how she's a spellbinder, how I'll do whatever it takes to keep her safe, and how my duíl magic doesn't even begin to explain the connection between us. If I'm lucky, she'll hear me out. If I'm blessed by the fates, she won't turn me to ash. I can't even imagine an end result better than that, not for a guy like me. Double agents like me aren't made for happily ever afters, we've done too much to stay alive; our hands will never be clean. But tonight? Tonight I can pretend that it's just us and the rest of Witchingdom and its messy problems don't exist.

I move from her mouth, trailing kisses down her throat,

and then take her hard nipple in my mouth, sucking the sensitive peak as she lets out the softest moans of pleasure. I love that sound. The surprised please-yes-more of it. I could spend a lifetime listening to her do that, but what I have is tonight, so I do it again and again and again as she murmurs words that don't quite make sense and yet do at the same time.

Lying next to her on the bed, I pull back. For a second, I'm mesmerized looking at her, so gorgeous with her red hair and pink lips parted just enough to make my dick harder than I thought possible. The image is burned into my brain forever. Her soft, round hips that are more than enough to grab ahold of. Her full tits are topped off with large, hard, pale-peach-colored nipples that I can't wait to roll between my fingers. Her long, strong legs that I'm willing to beg to have her wrap around me when I sink balls deep into her. And then there are her glasses—round, thick, and slightly off-kilter as always.

She rolls onto her side so we're face-to-face on the bed. "You like what you see?"

"Very much." I trail my fingers over the generous curve of her hip. "This right here might be my favorite." I move up to her nipple, rolling it between my fingers and tugging it just enough to make her eyes go dark with desire. "Of course, that's tied with this." Watching her bite down on her bottom lip as a flush of desire turns her cheeks pink, I kiss my way down her soft stomach to the edge of her reddish-brown curls, pausing as her breath quickens. "I bet I'd really love right here." I slide my fingers through her swollen wetness.

"You're all slick and wet. I already know you taste fucking fantastic." Eyes locked on her face, I bring my fingers up to my mouth and suck her off of them. Fuck me. Potent and addictive, she tastes so damn good. "Lie back so I can lick that pussy."

Tilda—who always has something to say—lets out a shaky breath and rolls back, spreading her legs. I'm between them a heartbeat later, kissing and teasing my way up to the promised land. I could get drunk on just the smell of her, but I'm a greedy bastard and I want to do a helluva lot more than make out with her inner thighs.

"Gil," she pleads as she lifts her hips up off the bed. "Please."

I'm an asshole, but not the kind that would leave her wanting when I could give her exactly what she needs. "I got you."

I get off the bed and onto my knees before grabbing her ankles and pulling her to the edge of the mattress and putting her legs over my shoulders. Then, I spread her open with my thumbs, stretching her wide as she lets out a soft mewl of pleasure, and skim her clit with my tongue. Fuck, she tastes so sweet. I take my time, slowly curling my tongue around it, circling her clit, licking it, lapping at it, and sucking on it while I circle her entrance with the tip of my thumb. At first, she's grasping at the bedsheets, fisting them as she makes encouraging moans. Then, I move from my thumb to my fingers, fucking her with one, then two, then three as I tease her clit with my tongue, keeping the pace slow and steady. I know I've hit the right rhythm when her breathing changes and she rocks her pussy against my face.

"Gil," she all but moans my name, her tone threading that fine line between desperate and I'll-murder-you-if-you-change-a-damn-thing. "Please."

I understand the assignment and keep alternating sliding my fingers home inside her warmth with working her clit with my tongue, feasting on her, worshipping her. She goes from holding on to the bed to threading her fingers through my hair and holding my face in place as if there is anywhere else in the world I'd want to be at this moment. I'm in heaven and she's about to break. I can feel it as her thighs quake on either side of my head. Her moans change when I speed up and increase the pressure on her clit. Going higher and faster, she all but turns my name into a mantra that even a fool could translate into "don't you fucking stop."

Then she's bucking against me, her legs squeezing my head as she comes, but I keep going, indulging in her orgasm and taking more than my fill. I lick softer now, a little slower and more gently, building her pleasure up again, pushing her right to the edge. She's almost tugging out my hair as she rubs herself against my mouth. I could be bald by the end of the night and I'd be more than okay with that—totally worth it to feel Tilda come apart beneath my tongue. Just the idea of it has my cock aching, and I reach between my legs, wrap my fingers that had been inside her around my dick, and give it hard stroke after hard stroke. Then, almost sooner than I'm ready, she calls out my name again a second before her body tenses again with another climax.

I'm harder than I've ever been before and I can still taste Tilda on my lips when I pull back and slide her legs off my shoulders. She's watching me, her eyes hooded with blissed-out desire and a satisfied smile curling her lips.

She straightens her glasses and lets out a happy sigh. "You made my glasses go wonky."

I shoot her a fake look of apology. "It won't happen again."

"That's too bad," she says, rolling up into a sitting position and leaning forward so her mouth is only inches from mine. "I was really looking forward to coming that hard again."

I cup the back of her head, tangling my fingers in her hair and pulling so her face is tilted upward toward me. "Greedy girl."

She just grins. "You bet your ass."

I crash my mouth down on hers, kissing her hard and thoroughly. She more than meets the challenge, teasing me with her tongue as she wraps her legs around my waist. It's good—so damn good—but my dick is pressed up against the mattress instead of her soft, slick slit. This is not gonna work, well, it would at this point, considering I'm more turned on than I have ever been before in my life, but me coming all over the sheets is definitely not how either of us wants this to go.

I snake my hands underneath her, cupping her ass with

the reverence that a gift of the fates like it deserves, and lift her as I stand up.

"Gil." She nips at my earlobe, then kisses it better. "Are we going to make out naked or fuck?"

"You say that like we can't do both."

"Challenge accepted," she says as she lifts her hips and reaches between us, encircling my cock with her hand and then lowering herself on it.

If there wasn't a wall behind me, we would have ended up in a pile on the ground, because the feeling of being inside her is so amazing that it doesn't just make my knees weak, it takes them the fuck out. If I were a better man and we were going to be together for as long as I am beginning to want, I'd ask about kids, begin the discussion about a pregnancy spell. The fact that I'm even thinking about it should scare the shit out of me, but all it does is make me want everything with Tilda that I can't have.

Then she yanks me back to the here and now by kissing me again as she rides my cock, planting her feet on the wall for better leverage as she fucks me hard and fast. It's good, almost too good, because if I don't take over, I'm going to blow before she comes again and that's not gonna happen.

Without breaking the kiss, I carry her over to the bed and lay her down on her back and pull out of her as I break the kiss. Losing contact, even though I know I need to, is like having an iceberg smashed against my skull. It hurts like almost nothing else I've ever experienced. Desperate to be back inside her, I flip her over onto her stomach, grab her hips, and yank her back so I'm there at her opening. On the inhale, I relish that anticipation of knowing what's coming next, and on the exhale, I'm sliding forward as her pussy grips my cock. I keep going until I'm balls deep. *Perfect* isn't the correct word for how we fit—neither of us is perfect, but it's as close to that as possible.

Her lusty moan and the way she grips my dick sends a jolt of oh-fuck-yeah right through me, and I rock back and forth, in and out of her before sinking all the way in again. Fuck me. The way she feels has me on the edge already and we've barely started.

"Oh my." She undulates her hips, arching her gorgeous back, and looks over her shoulder at me, one side of her glasses a little higher than the other and her red hair coming out of her half bun in the way it should on a woman who's had two orgasms. "That's good."

Forget out of my league, Tilda Sherwood is out of my galaxy.

"Just wait." And I pull back until all that's touching her is the head of my cock and stay there for a second as I glide my palm over the curve of Tilda's fabulous ass. "Are you ready to come again?"

She lifts an eyebrow high enough that I can see it over the top of her round glasses. "Three might be asking a lot."

"Challenge accepted," I say, throwing her own line back at her.

Before she can say anything else, I grab her fleshy hips and pull her back against my dick as I thrust, going deep. I withdraw and push forward before reaching around and slipping my fingers between her legs from the front. The second I stroke her clit while I'm inside her, she moans and fists the bedsheets again as hard as she's holding on to my cock. The color of everything in the room becomes more vibrant, the train speeds up and shudders as it rounds a bend on the tracks, and I swear the stars outside the window glow brighter as I circle her clit and fuck her from behind. Again and again I thrust into her and pull back, keeping the pace steady on her clit until I feel her tighten around me half a second before she comes a third time, and I know I'm only a few seconds behind her. I go one, two, three more times before my balls tighten as the ball of energy at the base of my spine explodes and my orgasm hits me, knocking out everything else but Tilda and me and this moment that is burned into my brain like a brand.

I collapse on the bed feeling like every bone in my body has turned to mushy oatmeal. All the happy hormones blasting my brain are making me so content. Then Tilda takes off her glasses, puts them on the small table next to the bed, and rolls over so she is right next to me, her body fitting against mine as if we were made to go together, and *content* isn't the right word, it's not enough for whatever this sense of absolute rightness is that's making me all floaty and happy.

"You're smiling," Tilda says as her eyes flutter shut. "You should do that more often. Of course, that wouldn't really be fair since you're already obnoxiously hot even when you're glaring."

I brush a kiss on the top of her head. "So, I'll only smile for you."

She chuckles, a happy little snuffle of a sound, but for once doesn't have anything else to say. Obviously, I'm not the only one defying gravity—or at least feeling like it. And as we lie there on the bed and my brain starts to come back online, I know that Griselda was right. My life has definitely just changed because of the woman I've been lying to since day one.

The truth is on my lips, but by the time I'm about to open my mouth and let it all out, get rid of the secrets between us, her breathing has steadied and softened. Tilda lets out a small, contented sigh and snuggles in against my side, already mostly asleep.

Tomorrow.

I'll tell her everything as soon as we wake up.

Am I being selfish or a giant chicken? Probably a little of both, but you already know what kind of asshole I am, and so do I—the kind who isn't made for someone like her. A few weeks ago I was fine with that. Now? I'd trade a decade back in The Beyond for twenty-four hours being the kind of man who is worthy of Tilda Sherwood, but there isn't a spell for that and there's no magical way that all of this will work out.

Chapter Twenty-Five

Tilda . . .

*W*hen I wake up a few hours later, I'm on my side and Gil is big spooning me, his exhales sending the ends of my hair flying so they tickle my nose. That must be what woke me up—well, that and the fact that I'd had three cups of elderberry tea to boost my courage before taking that nerve-racking walk down the train car to Gil's room armed with only muffins and a smile.

Who in the hell would have thought that would work? Not me, not really.

Why? Because despite everything, I know who I am—an outré in a world where the most important thing about a person is their magical ability.

Still, as I lie here with Gil's arm curled around me, holding me close enough to him that his chest hair brushes against my back when he inhales and I can feel his semi-hard dick pressed against my ass no matter what he's doing, all I can think about is the look in his eyes last night, the way he kissed me as if he'd never wanted anyone more in his life, and—yeah—the three orgasms that were their own kind of magic. The contradiction of what Witchingdom has conditioned me to accept as fact—that I'm not wantable—and the possibility that Gil has shown me that the rest of Witchingdom may just have it wrong has my brain buzzing more than a pair of beehives being used as maracas by a troll band.

I have to get out of here and get some answers.

Holding my breath, I slowly lift his arm from around my waist enough that I can do the slide-shimmy thing to get off the mattress. I lay his arm back down as gently as I can. He grumbles in his sleep, something about someone needing to believe him, and flops over onto his back. I grab my glasses off the little table next to the bed and put them on so I can find my clothes.

That's a mistake because now, instead of my usual non-corrected soft, fuzzy vision of a sleeping Gil in the semi-darkness of the room, I have a full twenty-twenty view. The sheets are down low around his hips, and my gaze goes from the defined lines of his abs up to his muscular chest and onto his face, so relaxed in sleep that it's like getting a look at his secret self, the one he doesn't share with anyone. It's intimate enough that I can't stop looking even though I know I should. That's when I spot them. Three jagged scars curling around the top of his right shoulder. They're dull and a pale pink as if they've been there for a long time, years at least.

The second realization hits me, I slap my hand over my mouth to keep from making a sound and waking him up.

No one talks much about exile. Why invite that kind of trouble into existence in your life, you know? But the one story every witch knows is the mark of the banished. Upon arrival in exile, three lines are drawn on the banished witch by a red-hot burst of magic that pulsates on the witch's skin for the first year, burning deeper and deeper into their skin until the scar goes all the way down to the bone. It's painful enough that it drives some witches to madness.

And Gil got it as a teenager for something he had no control over.

The barbarity and nonsensical cruelty of it all has me blinking back tears. I may be an outré, but I am still a Sherwood, and that means a level of privilege not available to most witches.

I grab my jeans off the floor and yank them on, then pick my sweater up off the lampshade it is hanging from and put it on before tiptoeing out of Gil's room. I hook a left outside of the door and head down to the lounge car. I know what I need to do.

The tarot cards are in an intricately carved wooden case in the middle of the single dining table. I unlatch it and take out the cards, my heart going a million miles an hour as I shuffle them and start to deal without even bothering to sit down first.

I'm still a null; I know I don't have what it takes to read the cards with one hundred percent accuracy, but anything seems possible tonight. There's a frisson of something extra in the air, as noticeable as the scent of chlorine when all the pools open up for the first time in the summer. Maybe this time, everything will click into place.

A tingly, scratchy sensation marches up the back of my neck and the hairs on my arms stand up. I flip the first card. The fool. Again. Okay, okay—new beginnings aren't bad. The next card is the eight of swords, then comes the knight of cups. This isn't just weird. It's unbelievable. Even for someone untrained like me, the tarot never turns out the same a second time. Sure, there could be a few of the same cards, but the exact same cards in the exact same order? Yeah. That isn't possible.

Of course, telling myself that and getting my hands to stop shaking as I hold the fourth card are two separate things.

Just like before, it is the ace of swords.

I don't mean to sit down at that moment, but my knees just kinda give out, and the next thing I know, I'm butt-to-velvet-chair-pillow, breathing like I just finished a marathon. So again, the cards are telling me about new beginnings, feeling powerless and stuck, being romantic and following one's heart, as well as a sudden opportunity and clarity.

The deck is as heavy as a cement block in my hand, and I'm as frozen as my family.

"You gonna keep going or are you too scared?"

I let out a yelp of surprise and jump up from my chair, my heart pounding in my chest, whirling around to see Vance standing in the doorway. His tatted-up arms are crossed and he's scowling per usual. He's wearing ratty gym shorts, a vintage Dead Kennedys T-shirt that he may have gotten at a concert a million years ago (unicorns and vampires share the whole live-forever thing), and a hot pink scarf decorated with rainbow-farting unicorns is wrapped around his horn.

"Vance!" I whisper-yell, hoping my chicken-butt scream didn't already wake everyone up. "You scared the crap out of me."

"Yeah, I picked up on that." He strolls over to the table and gives the cards another look. "Interesting."

Yeah. That is one word for it. I'd go with freakishly shitty and possibly literally cursed. "They're the same as the last time I did this."

He makes a *huh* grunt and then heads over to the bar, reaching over it and pulling a large bottle of hard cider out from underneath. He doesn't grab one of the glasses sitting on the bar but instead pops the top off of the bottle without the help of an opener. It sails across the room and ends up landing right in the middle of the fool card.

"So what do I do?" I ask.

"You flip the card or you don't," he says with a shrug.

"That's it?" I let out a frustrated groan. "That's all the advice you've got for me?"

I'd been hoping for some guidance. My mom would have told me exactly what to do, in detail, perhaps with a written outline. My sisters would have told me to go with my heart and gone on and on about how cool a repeat reading would be. Birdie and Eli would have advised me to put the deck down and walk away before it got any weirder. Griselda probably would have flipped the card over before I even got a chance to ask the question. And Gil? Well, a few weeks ago I would have said he'd make some cutting comment about outrés messing with magical things they had no business being involved in, but now I'm not so sure.

The seven-foot-tall unicorn next to the table only downs another long drink of hard cider.

I lift my hand holding the deck so the cards are as close to being in his face as possible. "Vance!"

He raises his hand, extends a finger, the nail paint black and chipped just a bit, and pushes the deck back down to my elevation. "I don't do advice—I've been alive too long to get involved in that kind of messy bullshit."

Ugh.

Where are the people who love to tell me exactly what to do when I need them? Oh yeah, I froze most of them, and the others are sleeping in the next train car on the way to a heist to steal the most important spell book ever so I can fix my icy fuckup. *Way to go, Matilda Grace. Stellar work. Really. Amazing.*

"What if I flip it and it's the same card as before?" I ask, the deck vibrating softly in my hand as its need to finish the reading manifests into physical movement. "Does that mean that the fates have set it in stone? Is there still wiggle room? Is the magic cast already?"

Looking bored, Vance sighs. "Flip it or don't."

"You're a giant pain in the ass, Vance," I say, but there isn't any heat in my words—how could there be, it's not like he's wrong.

He grins at me as if I've given him the biggest of compliments. Despite everything, it makes me chuckle. Unicorn shifters, what are you going to do with them?

Right now? I'm just grateful he's here, part of this ragtag group of misfits.

Acting on impulse, I give him a quick hug, squeezing him hard to let him know how much I appreciate his gruff, grumpy self. When I let him go and step back, he's lost some of the fuck-you scowl he always wears and his gaze is locked on the floor beneath our feet.

"Don't worry," I say, giving him a friendly punch in the shoulder. "I won't tell anyone we hugged."

"You hugged me," he says, still looking down.

Then he does the most unexpected thing and reaches out for me, pulling me into a bear—unicorn?—hug that ends with him delivering a few hearty backslaps powerful enough to have knocked some of my teeth loose.

"There," he says with a grin. "I hugged you back so it won't be awkward. Now, stop procrastinating and decide whether you're going to turn the tarot card."

I could walk away. Even if I were magic, the tarot wouldn't be complete without the fifth card. I can walk away and laugh about how silly it was in the morning. I could tell myself I was just being paranoid. I could—

No. I can't. I know myself better than that.

I have to know. Do I have any kind of future with Gil?

Letting out a deep breath, I sit back down at the table, clutching the tarot deck. I flip over the fifth card and I swear my heart stops, my lungs quit, and everything disappears except that damn decorative globe card.

Completion.

Celebration.

Power.

It's Leona's card again—or at least the one that represents the most powerful Sherwood sibling, which she is.

My throat is stuffed with emotion that makes it hard to breathe, my eyes are all watery, and I must make some kind of squeaky, distressed sound, because Vance's heavy hand comes down on my shoulder.

"I've been around for six hundred years and I can tell you one thing for sure—there are things in this universe that are more powerful than magic. Put your faith in those."

He punctuates that exceedingly rare bit of advice with a belch that smells like Lucky Charms cereal and hard cider. Whew, whatever the unicorn PR machine is doing to make everyone think unicorns fart rainbows and are nothing but polite sweetness is its own kind of magic.

"Whatever you do though," he continues, "don't let this fuck up tomorrow. Head in the game, Tilda. Whether or not you get to keep it attached to your neck might just be riding on snagging that spell book."

And yet, it is my heart that has me most worried.

Chapter Twenty-Six

Gil . . .

Tilda's pillow is cold, her clothes are gone, and her glasses have disappeared from the nightstand. She's probably down in the lounge car, but I'm still sitting here buck-ass naked in bed trying to figure out what to do next.

The smart move would be to get the hell out of here. Thanks to the protective dome around the Sherwood house, I doubt Cassius has realized I'm not in Wrightsville anymore. I know my parents are safe. It might take time, but I'll be able to track them down, and we could disappear forever on some small, unnamed island in the South Pacific where we could live our best lives without the threat of returning to exile hanging over our heads. You protect yours, and everyone else can fuck off. The only problem? Tilda is mine, so I can't walk away from her. And her circle includes her family and Birdie and Eli and Vance and probably a million other people who she looks kindly at—including, no doubt, the troll from the woods and the boar that led us to the mushrooms. That means I can't walk away from them either.

I grab her pillow and slam it down over my face to muffle my frustrated groan. That goes according to plan, but then I inhale, and the smell of Tilda's shampoo clinging to the pillowcase fills my nostrils, and it's pure fucking torture because all I want is to be with her again. Now. Later. Forever.

Fuck me. I never would have thought that life in The Beyond would be less complicated than falling in love with Tilda Sherwood.

I jolt up into a sitting position, the pillow falling into my lap.

Love?

No.

It's just the duíl magic, and now that's all taken care of, right? At least that's how it should work if desire was all there is to it. But it doesn't feel like last night ended anything. I mean, yeah, I know there's something extra mixed in there—probably because of her spellbinder magic—but it can't be love.

Love isn't magic, it's more terrifyingly powerful. It can't be controlled. It can't be fooled. It can't be outwitted. Love just is what it is, and there isn't a damn thing anyone can do about it.

I fall back and smother myself with Tilda's pillow again,

but that only gives me another hint of her scent, and I'm up and out of the bed, pulling on my clothes, and heading to the lounge car before I even realize where I'm going. Of course, I'm going to find her.

Where else in the world would I be if not with her?

I find Tilda—and everyone else—in the lounge car. Instead of the sweater and jeans she was in last night, she wears a pair of black leggings, an oversized hoodie, and a pair of woolly socks. She looks like she'd be perfectly at home in my rented house bingeing old movies on the couch, tucked up beside me as a fire crackled in the hearth. Not surprisingly, she seemed equally good standing in front of a hand-drawn replica of the Marie Laveau Museum in Salem, guiding everyone through their parts of the heist one last time. Tilda may not realize it, but she's in her element, heading up a team of people, leading a mission, and getting everyone on the same page. It is a gift that has nothing to do with magical ability or her last name and everything to do with the kind of person she is.

"Look who decided to show up," Vance says from his spot in the corner, where he's flipping through an issue of *Magical Mayhem.*

"Good morning to you too." I swipe a chocolate croissant from the tray of pastries on the table where I swear the tarot cards had been last night. My attention swings over to Birdie and Eli sitting together in an oversized yellow leather chair at the front of the room and give them a nod before turning my attention to Tilda. "Hi."

Her cheeks are flaming red, but her smile is anything but embarrassed. "Morning." She pushes her glasses a little higher up her nose and clears her throat. "So, as I was saying, Gil and I will provide the distraction while you two grab The Liber Umbrarum."

"Easy peasy," Eli mutters.

Birdie delivers a very unsubtle glare and elbow to his side.

"Well, this will help with that." Tilda picks up a brightly painted soapstone jar from the bar, slips free the hook holding it closed, and pulls out two small, round snuffboxes and hands one each to Birdie and Eli. "It's the agaric mushroom powder."

They both accept the boxes like Tilda is handing them live grenades. I can't blame them, no matter what Griselda said when she sent us out into the woods; something known as a death cap mushroom shouldn't be taken lightly.

Birdie takes a closer look at the snuffbox and seems to satisfy herself that the latch isn't going to pop open unexpectedly. "So we just take a pinch and toss it in the guards' faces?"

Tilda nods. "Yep."

"What happens if we inhale it?" Eli asks, a worried edge making the big man's tone sharp.

"Same thing as anyone else," Tilda says, calm as ever. "You'll become very pliant and relaxed."

Eli doesn't look convinced.

"Just hold your breath when you dose the guards and you'll be fine," Vance says. "You'd have to face-plant in it to actually die from it."

"Oh great," Eli says. "Very reassuring."

Vance curls his lips in what is maybe supposed to be a smile, but I highly doubt it.

"I'm a little ray of fucking sunshine," he says.

"Birdie," Tilda says, a little louder than necessary—no doubt trying to head off the giant witch and unicorn shifter from escalating, "you're going to pick Erik Svensen's pocket for the key to the case's analog lock."

The other woman nods and she plucks the round snuffbox from Eli's grasp and sets it down next to hers on a side table. "What makes you think he'll have the key?"

"From what Leona says,"—Tilda rolls up the sketch she'd made of the museum and pops it into the umbrella holder by the door—"he's the typical oldest son control freak who thinks he's the fates' gift to Witchingdom."

"So you figure there's no way someone like that will trust anyone else with the key?" I ask.

Tilda smiles at me. "Exactly."

That smile. It is all for me and I want more of it. The need to see it again and again and again is a gut punch. It's all I can do not to stride across the room, toss her over my shoulder, and take her back to my room. My cock thickens against my thigh and I'm two steps forward before I catch myself.

Not the time.

Not the place.

And I'm probably not the guy, but damn I wish I was.

Her cheeks a delicious shade of pink, Tilda continues. "Then you two will dose the guards protecting The Liber Umbrarum and grab the spell book. Gil and I will leave a change of clothes for you in this alcove near the entrance to the English gardens. You'll swap gala formal wear for dark green overalls that match the gardeners' uniforms and leave through the French doors. Follow this path to the back gate. There will be a motorcycle and sidecar waiting for you." She looks over at Vance. "You're sure your contacts can get that for you?"

He nods. "It'll work out perfect because everyone will be monitoring for magical activities. No one expects an outré getaway."

"And that's what makes us so perfect," Tilda says. "We have honed all of the skills they don't think are important, and that's what's going to make this heist a success."

She isn't wrong. In Witchingdom, everything is about power. Who has it? What kind? Can you get them to use it for your needs instead of theirs? Someone without magic or who can't get a spell out without sneezing or fucking up the words doesn't even manage to be a blip on most witches' radar.

"So after that we rendezvous back at the train?" Birdie asks.

"Correct. Then we head back to Wrightsville and save my family." She looks around at everyone. "Any questions? Did I miss anything?" When no one says anything, she looks over at me. "Is there anything we should know about The Liber Umbrarum?"

It's a solid question. Most spell books—especially the old ones—have their own kind of magic embedded into the pages from decades and decades of witch work being done around them. As far as the stories go, though, this spell book is more like Teflon than a sponge. Of course, that doesn't mean it isn't without its issues.

"Eli and Birdie, you should be prepared for The Liber Umbrarum to be heavy," I say. "It reportedly weighs close to fifty pounds."

Eli's eyebrows go up with surprise. "It has that many pages?"

"No, it has that much inlaid gold on the cover, golden threads woven into the pages, and gold ink was used to paint a scene of Druids' runes on the page edges of the book. Then there are the gems around the edge of the cover held there by a spell that supposedly can never be broken."

Birdie lets out a low whistle. "How much is it worth?"

"It's priceless, which is why witches have coveted it for centuries." The Liber Umbrarum's history is littered with stories about the lengths witches have gone to just to hold it. The fact that the Svensens not only figured out a way to possess it but are willing to display it for the world to see goes to show just how much juice that family has. "I've heard rumors of how much people are willing to pay for it—no questions asked—and it's enough money to equate to the GDP of a midsized country with a strong economy."

"Which is why," Tilda breaks in, presumably before I can really freak out the rest of our crew with some of the book's bloody history, "we'll be returning it to the Svensen family as soon as we unfreeze my family. We're not thieves. We're borrowers."

Vance snorts. "Yeah, I'm sure they'll recognize the distinction."

"And since Eli and Birdie will be in disguise," Tilda rushes on, "no one will realize that we're the ones who have stolen it, which means we won't have to worry about someone purloining it from us and hocking it on the black market for massive amounts of fast cash."

Vance leveled a hard look my way. "That won't be an issue."

I'd be offended if it weren't for the fact that the unicorn shifter isn't that far off from the truth.

My dad has told stories about The Liber Umbrarum for as long as I can remember. What it looks like. The power of the spells. How much a collector would pay for it, and how that kind of money could take us from a life of always looking over our shoulders to a peaceful existence on some speck of land in the ocean. I don't even have to concentrate hard to hear my dad's voice as he shares theories about who wrote the book and what all is in it—after all, that talk is what inspired me to go into historical spells and what garnered the interest of the Council in me. No one blinks twice at researchers going from town to town, except instead of gathering intel on historical documents, I was getting information about the most powerful witching families.

I meet Vance's glare with one of my own. I know who I am and it's not a good witch.

Tilda clears her throat and yanks my attention from the unicorn shifter. She takes off her glasses and uses the hem of her hoodie to clean them, the whole time watching me with concern. I shrug a shoulder and give my head a small shake. Smart woman that she is, she understands the message, slips her glasses back on, and continues with her briefing, answering the rest of Birdie's and Eli's questions.

I can feel Vance still staring at me, but I ignore it.

I don't need him to tell me what I already know—I have to do whatever it takes to keep Tilda safe. This isn't magic or a curse or a rogue spell drawing me to her. It's love, and that's so much worse.

But I don't have time to ponder that because the train is slowing down.

We've arrived in Salem.

Chapter Twenty-Seven

Tilda . . .

The Marie Laveau Museum is making me dizzy as I stand in the middle of the main gallery and look up ten stories to the glass ceiling. There aren't stairs in here. Instead, it's one very long, very smooth ramp that circles the main lobby, going higher and higher on its way up to the galleries on the other ten floors. On any other day, I'd love to lose myself in exploring all of the art, but tonight is all about stealing art, not appreciating it.

Straight ahead is the hall leading to the gallery with The Liber Umbrarum. The line for entry goes out all the way to the coat check and is filled with witches from the most connected families in Witchingdom dressed in their absolute best for the gala, who are being let into the room in pairs. Acting for all the world as if we couldn't care less about the book, Gil and I go from one work of art to another, admiring each for a few minutes and smiling at all of the witches who spot us and immediately start texting on their phones. If pics of us will distract them from the real action, then it's a perfect solution. And we are something to see—Gil is in a black tux that makes him look like James Bond, the hot Daniel Craig version, and I'm in my emerald-green sparkly dress that has just enough coverage to make me feel fully clothed but is revealing enough to have everyone's eyes glued to my boobs. It's definitely not my usual style, but it works perfectly for the purpose of being a glamazon distraction so Birdie and Eli can do their thing.

"Tilda Sherwood," says a man from behind me.

Gil looks past my shoulder and his eyes narrow. Turning, I look up at the black-haired guy with bluer-than-blue eyes and a killer smile wearing a navy tux that has to be custom-made.

"Erik Svensen." He holds out his hand in greeting, and like everyone else we've chatted with since walking in, his gaze never drops below my chin. "I hear you got tickets by bribing my brother Cy with enough juniper berries to fill a semitruck."

"That's exactly what I did." Really, what is the use in denying it? Plus, the only way we're going to carry this off is to lie as close to the truth as possible. And the fact that my palms are all clammy from nerves? Let's just hope Erik doesn't notice that as we shake. "What in the world does he need all of it for?"

"When it comes to Cy, I never know," Erik says with a chuckle. "Every family has one brilliant thinker, right?" He looks past me, scanning the crowd. "Did Leona come with you?"

Ah, there it is. "No."

"Pity," he says with a false cheer that doesn't do a thing to dim the genuine disappointment in his blue eyes.

And the mystery thickens. I have no idea what happened between Leona and Erik, but you can bet I'm going to find out as soon as she warms back up, because this guy is beyond just interested in her—no need for a truth spell on that one. His shoulders drop before he hitches them back up again, his friendly grin a little stiffer than it was when he first walked up.

He covers it up well though, stopping a waiter and getting a glass of champagne for each of us from the tray. "I don't believe we've met before, but you do look familiar."

"Guess I have one of those faces," Gil says as he accepts the champagne. "Gil Connolly."

They shake hands and do the puffed-chest dude thing where guys size each other up. What is it with guys? They really are beyond understanding sometimes.

"You requested four tickets," Erik says, turning his attention back to me. "Did you bring two of your other sisters?"

"No, just a couple of friends." I fight the urge to look directly at Birdie and Eli even though I've been watching their progress toward the target from the corner of my eye. "They're here somewhere."

At the moment, they're finally in line to see The Liber Umbrarum, but I'm not about to point that out to Erik.

"Well, it was good to meet you both. Be sure to tell Leona I said hello." Erik narrows his eyes and his gaze zeroes in on me. "You're not at all what I expected. LeLe always said you were something of a wild whirlwind."

LeLe? Oh wow. There is no way my very uptight, very by-the-books sister would like that nickname—or any nickname, for that matter.

I give what I hope is a convincing smile. "I promise to keep my gusts to a minimum during the party."

"That sounds perfectly boring and unlike any Sherwood in all of Witchingdom." He nods at Gil. "If you'll excuse me, as the family representative I have to go mingle, but I hope we'll get to chat again later."

Gil and I sip our champagne, the little bubbles popping against the roof of my mouth, and watch Erik make his way across the crowded gallery, stopping several times to chat with this couple or that group. He has an easy, friendly vibe to him, but I can't help but think that's just an act. The little voice in the back of my head is firmly against crossing Erik Svensen, but there isn't really a way around our night of thievery. I'll just have to ask for forgiveness and pray to the fates that our plan doesn't go south.

It isn't until Erik's past the large bronze sculpture depicting Moll Dyer outside of her ramshackle cabin in the Maryland woods that I let out a shaky breath.

Leaning in close to Gil, I whisper, "I thought for sure we were busted."

"Have faith. You've got this." Gil sets his empty champagne glass on the tray of a passing waiter. "Shall we get to work?"

I hand my glass to the same waiter and follow Gil to look at *The Musicians* by Caravaggio. While doing my best to seem as if I am admiring the lush colors and not-so-hidden sexuality of the painting, I keep sneaking peeks at Birdie and Eli as they chat with the couple in front of them in line. At the same time, I can feel what feels like a million sets of eyes on me as well as more than a few not-so-discreet camera phones aimed right at me.

Really, I should be used to it, and—between the past few weeks' accidental glitching in public with Gil—it's not like I don't give people the fool they're expecting. I can't blame them for expecting more of the same even though I hate it. That is my lot in life. The null who fucks things up. Imagine if they knew that I'd frozen my family. It would be a gossip-feeding frenzy. I know it's all part of the plan I came up with, but still . . . I hate it.

"They're all watching us," I mutter.

"I'm not surprised," Gil says, slipping his hand across my back and coming to rest on my hip. "You look amazing."

A blush heats my cheeks. "I don't think *that's* why anyone is looking at me."

Quick as lightning, he moves so he's in front of me, looking at me with an intensity that steals my breath. He cups my face in both his hands and kisses me like he is trying to tell me a million things in one all too brief touch. Then he steps back, his blue eyes stormy, and says, "Then they're fools."

My brain is still trying to catch up with what just happened when his palm is again resting on the small of my back and he guides me a few feet over to stand in front of the next painting, but I keep looking back to the spot in front of the Caravaggio where he just kissed me. In about five seconds he wiped my mind clean of everything but possibilities.

Is this what a future with Gil could be like? Not a life of crime, of course, but an easy camaraderie and teasing flirtation that gives me butterflies and all sorts of dirty thoughts? Breakfast out on the balcony together, drinking our coffee and sharing the paper? Date nights at the museum or the movie theater? Hours lost in the stacks at the Alchemist's Bookshop and Tea Emporium followed by road trips looking for rare spell books in little out-of-the-way bookshops in small towns? Holding hands as we walk down the sidewalk in front of Griselda's house? Picnics by the creek in the woods with the troll that eventually joins us and tells us stories about all the witches he's stopped with riddles? Adventure and comfort and fun and love.

Standing in front of *The Musicians*, seeing the everyday

heaven of the moment the bad boy Italian Renaissance painter captured, I realize how much I want all of that—and if we can carry off this heist, I can—we can—have it.

Together.

Arm in arm, we stroll over to the painting of Washington crossing the Delaware, which just happens to accidentally on purpose give us the perfect view inside The Liber Umbrarum gallery. Eli and Birdie are next in line. My heartbeat speeds up until it's banging against my ribs with enough power that I'm almost worried it will break through.

"I got you something," Gil says loud enough that the people standing nearby will hear. "I hope you like it."

We planned this next bit—a showy gossip fodder that is all but guaranteed to capture everyone's attention and pull focus away from the spell book. Still, I'm not prepared for the rush of desire that washes over me when Gil moves behind me, so close that I can feel the heat coming off his body.

His fingers glide across the bare skin of my arms as he reaches in front of me, a magnificent diamond and emerald necklace in his grasp. It's not real, of course, but unless someone rushes up with a jeweler's loupe, it's close enough to fool the witches in attendance. As he fastens the clasp, his fingers linger on my neck, tracing a line up the side of my throat. I know this is all for show, part of the plan, but it still feels real when he traces a path across my sensitive skin, then dips his head down and brushes a soft, barely-there kiss to my temple.

In the distance I can hear the not-really-whispers and

part of me realizes there are flashes going off from people taking pics with their phones, but all I can focus on in this moment is Gil.

"You're absolutely everything, Tilda Sherwood," he says, the low rumble in his voice moving down my spine like a shiver of anticipation. "No matter what happens, remember that."

He drops another kiss on that spot where my shoulder meets my neck that I feel all the way to my core and then moves beside me, taking my arm and putting it through his. We walk together over to Mary Cassatt's *Young Mother Sewing*. The little girl in the painting is leaning against her mom with her arms folded and her chin in her hand as she stares out, curious, open, ready for whatever comes next. There's not a single smidge of fear or worry or hesitation, just a confident stillness that seems to reach out and grab my soul. I know this girl. Maybe I was this girl, a million years ago, before I realized that I wouldn't be magical like my mom, but something else entirely.

I'm not sure I ever felt as confident as that girl when I was her age, but tonight after we carry off this heist and unfreeze my family, I can't help but think that I will find it again. Really, if my plan works, that will change everything. I won't just be the family flunky.

I can be more.

I will be more.

"They're on their way in," Gil says, pivoting to face me so that I can appear to be smiling up at him when I am actually watching Birdie's and Eli's progress as they walk calmly toward The Liber Umbrarum's gallery.

Birdie pauses in the doorway and leans close to the guard. Hopefully it's only because I'm watching them so closely when it seems like every other witch in the museum is looking at me, but there's no missing the small gray puff of a cloud that Birdie blows from the palm of her hand into the guard's face. His eyes go round and he reaches for the hard rubber baton at his waist, but then his jaw goes soft and his hand drops back to his side. Birdie whispers in his ear and he nods before moving over to the red velvet rope near the entrance and stringing it across the open doorway.

"Sorry folks," the guard says to everyone in line, his voice stilted but otherwise normal. "Fifteen-minute break."

Eli and Birdie don't look back as they make their way across the main gallery to the hall leading out to the formal gardens.

With all eyes on us, Gil and I stroll over to Winslow Homer's vivid painting *The Gulf Stream*, which depicts a man alone in a small boat surrounded by choppy waters and circling sharks. There's a storm brewing on the horizon, but a ship is coming too that may beat the squall. Hello, art imitating life, because it sure feels like every witch in the room is circling us like sharks.

That was, however, our plan all along, because if the attendees are watching us, eager for the next tidbit of gossip, that means they aren't paying any attention to Birdie and

Eli as they slip into the darkened alcove for the quick change of a lifetime.

Usually, I'd be sucked in by the painting's strong colors and the intensity of the composition as the man tries to survive the dangers that seem to be everywhere, but not tonight. Blood rushes in my ears as loud as the train we traveled into Salem on and adrenaline has my insides jittery even as I maintain the placid expression on my face while inside my head I am screaming, "Hurry up!" Whoever thought years of appearing calm and collected on the outside to deal with other witches' snide comments about me being an outré would come in so handy?

It's taking too long.

The guards are starting to blink and look around as if they're coming back to themselves.

Those standing in line for the exhibit begin grumbling about the wait.

My heart is in my throat as I desperately try to think of something—anything—that will give Eli and Birdie another few minutes.

"Matilda Grace Sherwood?" Gil says as he goes down to one knee in front of me, a small, square, velvet box in his hand.

Everyone around us stops even pretending not to be staring right at us. A bazillion cell phones get pointed our way. Several witches must have immediately gone live on WitchyGram, because they're talking into their phones like they're working the red carpet at the Oscars—a sound that I don't even have to strain to hear because the gala has otherwise gone silent. Still, no one is more surprised than I am.

Yeah, I'm bug-eyed and slack-jawed in front of the most influential witches in all of Witchingdom. My mom is going to be thrilled when we finally thaw her.

Gil opens the box, revealing the sapphire ring Vance had delivered along with a message from Gil's mom. Am I hyperventilating at this point? You bet your ass I am. Sure, I know it's not a real proposal. He's just buying time. The way he's looking at me, though, as if I'm the only person in the room— check that, in the world—has my heart fluttering in my chest.

"Tilda, will you do me the great honor of being my wife?"

I'm not faking my ear-to-ear grin or the explosion of happiness that has me about ready to take off like a rocket straight through the skylights at the top of the gallery. A cooler woman would be lying to you about all of that, playing it off like it was nothing. We've moved beyond that, though, and you know that this feels so damn good even though I know it's all pretend.

Gil slowly stands and takes the ring out of the box and holds it up so he can slide it on my finger.

My chest tightens enough that I worry my ribs will crack with the intensity of it all. I can do a lot of things, but I can't let him put that ring on my finger. My heart might be a lost cause already, but I still have to do what I can.

"Yes, I'll marry you," I holler loud enough for the pixies hanging over the top banister on the top level to hear me.

Then I throw my arms around him and kiss him the way I would if any of this was real.

Flashes are going off around us, but out of the corner of my eye I see two gardeners, the taller of whom has an oddly flat and rectangular chest under his coveralls, make their way from the alcove to the doors and out into the formal gardens.

The breath I'm holding escapes in a whoosh. "They made it."

Gil must be more nervous than he lets on, because his shoulders lower a few inches. "Two minutes and then we head for the doors."

He pockets the ring and presses his palm against the small of my back, more reassuring than pushy as we move to the next painting, closer to the hall leading to our escape out that back garden gate. Around us, people are whispering and taking photos, but no one approaches as we look at the painting by Elisabeth Louise Vigée Le Brun of a little girl looking at her reflection in the mirror and that reflection staring out from the canvas. At any other time I would look closer at the informational card by the painting, but I'm too excited to make the letters form words even as I pretend to read it as I count down the seconds until we can run out of here to go celebrate our engagement privately, as far as anyone in attendance knows.

Finally, I straighten and turn to Gil, absolutely everything in my body lighter and more bubbly than it has ever been. I swear, I could float all the way back to the train, my fingers intertwined with Gil's, and then once we got there we could celebrate—with Vance, Eli, and Birdie at first, but eventually back in his room, alone, naked, and orgasmic.

I smile up at him, too happy to hold it in. "I love it when a plan works out perfectly."

Of course, that's when a guard in front of the private gallery presses a button near the door and an alarm sounds, and all hell breaks loose.

Chapter Twenty-Eight

Gil . . .

The siren is high-pitched enough to stab a person right in the ear and yank out their soul.

There are guards rushing in from everywhere heading straight for us. Dressed all in black, they're the size of small trolls and armed to the teeth with nasty-looking long knives. Everything about them screams paid mercenaries. I push Tilda behind me into the curtained-off alcove where Eli and Birdie changed clothes.

Looking out between the narrow slice of space between the two curtains, I brace for whatever is coming next—not that it matters. My only mission at this point is to keep Tilda safe.

Another witch would let me take the risk of seeing what

the mercenaries are doing as they swarm the museum, but not Tilda. Instead, she sneaks in front of me and crouches down so she can look out without obstructing my view. A soft gasp escapes when she finally gets a peek at what is going on on the other side of the curtain. The mercenaries are stopping and frisking each witch. They've locked down The Liber Umbrarum gallery and are headed right for us, no doubt to secure the door leading out to the formal garden—aka our only way of escape.

We don't have many options, but one of them is far better than any other.

I step back from the curtain, taking Tilda with me. I don't mean to kiss her, but I can't help myself. It's not a nice kiss. It's hard, desperate, and ends too fucking quick. This may be the last time I see her. It's too soon. Hell, a million years from now would be too soon.

"I'll slow them down." I cup her face, memorizing every freckle on her nose as if I couldn't draw them all from memory already. "You get out of here."

She snorts and rolls her eyes. "I'm not leaving you."

"I'll meet you at the train," I say, letting go of her before I can't and forcing myself back to the curtain so I can time her escape.

"You didn't hear me," she says, her stubborn meter set to a million. "I'm not going without you."

"Tilda, we don't have time for this." I check the view through the curtain one last time. The mercenaries are all focused on the crowd gathered by The Liber Umbrarum's gallery. Only a few are stationed at this end of the museum. "The time to do this is now."

"Finally, we agree." She grabs my hand, intertwining her fingers with mine and holding on tight. "Guess we better go then."

This woman. This frustratingly stubborn, sweet, determined woman. I'd love to argue, because it's not that I *think* I'm right, I *know* I am. But I also know that this isn't an argument I'm going to win. There's a tilt to her chin I recognize from our not-so-by-accident dates, and I know her too well now to mistake her sweet face for belonging to a pushover. Tilda Sherwood is stronger than anyone realizes—sometimes I think even than she realizes—in ways that have nothing to do with magic.

And the mercenaries will turn their attention this way sooner rather than later.

"Fine." I open the curtain, winding my arm around her waist as if we had been in the alcove fucking instead of avoiding getting caught. "Let's go."

We no more than get out into the wide hall where the walls are covered in portraits of some of the most influential witches throughout history when an entire cadre of goons comes from around the corner past the door leading out to the gardens and heads straight for us. The world slows down and I fall back into old habits from The Beyond, picking out the likely opponents, identifying weaknesses, and bracing to take more punishment than the other guy is willing to suffer, because that's what it takes to win sometimes, being willing to endure the hurt.

I let go of Tilda's hand and sidestep so I'm in front of her, set my feet, and force my muscles to relax so I can absorb whatever blows are coming and respond. Then, at the last moment, the guards swerve around us and head straight for The Liber Umbrarum's gallery. Behind me, Tilda lets out a relieved sigh and lets her forehead relax against my back. Her soft breath tickles the back of my neck.

"I thought it was all over there."

"Which is exactly why you should have listened to me," I say, taking her hand and starting toward the doors to the formal gardens.

She shoots me an annoyed glare at the same time as we hurry down the hall crowded with witches watching the goings on with equal parts glee and horror. "I don't abandon the people I care about."

"You care about me, huh?" Not that her declaration makes my steps all that much lighter, but it totally does.

A quiet chuckle escapes as she straightens her glasses. "Do you really think *this* is the time and place for that conversation?"

I grin at her. "Excellent point."

We hustle as fast as possible through the throngs of witches staring agog at the paid mercenaries, who look like they're going to floss with the bones of whoever had the audacity to steal The Liber Umbrarum. Yeah, there is no way I am going to let Tilda be anywhere near these goons when they figure out the thieves aren't in the gallery anymore, which is why we are approaching the doors leading out to the formal gardens.

The cool fall air hits me like a blast of air-conditioning after a July afternoon spent cutting the grass on a five-acre plot with a push mower. It smells like freedom, but I'm not gonna stop and enjoy it, not while Tilda is still in danger.

"Just act like nothing is happening," I say as we head toward the back gate where, with any luck, Eli and Birdie, alerted that everything has gone sideways by the alarm, will still be with our getaway motorcycle. "We're just another couple checking out these beautiful gardens on a clear fall evening."

Side by side, we quick-walk down the path toward the gate while pretending to admire the gardenias, the mums just starting to bloom, and the boxwoods trimmed into tight, compact squares even as adrenaline rushes through me. I'm on hyperalert for any sign of danger. Well, any sign of additional danger.

Ten steps to the gate and my sense of dread starts to abate.

Eight steps and Tilda grins at me. We just might carry this off.

Six steps and the alarm goes silent. Tilda's hand tightens on mine.

Four steps. "Hey, you," someone shouts from behind us.

Two steps, and without having to say anything, we pick up our speed.

The gate bursts open, revealing Eli and Birdie standing next to a motorcycle with a sidecar. He's got The Liber Umbrarum strapped to his chest, wrapped up in oil paper and secured with a mix of magic and duct tape. They're holding hands, and Birdie is murmuring a cloaking spell. The air around them sparks with light but fizzles out within seconds, punctuated by Birdie's sneezes, one right after the other in quick succession that snaps the spell.

"Tilda!" Erik hollers as he sprints from the museum door, flanked by a dozen mercenaries. "Stop!"

There's no time for explanations, no matter how much she deserves one—not if I'm going to get her out of here. Rushing forward, I grab Birdie's hand. Her eyes go wide, but she keeps up with the spell casting as best as she can. Around us the air thickens, a fog gathering out of the magic, trying to build up enough density to shield us from view but evaporating within seconds as another sneeze fit hits Birdie.

Turning to Tilda, I ask the one question that should definitely be answered with a no. "Do you trust me?"

Tilda nods, and it's the best-worst thing to ever happen to me. I may love her, but I sure as hell don't deserve her, not with the lies I've told and the secrets I've kept from her. But that's for later. Right now the only thing that's important is keeping her safe, and I can't do that without her help.

"We all have to hold hands." I take her hand, already feeling the sizzle of magic just under the surface. "Whatever happens next, just don't let go."

I add my voice to Birdie's as she takes Tilda's hand. The

moment the circle closes, the wind whirls up out of nowhere as the spell gains power. Thunder cracks. Lightning flashes. Rain pours down. It's as if there is so much magic crackling around us that the earth has to shed some of it or we'll all explode.

Then Tilda adds her voice to the spell and the ground shifts under my feet. It's quiet, and I can barely hear her above the whipping winds, but it's there, calm and centered. Her eyes are closed and there's such an ethereal vibe to her in that moment that I'm not even sure she realizes she's doing it.

But the magic does.

I can smell it in the air building up to a gale, feel it zipping along my skin, see it in the soft glow around Tilda that's visible between the flashes of lightning. The extra-buttery popcorn I'm used to when my magic mixes with Tilda's is amped up by the honey and cinnamon sugar that must be Birdie's and Eli's. Together, we're powering the cloaking spell, overwhelming Erik and his mercenaries, who are fighting against the gusts to get to us before the fog fills the space completely.

Suddenly, Erik jerks to a stop. I can see his lips moving, but the crash of thunder temporarily steals my focus from whatever spell he's spinning with enough power even by himself to make every pale yellow piece of gravel lining the paths of the formal garden go airborne as he throws up his arms.

"Tilda," I holler over the cacophony of the storm. "Finish it."

Her eyes snap open, a confused look on her face.

"The spell, really mean it." I squeeze her hand. "Trust me."

She hesitates for the briefest of moments, but then her demeanor changes. Her shoulders straighten. She stands taller. Her gaze sharpens. She lets out a deep, cleansing breath and begins to purposely chant with Birdie, Eli, and I.

"Tuere. Celare. Liberate."

The fog thickens, forming a fluffy barrier between us and Erik. It's good, but not enough to stop a million pieces of gravel that will be flying straight for us at any moment.

"Tuere. Celare. Liberate."

I squeeze Tilda's hand. We lock eyes. A wall of blue-flame-level heat slams into me as she straight up starts levitating a few feet up off the ground.

"Tuere. Celare. Liberate."

The rain picks up, slashing at us as the wind tears at our clothes. It takes everything I have to hold on to her as her power tries to take her higher.

"Tuere. Celare. Liberate."

A huge boom of thunder crashes against us, a tangible sound wave that blows my hair back half a second before a bright flash of lightning nearly blinds us all, and then we're flying, rocketing through the night air. We're high enough that ice crystals form on my eyelashes. I sneak a glance over at Tilda. Her red hair flies behind her like flames, her glasses are askew, and she has the most excited-but-unsure smile on her face.

It's fucking adorable. I couldn't possibly love her more—not because she's a spellbinder or because she can do anything for me but because she's Tilda.

What I wouldn't give to think that it could work out between us, but you don't get to survive The Beyond by believing in the impossible.

The realization has my chest aching as the magic does a controlled burn, slowing us down as we approach the train yard. It lets us down on the platform on the last car of our train.

We're all soaked from the rain, but we're alive. In a matter of minutes we'll be on our way back to Wrightsville on the least likely form of witch transportation that anyone can think of so Tilda can use the novis spell to unfreeze her family. We're not home free yet—no doubt Erik is already looking for us—but we're a helluva lot closer than we were an hour ago, and in this world I'll take that as a win. In this life, you have to take the Ws when you can. Arm in arm, Tilda and I follow Eli and Birdie inside the lounge car.

As soon as we step inside, Vance looks up from the bowl of Lucky Charms he's eating at the bar and lets out a sigh that all but screams "what did you fuck up now." "I take it things did not go according to plan."

Yeah, that's putting it mildly.

"We gotta go," Tilda says. "Now."

Chapter Twenty-Nine

Tilda . . .

$\mathcal{M}$y feet may be planted firmly on the train's floorboards, but I am still flying, and the fact that I don't have electricity shooting out of my fingertips like laser beams blows my mind. That was petrifying and thrilling and not something I want to do again *exactly*, but wow what an experience.

I'm dripping all over the floor and all four of us look like half-drowned witches while Vance uses the train's intercom to tell the engineer to get us back home like the dogs of hell are nipping on our heels. I don't think Erik is quite that bad, but he is definitely not a fan of ours right now. Once I get back home and unfreeze my family, I'll return the book immediately. I'll have it back by dawn at the latest.

Part of me can't believe we pulled it off—especially with

all of that chaos at the end there—and part of me is all fuck yeah! And judging by looking around, I'm not the only one feeling like a can of soda that has been tossed in the passenger seat of a car and then driven down a pothole-heavy dirt road at a hundred miles an hour. Birdie's eyes are wide with excitement, her cheeks are flushed, and she is talking a mile a minute bringing Vance up to speed about what went down at the museum. Eli, meanwhile, can't keep his eyes off of Birdie, tracking her every move as she paces the train car, moving closer as the train starts rumbling down the tracks, no doubt so she has someone solid to hold on to in case we have a bumpy ride.

I look over at Gil and catch him watching me from his spot across the room. Something shifts inside me, a comforting warmth filling me right up—that is, until the moment I spot the tarot cards on the table spread out in the five-card formation I left them in after my last reading. The decorative globe, pure power in card form, sits in the middle of the circle formed by the other four cards.

Leona.

How in the hell could I have forgotten about my sister? How could I be that selfish? They were destined to be together, at least according to the cards as I dealt them. But really, if it wasn't true, how would I have ended up with the exact same cards in the exact same order twice in a row? Suddenly, all of the excitement fizzing inside me goes flat and the effort of keeping my shoulders straight and my chin up becomes too much.

That's when Gil moves from his spot by the bar over to the tarot table, where he moves the globe card from the center of the spread to the top right.

I hustle over. "What are you doing?"

"The order was messed up," he says, his attention focused on the cards. "The world card, it's in the personal identification spot when in a five-card spread like this it should be over here in growth." He looks up at me. "Did you do this?"

I nod.

He grimaces and rubs his palm hard against the back of his neck as he contemplates the spread on the table. "Makes sense."

Well, ouch. Forget being a two-liter bottle that someone left the cap off of, now I'm the drink dispenser that ran out of soda syrup. "Because it's wrong?"

"No." He shakes his head. "It's because of what happened tonight. That was your power, didn't you feel it?"

Feel it? I could probably have powered a small town with the amount of their excess magic rolling through me while they did the spell. "I was just completing the circle."

"It wasn't that and you know it." Gil takes my hand, sending off sparks of awareness, anticipation, and something that feels a lot like home. "Tilda, there's so much we need to talk about."

Yeah, it is definitely beginning to feel like that, but it is so much to process. If I'm wrong about the tarot cards pointing to Leona—Griselda all but said I was—what else am I wrong about? The power part is sweet, but I spent years trying to cast spells on my own in my room. I memorized the most popular spell books from front to back and in some cases, back to front. I wasn't even able to make a feather float. It took years of going to my magical misfits group sessions to start to accept who I am—a null, a dud, an outré.

I'm about to tell Gil exactly that when Vance lets out a belch loud and long enough to set a record, a gross record but still a record.

"Okay children, go get out of those wet clothes before you all catch your deaths. We'll be back in Wrightsville in the morning." Vance unwraps the oil paper from around The Liber Umbrarum and settles into a reading chair with it. "Go on. Get."

Hand in hand, Birdie and Eli head off to the sleeping car in front of the lounge car with their rooms in it. Meanwhile, Gil and I go in the opposite direction to our sleeping car, leaving a trail of rain droplets in our wake.

"What did you mean out there, about my power?" I ask as soon as we cross the gangway into our car.

"Tilda, you know that was because of you. You made all of that magic happen."

He says it with such sincerity that I want to hug him as we walk down the narrow hallway and stop in front of his room. I know all I added was moral support, but the magic rubbed off on me anyway, leaving me all tingly and desperate for an outlet for all the adrenaline coursing through me.

"Gil, I need something from you." I reach behind him and open his bedroom door, slipping around him and going inside before I lose my nerve. "Can I stay the night?"

"You don't believe me about the spell and your power," he says, his disappointment evident as he comes inside the room, his shoulders slumped.

I can understand. From the outside, the idea of me being magical probably seems like a mix between a miracle and the most amazing gift from the fates ever. I'm sure he expects me to be thrilled at the possibility, to clap my hands and dance in celebration. The thing is though that I've spent my life thinking that the only thing that could possibly make me special was the one thing I didn't—and could never—have.

But I've been wrong.

"If this whole disaster has taught me anything it's to be honest with myself and others. I like you, Gil. No, I more than like you." Okay, I didn't mean for that bit to come out, but I'd already asked him to bang me, so in for a penny, in for a pound. "And for the first time in my life I don't feel like a dud. I may not have all of the magical skills my sisters have—and definitely not that my mom has—but that's okay." The truth of it fills me back up with that bubbly sense of expansive excitement. "I have talents. I can do things. I can help carry out a heist that Witchingdom will be talking about for decades. I wasn't just a part of all of this out of pity or a sense of family responsibility but because I had something to contribute." Something that went beyond scheduling social media posts and taking casual photos of my mom that she absolutely hates. "Do you know how rare that is for me? To be needed? To be wanted? To be an equal? It's really fucking rare. Tonight showed me that it doesn't have to be. And I have you to thank for that. Not because of how I feel about you, but because you and Birdie and Eli and Vance opened my eyes. Now I understand that I don't have to be what people expect. I can be more. I can be me."

There is something freeing to the realization, a power to knowing that being myself is enough. It's like being in the air again, flying so high the air is frigid and the view stunning. I'm not gonna lie, I'm scared out of my mind, but *wow* what an opportunity.

"Tilda,"—Gil takes my hand, brings it up to his mouth, flips it over, and kisses my wrist right where my pulse is going faster than a race car with a nitro booster—"you are a pretty fucking fabulous person to be."

And I thought my heart was speeding before.

"Are you sure I was wrong with the tarot cards?" *Please say yes.*

He nods, his gaze intense as he watches the water droplets dripping from the ends of my hair, traveling down my neck, and from there sliding down the valley between my boobs. Thank the fates for the wall behind me, because it's suddenly so hot in this room that I am worried about passing out from sexual tension. You doubt that's possible? Oh honey, trust me, it is.

"I've never been more glad to have shitty witchery skills in my life."

He manages to force his gaze back up to my face and cocks his head to the side. "Why?"

"Because I'm falling for you and the cards kept showing you and Leona being together. She's the most powerful out of us sisters, and I just—" Really need to shut up because he's gone from looking at me like he's going to lick me wet before he licks me dry to laughing out loud.

"Leona." He steps close enough that my breath catches and my hormones go haywire. "Isn't." He plants his hands on the wall on either side of my shoulders. "My type." He dips his head, bringing his lips close to my ear, and whispers, "You are."

So there's only so much a woman can take before she snaps. I have reached that limit.

The next thing I know, I'm kissing Gil with everything I have—and he's kissing me just as good right back.

It's amazing, but it's not enough, not after last night. I need more. I need him naked and inside me. Now.

The wet buttons of his shirt slip in my grasp and it takes me a few attempts, but I manage to undo his white tuxedo shirt while kissing the ever-loving hell out of him. I can't help it. I want all of him and I want it now. I want to taste every inch of him, hear him groan out my name as his fingers tangle in my hair while I'm kneeling between his legs, feel him come so hard that it makes his knees buckle. I want all of that. Then I want it again. Tonight. Tomorrow. The day after and the day after that to infinity.

That's not a lot to want, right?

Yeah, I know, it's everything, but after tonight it seems like believing this could be that isn't such an out-there thought.

"Is this too fast?" I ask as I pull his shirt free from his tuxedo pants and yank it down his arms as he kisses his way up my throat.

"Afraid of scaring me off?" He sucks my earlobe into his hot mouth. "Not possible."

My hands go to the button on his pants. I'm so desperate for him to be naked, it's like I am barely in control—but I still am, so I stop even though it goes against my every instinct and look up at him. "Gil."

A plea? A promise? Both. Definitely it's both.

Instead of answering though, he pushes the straps of my slinky green dress down. The sequined gown slides down my body to pool around my stilettos. He glides the back of a knuckle down the satin straps of my bra, over the unlined lace cups, coming so close to my aching nipple but not quite touching it. My breath is coming in pants and I'm so turned on that my core clenches with anticipation. After teasing me to the point that I'm biting down on my bottom lip, Gil trails his fingertips over the gentle rise of my belly and to the edge of my panties' waistband. Desire, hot and needy, has me on the edge of coming, and the man hasn't even touched my swollen, desperate clit.

The man is pure evil with this kind of blissful torture, and I can't fucking take it. I reach down and hook my thumbs around the elastic waistband, ready to shove the lace down over my ass, but Gil has other plans.

He wraps his fingers around my wrists and hauls my arms up over my head. "You're impatient."

Well, yeah, has he seen him naked? It's a whole thing.

Still, I try to play it cool by shrugging a shoulder. "I want what I want."

He draws teasing circles around my hard nipple without actually touching it. "And what is it that you desire?"

"You." So much for trying to play coy.

My arms still up in the air, he twirls me around and spins me into the slipper chair by the window and then he steps back. "Spread your legs."

I don't hesitate, widening my legs. His gaze immediately drops to the black lace at the juncture of my thighs. Judging by the way his eyes darken with lust, he didn't miss the growing damp spot soaking through the material. I slide my hands up my thighs, going slow as his hungry gaze tracks my progress. By the time I skim my nails ever so lightly across my hot center, he's kicking off his shoes and shoving his pants and boxers down in one move. Fuck, I love looking at this man's dick. I know, the prevailing wisdom is that they aren't so pretty to look at. Those folks who think that haven't seen Gil Connolly's cock. Thick, long, curving just a little to the left, it's a work of fucking art. And when he fists it, squeezing the base so hard I can practically feel it? It's all I can do not to give in to the urge to slide down off the chair and crawl over to him so I can suck that pretty, pretty dick of his.

"Take it off. All of it," he says, his voice rough with lust. "But stay on the chair."

The thought to object doesn't even enter my head, and I'm past the point of teasing him, so it takes what seems like all of about fifteen milliseconds for me to be naked—except for my high heels—on the chair, my legs spread open for him, giving him the perfect view of my slick, swollen folds. The cool night air against my core and his hot gaze are more than I can take.

He sucks in a harsh breath. "You're so fucking beautiful."

Closing my eyes, I arch my back, cup my boobs, and roll my nipples before pulling them hard enough that I know they'll be red and the exact right kind of tender. Gil's throaty groan only encourages me to do more. Touch my tits the way I do when I'm alone, teasing them, toying with the stiff nipples, tugging and twisting with just enough pressure that my thighs are getting wet.

I rest a hand on my leg so my fingers brush against the last spot of my inner thigh before it becomes something else entirely, something hot, something pulsing with want, something practically dripping with desire. "I'm gonna touch myself now."

He lets out a strained hiss of breath and strokes his cock with slow, steady movements, his attention never moving from me. "Fuck yes."

I haven't even touched myself and I am already so close to coming. I slip my fingers between my legs and nearly bliss out just from that first touch. I circle my clit, slide my fingers lower to my opening, and go back up. Gil follows my moves with a fierce gaze that pushes me closer and closer with every stroke of my fingers. This isn't a show so much as it's a shared experience, not touching but together. Honestly, it's hot as hell and there's no way I'm going to be able to draw it out. So I don't bother. There will always be the next time. We can tease and torment each other then for the absolute best of reasons. Right now though, I just want to come while he watches and strokes his gorgeous fucking cock. And I do, the tension building and building in my core until I can't take it anymore and it explodes inside me, pleasure washes over me, and my bones melt to Jell-O.

"Gil." I'm still floating down from the high of my orgasm, but I'm not even close to done yet. "I want you inside me."

"Good," he says, "because there's nowhere else I'd rather be than with you."

He takes my hand and helps me up from the chair. My legs are shaky and I'm still trying to catch my breath, but Gil's a steadying presence, and I know he's not gonna let me fall even with the train running faster than normal so we can get back to Wrightsville as soon as possible to save my family.

"You don't have to worry with me," he says, sitting down on the chair I've just vacated and bringing me with him so I'm straddling him. "I've got you."

I don't have a single worry in my head about that. How could I? You can't doubt the person you love.

His hands are on my hips as I reach between us, wrapping my fingers around his hard cock and lowering myself down on him, letting him fill me up. It's not perfect—we're not perfect—but when we're like this in this moment, it sure feels like we're as close to it as we can ever be.

"I love you, Gil Connolly."

I don't mean to say it, but the words just slip out. I have half a second of oh-fuck-what-did-I-just-do panic running through my head before his mouth comes crashing down on mine while at the same time he lifts his hips, fucking me from underneath with such glorious power and delicious intensity that the ability to form thoughts doesn't seem so important anymore.

He cups the back of my head, his gaze locked on my face, and I can't get a read on his expression. He pulls my head lower.

"Tilda," he says the second before our lips meet in a kiss that melts my brain.

It's not "I love you," but to my ears in this moment it sounds a lot like it. I undulate against him, riding him as we chase the orgasm we're both reaching for. It's so close, like the storm I can hear outside the train's windows, turning the sky into one bright flash after another. Again and again I impale myself on him, sliding up and down his length as I rock my hips. I plant my hands on his thighs behind me to change the angle, take him deeper as the ball of electricity in my core builds, tightening. One of his hands sneaks up from my hip, slides up my back, and pulls my hair, sharpening the arch of my back, and it's more than I can take. My nails sink into his muscular shoulders as I break apart into a million waves of pleasure that make the whole world disappear before bringing it all back brighter than before.

Letting out a muttered curse, he picks up the pace of his

upward thrusts at the same time that he slams me down on his cock. The world around me is electric and it's like I can feel every part of the universe as I roll my hips, smoothing the hard edge of his need. His breaths are ragged and his body tense as he fights the inevitable as if he can make this single moment last forever. But it doesn't work like that, life never does.

"Tilda," he says, "I—"

Everything else is lost though when I take him in deep one last time and he comes.

A million years or a few seconds later, our breaths are still coming in hard, and his arms are around me as he holds me close to him on the chair. I'd get up if I could, but my legs are mush and the rest of me is awash in happy hormones.

"I got you," he whispers, and then scoops me up in his arms at the same time as he gets up from the chair and carries me across the room to the bed.

Tucked up against him under the covers a second later, his arm wrapped around my waist as he spoons me, I don't even try to fight falling asleep. Tomorrow I'll freak out about what I said, but now I'll take this perfect moment. Life doesn't give someone like me many of those, so I'm going to appreciate it.

Chapter Thirty

Gil . . .

Hours later, the sun is just starting to peek over the horizon when I tiptoe back into my room carrying an armload of plundered goodies. Tilda is sitting up in our bed, staring out the window with the unblinking blank look of the non-morning person who has just woken up.

"Morning, sunshine," I say as I close the door with a backward foot shove.

"Morning." Her gaze is unfocused as she glances over and her smile shy. She picks up her glasses from the bedside table and slides them on. She glances at the box tucked under my arm and her jaw drops. "Are those Vance's Lucky Charms?"

"I'll get him more when we get to Wrightsville." Okay, I'll probably end up buying him a case of the sugary stuff and have to pay some kind of embarrassing penance for snagging Vance's favorite food, but it's worth it to make sure Tilda is taken care of. Fool in love? Yeah. Guilty. "You needed sustenance after last night."

She shifts in the bed and the sheets fall down to her waist. "You're either incredibly brave to take a unicorn shifter's food or—"

"It's that." Walking over to the small table in front of the window, I nearly trip over my own feet because ninety percent of my brain function is taken up with checking out Tilda's perfect tits.

Tilda smothers a giggle as she leans forward, giving me an even better view of her breasts, obviously more than aware of what is distracting me from the basics of putting one foot in front of the other. "You didn't hear the other option."

"Don't need to, it's definitely brave," I say as I lift my arm and let the cereal box drop to the table and then set down the tray loaded with our bowls, spoons, and one very large, very heavy book.

Her glance drops to the items I'm unloading and her flirty smile disappears. "You brought the spell book."

"Yeah." I'd spent most of the night trying to figure out a plan for how I am going to tell her the truth and how long I've known about it. Brainiac that I am, I still don't have one, but I can't put it off anymore—not after last night. She needs to know. "I have to show you something."

Still, I delay for as long as possible by pouring her a bowl of cereal and bringing it to her along with a cup of elderberry tea on the tray. While she eats, I sit next to her on the bed and flip through the The Liber Umbrarum.

It's more than just a magic recipe book like some spell books. There are highly skilled illustrations that go along with semi-fictional fairy tales, profiles about historical people, encyclopedic descriptions of various magical creatures, studies of different types of witches, deep dives into the hows and whys of specific ingredients, and—finally—spell after spell after spell. There are hexes for everything from painlessly extracting newts' eyes to turning your annoying neighbor into one. No wonder the thing is so heavy.

As Tilda finishes up her cereal, I turn the pages past a ton of entries to a double-page spread where the words all curve around a gorgeous watercolor of a witch in old-timey garb, complete with a black pointed hat and a purple robe that the artist has painted so it looks like it's in motion on the page and the witch might just fly off of it at any second. The title *Spellbinder* is written in calligraphy and stretches from one side of the left page to the other side of the right.

Tilda sets the tray with its empty cereal bowl and half-drunk cup of tea on the bedside table.

It's now or never.

Nerves eating away at my stomach lining, I smooth my hand over the pages. "This is what I wanted you to look at."

She tucks her hair behind her ears and then straightens her glasses before peering down at the book as if she's looking at one of those hidden items pictured and needs to locate the golden hammer. "Why?"

"Read the description."

Yeah, my vibe is getting to that weird intensity that makes my skin all itchy, but I have to push forward. Tilda needs to know who she is. She needs to understand that what happened at the museum wasn't a fluke. It wasn't me. It wasn't Eli and Birdie. It was her. As a spellbinder, she alone can take a spell and juice it to its most powerful form. She's not just the rarest kind of witch out there, she's also the most powerful.

Holding back as she reads the entry is pure torture, but it doesn't take her long to read all of the cramped writing on the page. By the time she's done, her eyes are wide with shock and her hands are shaking as she reaches for her cup of tea and takes a long drink, draining it.

When she tries to take another sip from the empty cup, I take it and put it back on the table. "You see it, right?"

"See what?" She tries to play it off, but she can't fool me.

I pull her onto my lap and wrap my arms around her, tucking her in against me. "Denial won't change anything."

"It can't be right," she says into my shoulder. "My family, they'd know."

I brush a kiss across the top of her head. "Who says they don't? Griselda—"

"She knew?" Her face falls. "Of course she knew. It's her job to ferret out the magical talents of Sherwoods on their first birthdays." Her pitch goes higher with every word as reality settles in. "There's a whole ritual with incantations and special tea and—"

"Tilda." I cut her off before the panic eating away at the edge of her voice can gnaw its way inside.

Once that happens, once the panic infests your soul, it's hard if not impossible to strip it out. That's why on cold nights, the kind where the chill settles deep inside you, I still hear the creaks and the groans of my first boarding school in The Beyond.

"No, it can't be right." She scrambles off my lap, out of the bed, and begins to grab her clothes from where they'd fallen the night before. "My parents would have had to know. They wouldn't lie to me about something that important. They wouldn't have let me think that I was a null." Looking at the sparkly green dress in her hand with annoyance, she throws it onto a nearby chair and snags a pair of my sweats from my duffel bag on the floor. She looks pissed off, but there's no missing the red flush at the base of her throat or the way her bottom lip trembles or the fact that she's blinking her suddenly watery eyes a mile a minute. "And Griselda! She would have had to have known if this was true. She was there when I was born. She was the one who confirmed I am an outré. She doesn't lie. Not for anything."

"To protect you she would. They all would. An outré is the perfect cover for a spellbinder since they can't start their own spells."

"Protecting me from what?" She yanks one of my T-shirts over her head with enough force to hand start a stubborn lawn mower. "Why would they do that to me?"

As she paces, working through all of the information bombarding her, I turn the page in The Liber Umbrarum. On the next double-page spread, there's another watercolor of the witch from before. This time, however, she's tied to a stake set in the middle of a pyre. The fire is just starting to lick at the witch's purple robes as a crowd of magical creatures and witches holding torches celebrate in the background. My first instinct is to slam the book shut so she doesn't have to see that, but I can't do it to her. She's lived her life in forced ignorance. From now on, she has to be able to access the information she wants and use it how she sees fit.

"We learned about the purge edict in The Beyond," I start. "Any witch who stood out, anyone who broke tradition, anyone who went beyond the Council's strict definitions of what a witch could or should be was burned."

"All of that is in the past though." She stops her pacing and stares at me from the foot of the bed, her hair going in a million directions, denial obviously pushing her away from accepting the truth. "No one is out here burning spellbinders."

"That's because they only come along every few generations." I get up and cross over to her, wanting to gather her up in my arms and act as some kind of protective barrier against the world opening up to her. "Their power, *your power*, scares the ever-loving shit out of the people who like to think they hold the most sway in Witchingdom. That's why the Council puts so much effort into researching every witch who doesn't conform to their expectations."

"Like outrés," she says, sounding defeated.

Guilt, heavy and acidic, burns a hole in my gut. "Like outrés."

"That's why we kept getting set up together on dates." She sinks down into the slipper chair, her shoulders curled forward. "The Council had you doing research ops on me."

What can I say to that? It's the truth. Shame burns a hole in my gut.

"I don't think Griselda believed I'd figure it out." I mean, it's not like people go around expecting to run into a spell-binder. Even among researchers like me, it's more theory than reality. "And when I did, the Resistance had already rescued my parents from The Beyond and—to keep them safe—stashed them somewhere the Council couldn't find them. And neither could I."

"That's blackmail!" Tilda's jaw drops and she shoots up from the chair, wrapping her arms around me in a fierce hug. "How could they?"

Before Tilda, I would have said they could because of greed or malice or just plain old evil intent, but now I understand better. "Sometimes we do the wrong thing to protect the people we love. Griselda, your family, they just want to keep you safe."

"I know that, but fates alive, I really wish people would realize that I should have a part in all of this." She throws her arms up in the air with frustration and starts pacing in front of the window again. "That them bypassing me in these decisions in the name of protecting me is just bullshit." She whirls around, a fierce determination emanating off her that screams "don't fuck with me I'm a Sherwood." "I swear, if I didn't love them so much, I'd let them stay on ice for another couple of years for this."

"Really?" I scoff.

"Fine." She rolls her eyes and crosses her arms. "I wouldn't do that, but I'm still mad. As soon as we get The Liber Umbrarum home, I'm going to melt them down, and then you can let them know exactly what I think about this whole keep-Tilda-in-the-dark security plan." She pauses, shaking her head as if she doesn't even believe all of the venting she is doing. "I'll do it right after I get done hugging them and apologizing about a million times for freezing them."

Yeah, that part sounded exactly like the Tilda Sherwood I know and love.

I glance over at the clock. We are only a few hours away, outside of the window of being able to use a transport spell to poof from the train to the Sherwood house without a miracle. Even in the best of circumstances though, that spell doesn't come without serious risks. Witches have been known to arrive at their destination with fingers on the wrong hand or a nose where their ear should be. Tilda's spellbinder magic wouldn't help avoid any of that.

"You start planning what you want to say, and I'll take care of securing The Liber Umbrarum until we get to Wrightsville." I glance out the window, the survival skills I'd learned to listen to in The Beyond starting to itch.

"What?" She lets out a melodramatic gasp and presses her hand to her chest. "You think one of us is going to abscond with it and sell it to the highest bidder for fabulous riches and infamy, or is that your plan?"

My whole body goes cold. She's joking, logically I know this, but still, it's exactly how it works with the Council. Like any great narcissist, the organization is all about projecting their bad deeds or nefarious plans onto others. Surviving them means always being on the lookout for what they're plotting next.

Tilda cocks her head and laughs. "If you could only see your face right now. I'm kidding. Jeesh."

"Sorry," I say, "old habits."

She looks up at me in confusion.

But, before I can explain, the entire train jerks to a stop, throwing us forward. Acting on instinct to protect Tilda no matter what, I magic The Liber Umbrarum to my chest and grab her, pulling her close so that the spell book acts as a kind of bumper for her as I turn my body so that when I slam into the wall, I absorb most of the tooth-rattling blow.

She skims her hands over me, her face squished up with concern. "Are you okay?"

"I'm good." As long as Tilda's okay, my aches don't really matter. "I'm gonna go see what's going on. You stay here. Eli and Birdie will come looking to you for answers."

I'm halfway through the caboose on my way to the platform so I can get a good look at things, when I realize I still have The Liber Umbrarum glued with magic to my chest like a shield. There's not enough time to undo the spell before I burst out onto the platform and climb the railing to get a better look. There's a yellow-tinted protective dome spreading outward to cover the train, and standing underneath the middle of it, on top of the lounge car, is Erik Svensen—and he's not the only one there.

I can't see the Council agents, but I can feel their presence like the shiver that goes up your spine in the dark when you know you aren't alone. It's a skill you develop in The Beyond, a sort of sixth sense that becomes instinctual. They're watching and waiting, willing to just observe until they can make their move.

Icy realization freezes me. I did this. I failed Tilda and brought the Council right to her. There's no way the show of power at the museum would go undocumented by the Council's spectrometers, and now they'll do whatever it takes to force her to their side or destroy her.

I can't protect Tilda from this on my own. Even though it goes against every survival lesson I learned in The Beyond, I have to go get help—and not just any help, I need the Sherwoods.

As the protective dome covers the train, coming toward me like lava pouring down a volcano, there's no time to say anything to Tilda or weigh the odds of actually getting to the house in one piece with all the parts where they're supposed to be. Not that the last bit matters. When it comes to saving Tilda, I'll do whatever it takes.

It's not until I'm airborne and about to make the magical jump to the Sherwood house that I spot her in the window of the sleeping car. It's too late to stop the transport spell, though, and I'm gone in the next breath, the look of betrayal on Tilda's face etched into my brain forever.

Chapter Thirty-One

Tilda . . .

$\mathcal{S}$ tanding there by myself in Gil's room as the train starts chugging down the tracks again, I can't move. The betrayal cuts me like a rusty blade. I am alone and everything hurts.

No, that's not good enough.

It doesn't just hurt, it aches, burns, screams in agony.

He left. Gil Connolly just took The Liber Umbrarum and poofed out of here without a goodbye, an explanation, or anything else. And while *some people* would take the opportunity of the crash, boom, BANG of this disaster to dis-the-fuck-appear, I am not that person. I'm a Sherwood and that means something.

So without second-guessing what needs to be done, I head toward the gangplank leading to the lounge car as the train continues to speed down the tracks, swaying and rumbling under my feet, on its way to Wrightsville. I make it as far as the doorway leading into the car before I freeze.

This isn't just bad, it's a fucking disaster.

Eli and Birdie are in the corner by the tarot cards. Vance is duct-taped to a chair, his chin touching his chest, his jaw slack with unconsciousness, but he's still breathing. The amount of sheer muscle it must have taken to knock out a unicorn shifter is a lot. They aren't immortal beings without having learned a few million tricks of the bare-knuckles brawling trade, subterfuge, and general badassery.

As soon as I walk in, Birdie rushes forward but doesn't get more than two steps from the table before slamming to a stop, her feet locked in place by what has to be some kind of containment spell. For his part, Eli looks like he's about to eat the gizzards of whoever has the audacity to do this to Birdie.

That person is none other than Erik Svensen. He is, surprisingly, by himself without a goon-sized magical minion in sight.

"I assume you know why I'm here," Erik says, his shoulders slumped as if he was the one being held hostage as opposed to being the one holding all of the magical power. "Hand over The Liber Umbrarum."

"I don't have it." And for some unknown reason, I don't immediately give up Gil Connolly as the one in possession of the world's most powerful spell book.

Why?

Because, it seems, I'm a fucking sucker right to the end.

"Please do not make me do this the hard way." He pinches the bridge of his nose and lets out a tired sigh. "Come on, Tilda," he pleads, "be smart about it. You can't win."

Fuck that. I've had it.

Yeah, Gil was probably lying about me being a spellbinder, but I can't shake the idea that maybe he wasn't. Maybe part of it is because there's a good percentage of my heart—like all of it—that wants to believe the man I love isn't completely full of shit, but it's more than that too. What happened between Gil and I at the coffee shop. The dragon's blood tree's obsession with me. The fact that I was able to kiss Gil when he was body walking, which is pretty close to—but not totally—impossible. The glitch that froze my family. The blast of energy when we escaped the museum. All of it would make sense if I am a spellbinder.

The chance that I'm a spellbinder is small—there's only one every three to four generations according to The Liber Umbrarum—but it's not zero.

Anyway, what have we got to lose by trying to juice a spell and seeing if me being a spellbinder is not a total fucking lie?

Gil will still have dipped out with the most powerful spell book in all of the Witchingdom.

Vance will still be unconscious and strapped to a chair.

Erik will still be staring at us as if he can't decide whether to thunk us upside the head or forget he ever tracked us down in the first place.

And I'll still be me—weird, doesn't-fit-in Tilda Sherwood,

who is lucky enough to have two of the best friends in the world. They risked it all for me. I couldn't live with myself if I didn't do everything in my *maybe* power to get them out of the mess I made.

"Birdie. Eli," I whisper, "start the freedom spell."

"Are you serious?" Erik scoffs, because obviously whispering is not one of my super skills. "You three are going to overpower *my* spell, two magical misfits and an outré." He narrows his eyes and tries to look all badass, but there's no missing the pity in them. "Look, I just want the book. I have no interest in hurting any of you. However, if I don't get The Liber Umbrarum back before my dad or the Council realizes that you have it, even The Beyond won't be a safe enough place to hide from them."

He starts to pace in front of Vance, who is still passed out, and opens up a small communications portal that is situated so that neither we nor the unicorn shifter can be seen. "I told you I'm on it, Dad," Erik says on the other end.

Eli, Birdie, and I huddle together as Erik and his dad go from general check-in to micromanaging of how exactly to get the spell book back.

"You guys," I say, hoping my whisper won't be overheard since it sounds like Erik is arguing with his dad, "we've gotten this far, we can do this."

"But, Tild—" Birdie's sneeze cuts off the rest of my name.

"It's okay." I take her hand and I swear I can feel the sizzle of magic waking up in the air around us, a live, palpable thing. "We can do this."

Neither of them looks convinced, but Eli takes Birdie's hand. "Maleficas omnium magicas veterum ac novorum nostram appellamus ad libertatem."

The invisible electric magic shifts around us, and one of the tarot cards on the table flutters in the air before falling back down. Erik glances over and glares at us before turning his attention back to the communication portal.

"Close." Birdie looks up at Eli and gives him a soft smile. "Maleficas omnium veterum ac novorum magicas appellamus . . . ah . . . ah . . . ah—" Birdie fights back the sneeze, her eyes watering as she goes still trying to fight it off, but she can't. "Ah-choo."

The lights in the train car get blindingly bright for a second before flashing out and leaving us all in the dark. Yeah, it feels a little spot-on for me too, but the universe is like that sometimes. You feel like you're in the pit of despair and it can't get worse? "Oh here," the universe calls out, "let me prove you wrong." And that's how you end up standing in the dark facing down one of the most powerful witches in Witchingdom with absolutely no hope of making it out of there.

"Dad, everything's under control. I've gotta go." There's a soft yellow glow around the portal and then it disappears right before Erik waves his hands and sets off a spell without even having to utter a word.

There's a whoosh of magic, and the scent of fresh-brewed coffee fills the train car half a second before the lights blast back to life. Eli, Birdie, and I all exchange what-the-fuck eyebrow raises. Vance is still knocked out and magically duct-taped to a chair. There's power and then there's *power*. The oldest Svensen sibling definitely has the second one.

"Look." Erik shoves his fingers through his dark hair roughly enough that it's all spiked up. "I don't want to do this. LeLe would—Well, that doesn't matter, does it? Where's the book?"

"I don't know." It's the truth. For all I know, Gil is taking it to some undiscovered island in the Pacific Ocean to prep it for auction to the highest bidder. "Gil took the book and magicked his way out of here right after you got here."

Erik starts pacing in front of Vance's chair again and lets loose with a string of delightfully creative curses about Gil that I mostly agree with. The man does deserve to attend a troll dinner party as the main dish. Of course, none of that is going to get Birdie, Eli, Vance, and I out of this mess. My family is still frozen. Gil is gone. There's no one left to help. We have to come to our own rescue.

That's when I spot two of Birdie's allergy pills from Griselda on the tarot table next to a glass of water.

Leaning in close to her, I lower my voice. "Your pills, you gotta swipe them."

Her eyes go wide. "He's watching."

I lift an eyebrow in challenge. "And here I thought you had all sorts of sleight of hand skills."

One side of her mouth curls up as we all brace our legs as the train takes a bend in the tracks at top speed. Yeah, that's the Birdie I know and love.

"Sorry," she says.

I have half a heartbeat to wonder what about before she stumbles forward, her foot landing hard on my bare toes. My yelp of pain is genuine and just enough to snag Erik's full attention as Eli shifts his position to give Birdie cover as she reaches behind him and grabs the pills and downs them dry.

"What's going on?" Erik asks.

"Nothing, just lost my balance," Birdie says with a ditzy giggle. "I'm good now."

"Well, thank the fates for that," Erik grumbles as he resumes what seems to be his life's mission of wearing a hole in the lounge car's carpet, "since everything else has gone straight to shit."

All but ignoring us since he's no doubt decided we aren't really a factor in the whole magical-power thing, he continues to pace and wonder out loud to himself about what in the hell he's going to do now and something about how LeLe is going to kill him. Honestly, as a fellow talk-to-myself person, I kinda feel for him on this. Beyond the whole knocking out Vance and trying to steal back his own property, he seems like a nice enough guy. And if Leona is going to kill him, she's gonna do it slow, so he is in for a world of misery. She looks sweet and innocent, but in reality, my next-to-oldest sister is mean as hell. Seriously.

Birdie starts, her voice barely above a whisper. "Maleficas omnium veterum . . ." She pauses, the tip of her nose twitching.

I'm holding my breath and trying to watch her fight off

the sneeze with one eye while keeping watch on Erik with the other, which is about as easy as you'd expect.

Eli takes Birdie's hand and continues the spell, "Ac novorum magicas appellamus ad ... ad ... ad ..."

Birdie smiles up at him and leads the final part of the incantation, "Ac novorum magicas appellamus ad libertatem."

Watching each other, they start again as the softest flickers of magic start to glow in my peripheral vision. I take Eli's hand and start to recite the spell with them.

"Maleficas omnium veterum," we say, our voices growing more confident with each Latin word, "ac novorum magicas appellamus ad ac novorum magicas appellamus ad libertatem."

Birdie closes her eyes, going into that witchy trance I've seen my mom fall into a million times as she gives over her full concentration to cooking up a spell in our kitchen cauldron.

"Maleficas omnium veterum ac novorum magicas appellamus ad ac novorum magicas appellamus ad libertatem."

My whole body is humming as the scents of honey, butter, and cinnamon sugar fill the air, making the lounge car smell like a fresh-baked sweet bun. The power is filling me up, lifting me, making my hair float around my head as if gravity doesn't exist, and knocking my glasses cockeyed—something I hadn't realized until this moment always seems to happen to me when magic is brewing around me.

I might hate him, but Gil is right—I am a spellbinder.

The power has been in me all along, waiting to come out, and this is the most perfect opportunity to unleash it all.

I take Birdie's hand, completing the circle. It's like touching a live wire, and I can barely hold on. My hand starts to slip, but Birdie holds tight, giving me the extra oomph needed to settle all of the buzzing inside me and finish what we magical misfits have started.

"Maleficas omnium veterum," we say as one, the air around us sparkling with magic, "ac novorum magicas appellamus ad ac novorum magicas appellamus ad libertatem."

The lights in the lounge car go from regular strength to sun-level brightness to peak supernova before thunder cracks loud enough to make me wonder if I'm about to be struck by lightning, and then all the bulbs shatter, sending tiny shards of glass everywhere half a second before the freedom spell explodes, breaking Erik's containment hex in half as he stares slack-jawed.

Great, right?

Well, yeah, except for one small thing. You see, with great power comes great, unexpected consequences (example: me freezing my entire family)—in this case, the power of the magical blast makes the train jump the tracks and hurls it into the air.

Sheer panic rips through everyone and we scream, waking up Vance half a second before his chair goes airborne. Then we're all in the air, with what seems like miles between our feet and the floor. Before any of us have a chance to even yell out again in terror, though, the train goes from flying to float-ing and then to a soft landing next to the tracks.

Beyond the sound of my blood rushing through my ears, the inside of the dark train car is absolutely silent—until I hear *her* voice.

"Brace yourself, Svensen," Izzy Sherwood yells from out-side the train, all of the mom-voice scariness in her tone dialed up to infinity. "If even a single red hair on my daugh-ter's head has been harmed, you are in for a world of abso-lutely devastating pain and misery."

Chapter Thirty-Two

Tilda . . .

*B*irdie, Eli, and I rush toward the door. I'm running so fast out of the train that I nearly face-plant on the gangway in my haste to make sure I'm not imagining it all. My heart's in my throat, and I'm seconds away from crying when I spot my parents standing shoulder to shoulder looking prepped and ready to face off with whoever emerges from the derailed train. My sisters are all standing with their backs to my parents watching the orchards as if they expect someone more powerful than Erik to come rushing forward.

"Mom! Dad!" I freeze to the spot, my fist pressed to my belly as I dig my nails into my palm, trying to convince myself that since I feel the pain but am not waking up that this isn't a dream.

It's not just my parents and my sisters here though. Griselda is here. My aunts and uncles, my second, third, and fourth cousins, Grandma Louise, and even Barkley, my rooster nemesis, are all gathered in the clearing by the train. I want to wrap my arms around each and every one of them at once. I want to scream and holler and thank the fates for all of them, but I can't. Emotion blocks my throat and for the first time in my life, I can't even begin to figure out where to start.

"But how?" Birdie asks from behind me, saying the words running through my head that I can't get out.

"A very handsome professor-looking type," Grandma Louise says, doing what she considers her most suggestive eyebrow wiggle. "You should hold on to that one, Matilda Grace."

Yeah, that isn't going to happen—partly because he's already gone and partly because I might be feeling a wee (a lot) bit murderous about the fact that he abandoned my friends and I at the absolute worst possible moment, after promising me how many times that he got me? A billion and one.

My sisters rush me, their arms wrapping around me, hugging me as Barkley does his weird cock of the walk thing in a circle around us as if daring anyone to try to take a shot. As if anyone would, looking at this crew. It's not just the pure number of Sherwoods that should make Erik quake in his several-thousand-dollar bespoke tux, it's the fact that they broke open the armory. Every member of my family is there. They are armed with wands, ritual double-edged knives, white-handled bolines with hooked blades, long-tailed whips, and spears. Grandma Louise has her travel cauldron, engraved with her address in case she accidentally forgets it—which with her, happens more often than you'd think. Barkley even has deadly sharp metal armor over his spurs.

The show of support has me close to tears. "You came to save us?"

"No," my mom says, steel in her voice.

My sisters part like they're in a synchronized dance from the 1800s and my mom walks down the aisle, looking as regal and scary as always.

"We came to help, *but* only if needed," she says as she wraps her arms around me in a tight hug that warms me up all the way from my toes to the ends of my hair. "I figured you'd have everything either taken care of or close to it by the time we got here." She looks over her shoulder and glares at the night. "And if there are any other moves tonight, I pity the witch who tries it, no matter what power they think they have."

There's a rustling sound, and then a blast of hot air falls over us like a tsunami before half a dozen shadows take to the night sky, disappearing among the stars.

"Don't worry," my mom says, giving me another squeeze. "The Council's gone for now. They'll be back once they regroup, but we'll deal with them later. Right now I just want to hug you."

She does, holding me so tight that I'm not sure she is ever going to let go.

And that's when I realize Gil wasn't lying about my family.

My mother had known. They all must have known. I'm stuck between hurt and shock, but I'm too damn happy to have my family back to say anything, but it has to be written all over my face, because my dad joins in on the group hug. My sisters join in and even Barkley delivers a friendly peck to my toe.

"I was wrong to not tell you the truth, Tilda," Mom says when the hug breaks up, uttering the words I don't think anyone has ever heard from her before. "We've known since you were born that there was something different about you. But it wasn't until Griselda told us you were a spellbinder that we decided the best thing we could do to protect you until you were ready was to keep it a secret—even from you."

"We should have told you before now," Dad says, giving me an apologetic grin. "I guess it's just hard to recognize that the baby of the family has grown up."

"But you sure did," Mom says, a proud smile on her face. "Look at what you made happen. You know, there's a reason why I put you in charge of our family social media."

"Because it was the only thing I am qualified for?" I ask.

"No." She gives me the mom look. "I put you in charge because there's no one I trust more with the Sherwood image and legacy than you. Tilda, you had it in you all along. And just look what you accomplished when you put your mind to it."

"No thanks to this one," Vance grumbles as he walks out onto the train platform. His unicorn horn is glowing a mean shade of red and he has a white-knuckle grip on Erik's arm.

Leona's jaw drops in surprise and her cheeks turn pink.

"Hi, LeLe," Erik says, cocky even under the circumstances.

Leona stalks over to the platform, smoke—yes, literal smoke—coming out of her ears. "*You* threatened to hurt my sister?"

All of the Sherwoods take a step back in unison. Leona's temper and refusal to suffer fools is legendary. No one wants to be in the way of one of her pinching spells. My sister is very creative in her target areas.

"I was trying to help," Erik shoots back, shaking off Vance's hold. "She *did* steal The Liber Umbrarum. My dad spent years planning the security for the gala and making sure all magic was null and void inside the museum."

"Well done, Matilda Grace and friends," Grandma Louise says with a delighted chuckle. "I knew you had it in you. You take after your grandfather. He was quite the troublemaker in his younger days, you know." She claps her hands together with glee. "I can't wait to hear all the details over eye of newt muffins and a cup of piping hot elderberry tea."

I would love to say yes, and I'm so damn happy to have my family back that I'm so tempted to go along with Grandma and play the whole thing as an amusing adventure, but I can't. People I love got hurt because of me.

"I'm so sorry, everyone, for the mess I caused," I say, making my voice loud enough that everyone can hear. "I understand it may take some time, but I really hope you can forgive me."

"On one condition," Mom says, a soft look in her eyes.

I don't hesitate. "Anything."

The tip of her nose is red and there are unshed tears in her eyes. "You forgive us for keeping the truth from you. We thought we were protecting you, but the universe knew you were ready."

"Even when I froze you?" My voice breaks on the last word, and then my tears are spilling over, because how in the world am I supposed to stand in the middle of this field, next to a derailed train, surrounded by the people I most love in the world, and watch my mom tear up without getting all emotional?

"I never worried, not even while we were frozen; I knew you'd find a way to fix everything. You're a Sherwood, after all." Her eyes narrow. "However, if any of you ever puts a kitchen dish towel over my head again, there will be uncomfortable consequences."

All of the color drains out of Birdie's and Eli's faces. No one—and I mean no one—wants to be on Izzy Sherwood's shit list. Then my dad gets the giggles, the kind that takes over your whole body and you can't stop no matter how hard you try. Mom plants her hands on her hips and glares at the love of her life, but she's pressing her lips together so hard there's a line of white around them. Her shoulders start shaking. A chuckle escapes that she tries to play off as a cough, but she can't do it. The whole thing is too ridiculous. She busts out laughing, an infectious sound that has everyone joining in.

I'm wiping away giggle tears a minute later and taking in

the rough and ready gathering of Sherwoods. "I can't believe everyone came *and* that they came so well armed."

"We may have overpacked," Mom says with a whatcha-gonna-do shrug. "We Sherwoods do have a tendency to do that."

"I hate to be the bearer of bad news, but you may need all those weapons," Erik says as he and Vance walk down from the train platform to where Leona and I are standing with our parents. "My dad is absolutely livid and ready to go to war—but if I can get the spell book back tonight, there's a chance I can talk him out of emptying our armory."

Looking as bored as she most definitely is not, Leona crunches a pile of fallen orange leaves under her tennis shoes. "So we take it back."

"We?" he asks, one of his dark eyebrows shooting up.

Leona gives him a dirty look that would send most witches for cover. Erik doesn't even flinch. "After what happened last time, there's no way I'd trust you to make sure your dad understands that war is not on the table."

"How many times do I have to tell you the same thing?" Something that looks a lot like annoyance at having what seems like the same argument for the fortieth time flashes in Erik's bright blue eyes. "Last time was not my fault."

My sister's smirk back at him is anything but sweet and friendly. "Whatever helps you sleep at night."

Leona and Erik continue to bicker, but it fades into the background along with the rest of the world because that's when I realize Gil is here. He's been here the whole time, hanging out on the edge of the crowd. It takes two beats of my broken heart for all of the pain to come rushing back, vicious and raw.

If he has any idea of the danger he's in at the moment, he doesn't show it as he walks confidently over. "I knew you could do it if you only gave yourself the chance."

I'm shaking with a whole tornado of mixed emotions at seeing him—anger, hurt, relief, excitement. Even now, after he abandoned Birdie, Eli, Vance, and I to our fates, I can't help but want to throw my arms around him and be forever grateful that he came back. What kind of weak fool am I? Gil Connolly is a know-it-all jerk who couldn't even be bothered to trust me with his plan. And that was it right there, why all of this hurts so bad. He'd asked me a million times to trust him, but when it came down to it, he didn't return that trust.

"Trust me," I throw back his own words at him before adding a few of my own, "you're about to find out exactly what I can do."

I grab Erik's forearm, the power of his magical abilities a perceptible humming in my head as soon as I do. "I need a banishment spell."

"Are you sure?" he asks, glancing over at Leona for support or guidance or who the hell knows.

I sure don't. I'm not sure I know what I want right now, but seeing Gil standing with my family as if he belongs, as if we belong together, has me hurting so bad all over again by showing me everything that could be.

I tighten my grip. "Just do it."

Erik inhales a breath, summoning his family magic and the unique flavor that's all his own.

"Tilda, wait!" Gil pleads, his hands palms up in surrender. "Please. Can we talk?"

But it's too late for that, the wind is already whipping around me and the scent of butter and fresh-brewed coffee is in the air. Magic rushes through me, a blast of power with only one target.

Chapter Thirty-Three

Gil...

$\mathcal{T}$here isn't time to duck and, honestly, I already know there isn't a need—not with Tilda. She may have enough power in her little finger to flatten half of Wrightsville, but she'd never actually do it. Still, that doesn't mean the little hairs on the back of my neck don't stick straight up and my balls don't tuck up when she tells me it's too late for talking.

I'm confident in Tilda, I'm not stupid about my ability to piss her off.

A blast of magic makes a sonic boom in the meadow and an entire hundred-acre orchard of apple trees that was on the top of the hill behind me disappears in an instant.

All of the Sherwoods fall silent—something I wouldn't have believed possible—and those of us non-Sherwoods stand there for a second, our mouths agape. There's power and then there's banishing more than 3,500 apple trees with the flick of a wrist.

This is when a better man might approach the love of his life with some caution. As you know by now, though, I'm not a better guy. I'm a double agent. I've lied, cheated, snuck around, double-crossed people, and—up until I met Tilda—was more than satisfied with that life. Of course, now I can't imagine being that guy any more than I can imagine spending the rest of my life without Tilda.

Eyes wide with shock, Erik makes a tactician's surrender and walks over to Leona, who, while surprised at the power move her sister made, is still obviously annoyed enough with the Svensen heir to shoot him a 9.5 glare on a 6-point scale.

Heart hammering against my ribs, I close the distance between us, needing to be near her the way I need oxygen to breathe. "Did you just send a bunch of apple trees into The Beyond?"

She straightens her glasses and gives me a what-are-you-going-to-do-about-it chin lift. "Until we can put a stop to what the Council is doing, I thought it might help add to folks' food stores so they don't have to work as hard as your parents did to feed you."

Only Tilda would exercise her anger by making sure a bunch of strangers had enough to eat.

"Why?" She crosses her arms, the move drawing my gaze to the way her tits look in my old black T-shirt and the little points her nipples make as they strain against the cotton material. "Did I scare you?"

"Yes," I say, playing along. "You are petrifying. I think it's the glasses."

She throws back her head and laughs. "They do have that effect on people."

We stand there for a second. Neither one of us sure what to say next. There are a million things I want to explain, a billion promises I want to make. But first I have to apologize. "I'm sorry I didn't have time to let you in on my plan."

Her chin trembles. "I thought you'd left."

Fuck. It really doesn't get worse than the disappointment and hurt in her voice. "Never. At least not permanently." I take her hand in mine, intertwining our fingers, my thumb brushing over the spot on her ring finger where a band will go. "You're stuck with me, Tilda Sherwood."

"Look, about what I said last night." Her whole face is the color of one of the apples hanging in the part of the orchard that is still here. "It just sort of slipped out. I know it's way too early for anything like that and—" She stalls out for a second, turning even redder as she gnaws on her bottom lip. "I know it doesn't make any sense, but Griselda always says you know when you know. Well, I know. I realize that this may be coming from way out of left field, and after everything I've said on our dates may seem way out of character for me, but it is what it is. I love you. I realize this could be influenced by the adrenaline ride of the past few days or your family duíl magic, but that doesn't mean it's not real. I'm not asking you to love me back. We can take it one day at a time. No pressure. I just—"

"You're right." She always seems to be. I mean, I'm sure I'll find something she's wrong about. Someday. "Everything's happened in a rush and maybe we should take it slow. That would be the smart thing."

"Yeah, of course," she says, her voice a squeak of a sound. "Right. Perfect."

"But the thing is,"—I dip my head lower so that our lips are practically touching, and the urge to kiss her nearly overwhelms me, but I have to get the words out first—"I don't want to be smart about this. I don't want to think cynically about the possible outcomes. I just want to keep on loving you."

She blinks several times before one side of her mouth curls into a smile. "You do?"

"I do." Unable to wait any longer, I kiss her, brushing my lips against hers in a promise of what's to come since we are surrounded by her entire family, and they are all watching us. "I'm gonna tell you a secret about the duíl magic. It can't make something out of nothing. The desire has to already be there. We might let folks think that it can create a want or need that wasn't there before, but it can't. Like your spellbinding magic, it only amplifies what's already there. I may not have realized it, but I was already half in love with you in that coffee shop when the dragon's blood tree went after you. That's not gonna stop, with or without the duíl magic, because there will never be an end to me wanting to love you. It'll be there forever."

She toys with the buttons on my shirt, bringing back memories of last night and sending all of my thoughts to exactly where they don't need to go at the moment.

"And the adrenaline factor?" she asks.

Oh, the woman is just fucking with me now. "Tilda, I have absolutely no illusions about living with you. It will always be unexpected, exciting, and everything I could ever want."

"I snore."

I shrug. "I'm a hard sleeper."

She bites her bottom lip, looking up at the sky as she tries to come up with another warning for me. "I take really long showers and use up the vast majority of the hot water."

"Looks like I have a reason to join you then." Tilda soapy and naked in the steam? Yes please.

She glances back at the crowd of Sherwoods watching us. "My family is a lot."

"Just wait until you meet mine." There aren't as many, but they are definitely just as nosy.

"For the love of pixie dust," Vance hollers from the train platform. "Will you just put the man out of his misery already and tell him you really do love him too?"

Griselda, who is standing next to him, rolls her eyes. "Vance Eldridge, you have the manners of a unicorn shifter."

"I *am* a unicorn shifter," he shoots back.

"Believe me,"—Griselda pinches her nose—"we smell that."

"Watch it, Griselda, or I'll get your future godson-in-law to use that duíl magic on you."

She lets out a bark of a laugh. "I already have everything I want."

"Only on Thursday nights," Vance says with a wink.

Griselda turns six shades of red and disappears in a poof. Vance lets out a low, rumbling laugh.

"Don't worry, G," he says to the empty spot where Griselda was. "I'll still be there at the usual time."

The exchange between Vance and Griselda breaks the moment and the Sherwoods stop watching us as a live reality show and start to share theories about what's really going on between the unicorn shifter and the baddest old-school witch in Wrightsville. Witches, you can always count on them to get distracted by the latest gossip.

"So, is it true?" I ask Tilda, pulling her close.

"Yes." She nods. "I love you too."

There aren't four words in the world more magical than that.

Part of me wonders how I went from being such a cynical jerk to the biggest sap on the planet, but really, it doesn't matter. All that does is that Tilda loves me as much as I love her. Life doesn't get better than that.

"You ready to get out of here?" I jerk my chin toward the nitro-powered magic carpet floating nearby. "I know this place that serves great tea and happens to have a private table next to a really friendly, very smelly, and very lonely dragon's blood tree."

"I thought you'd never ask."

We make a run for it and are gone before her family even realizes we've stolen one of their magic carpets. Not that we're going to make a habit out of thievery, but, well, we do have a certain talent for it.

Epilogue

Tilda . . .

*T*he hottest man I've ever known is heading my way with a double paper plate loaded down with enough food to feed six of me. Needless to say, Gil takes his job as husband to the pregnant witch very seriously. Meanwhile, I am happy just to be able to keep food down again in time for the annual Sherwood Samhain BBQ, complete with limbo contest, my dad in a ridiculous Kiss the Pit Master apron at the grill, and various relatives and friends laughing, eating, and having a great time.

"I wasn't sure what you'd be craving," Gil says—he gave up know-it-all-ness with my first pregnancy, smart man. "So I brought some of everything."

"What I could really use is a kiss." I lower my glasses and give him a flirty wink. "You know how the second trimester is."

He shoots me an evil grin. "I love the second trimester."

Yeah. Him and me both. There's just something about being amazingly horny all of the time that puts a woman in a damn good mood—especially when there are so very many orgasms.

Priorities.

I've got 'em. The family I love. The social media management company I started that is about to open up a satellite office in Salem. I'm definitely living my best life and even using my spellbinding powers when needed, which isn't that often since my sister Bea delivered the absolutely most perfect death blow to the Council. Who would have ever thought her rooster familiar could ever be helpful in any situation, let alone one as massive as that? Well, he was and now we're all big Barkley fans around here.

Any thoughts of obnoxious roosters fly out of my head though the second Gil leans down, hands me my plate, and gives me a toe-curler of a kiss.

Deviled eggs and phenomenal kisses, really, does life get better than that?

"Can you two keep it down over there?" Vance grumbles from his nearby lawn chair where he's holding my firstborn in his huge hands. "The baby is trying to sleep."

Griselda sidles up to the unicorn shifter and tiny toddler to get a closer look at the half-asleep child, but Vance shifts

Marisol to his other side and shoots Griselda a so-there grin. Those two have been like that with the girls since the night they were born. Coincidentally—or not—that night there had been some of the most fantastic lightning storms over Wrightsville, as if the whole sky had gone electric.

Yeah, labor is like that.

I take a bite of potato salad and watch the fireworks of the metaphorical kind between my godmother and the triplets' godfather.

"Who appointed you the nanny overlord?" she asks.

"I appointed myself." Vance continues to rock back and forth in a move guaranteed to put even the most stubborn child—even a half Sherwood—to nap. "You can't expect just anyone to be able to handle a baby like Marisol, she's special."

Griselda gasps and gives him the evil eye. "What about Thea and Zita?"

"Just as special," Vance says. "Triplets are always extra luck."

"For once, you aren't completely wrong," Griselda grudgingly admits. "Triplets are always lucky, but these three, oh the fates have something fantastic planned for them."

"What's that?" he asks.

Now it's Griselda's turn to so-there him with a don't-you-wish-you-knew smirk. "A good witch never tells. The fates will unravel it all when it's time."

"Bunch of riddles and poppycock," Vance grumbles. "These three are perfect and they'll be telling the universe what's good, not the other way around."

Griselda rubs her hands together with glee. "Bet on it?"

Vance doesn't hesitate. He sticks out his hand to shake on the deal. Griselda cackles in triumph and uses her considerable magical powers to snatch Marisol from his burly arms and disappear in a poof only to appear again a second later on the other side of the dragon moonstones, cooing and making faces at the baby. Vance—who has three new names tattooed over his heart in a scary font—glares at Griselda as if she wouldn't mow down heaven and earth to protect the girls from any and all dangers.

Good luck to both of them on that. Trouble always tends to find us Sherwoods—and we handle it. Okay, fine, it may take us a while to do it and we make a ton of mistakes in the process, but if there's one thing I've learned, it's that there is a core of power within each of us, we only have to get out of our own way and figure out how to tap into it. After that? Witchingdom doesn't stand a chance.

Gil shakes his head at Vance and Griselda as he sits down in the pink-and-purple-striped lawn chair next to me. "Those two are going to spoil the girls rotten."

"Only Vance and Griselda?" I scoff and scoop up a bite of potato salad. "Both of our parents are already locked in an unspoken battle to be the grandparents supreme."

We both look over to where our parents are chatting by the lavender bush. Gil's parents smile more than I'd ever expected, but I guess surviving exile and helping to take down a band of asshole fascists tends to make a person appreciate all of the small bits of happiness in the world. And my parents haven't stopped smiling since the wedding. Fine. That's a slight exaggeration, but you understand what I mean. I think keeping my spellbinder secret weighed on them and having everything out in the open is allowing them to relax their guard for the first time in a long time. Well, that and the fact that the Council's master plan to take out our family didn't come to fruition. You know, just the little things.

Wait, you don't know that part yet? Not even about the demon dog, the pixie kidnappings, and the only-one-bed incident?!? Well, my sisters are going to have to share all of that with you. After all, those are their stories to tell. You're gonna love them. Trust me.

Still, after the past few years' excitement, I could really go for a little vacation.

"Do you think we can still find our way to that uncharted island in the Pacific?" I whisper to Gil. "Just you, me, and the girls?"

Gil puts down his empty plate—how did he manage to eat it all so fast? Men! "We can go wherever you want."

Best. Answer. Ever. "Today?"

"Or tomorrow, or whenever." Gil snags my plate and then magicks me so I'm floating one minute and sitting on his lap in the next. He wraps his arms loosely around my waist. "As long as we're together. It *was* in the cards for us all along, you know."

Ugh. This man loves to bust my chops about that. I haven't given up on reading tarot, but I still stink at it. Turns out that there are some things even a spellbinder can't do.

"You're never going to let me forget that I thought you were going to marry Leona."

He tucks a few strands of hair behind my ear, gliding his fingertips over the shell of my ear with just enough pressure to send a shiver of desire through me that I can't blame on second-trimester horniness. Truth of it is, I cannot get enough of my husband. Luckily for me, he has the same problem when it comes to me.

"Yeah," Gil says, his tone teasing, "even if I wasn't against it being anyone but you, I think Erik would have something to say about that."

"He's not the only one." A more-than-satisfied happy sigh escapes and I settle back against him, letting my head rest against his shoulder. Who would have thought that my know-it-all dating nemesis would turn out to be the one I'd fall for? "I love you, Gil Connolly."

"I love you right back, Tilda Grace Sherwood Connolly." He brushes a kiss against my temple. "And I always will."

Cheesy? Completely. Who knew the sexy double agent with the metaphorical stick up his butt would be such a softie under it all? Don't even get me started on his love of old rom-coms and the tearjerker commercials they show during the Super Bowl—he'd deny it anyway.

Across the garden, Zita, who is climbing Vance like he's a jungle gym, starts babbling to Marisol in their shared triplet language and Thea joins in on the conversation. There's a shiver through the atmosphere half a second before flowers from the garden start floating and dancing in the air. The girls all start giggling and clapping their hands. Oh man, the Witchingdom is very much not ready for whatever these three are going to cook up.

I can't wait to see how it all turns out.

"You're plotting again," Gil says as he kisses that sensitive spot where my throat meets my shoulder.

"Maybe I'm plotting how we can sneak out of here and get at least a few minutes of mommy and daddy alone time." I mean, I wasn't half a second ago, but with that kiss I definitely am now.

"Already ahead of you." He snaps his fingers and poof! We're gone.

I really do love it when a plan comes together; almost as much as I love Gil, my girls, our baby on the way, and the happily ever after we have together.

Life's kinda magic like that—even when you don't think you are (but trust me, you—yes, you—totally are) a magical badass.

xoxo,

Tilda

Acknowledgments

The devil works hard, but copyeditors work harder—especially on this book. Trust. A huge thank-you to the entire team at Berkley for helping to bring Witchingdom to life: Kristine for asking if I'd ever thought about a witchy rom-com, Leni who created the most beautiful illustrated cover, Tina and Bridget for their hard work getting it in readers' hands, Mary for being a true force for good, the copyeditors and proofreaders who are magic, and the rest of the team who helped bring Tilda and her family to life. A huge thank-you to my agent, Elaine, for being with me on the journey and being just completely awesome along the way. As always, I couldn't do any of this without the support of my family (who are all against getting dog number six, spoilsports). I love y'all so much. However, the biggest thank-you goes to the readers. THANK YOU, FELLOW BOOK NERDS!

xoxo,
Avery

Keep reading for an excerpt from
Avery Flynn's next novel . . .

Resting Witch Face

Available soon in paperback from Berkley Romance!

Leona . . .

*E*rik motherfucking Svensen.

He is the last man I ever want to see again in this lifetime or any others that might happen to follow. The man is a cocky, smooth-talking jerk who is too hot, rich, and smart for his own good.

Even worse, he's technically my husband.

My *secret* husband that no one—and I mean no one—knows about. Well, except for him, and I've already told him the magical miseries I'll rain down on his head if he even hints at our matrimonial status. It is enough to drive a good witch to drink, and I am no good witch, at least not when I'm around Erik Svensen. He brings out the bad witch in me.

Don't judge. We all make mistakes. Mine just happens to be of the six-four, broad-shouldered, eight-pack abs, black-haired and blue-eyed with a mouth that did things that still have me waking up in the middle of the night from a hot dream on the verge of orgasm variety.

I've spent the past year outmaneuvering him, working on the down low with attorneys to break the secret handfast marriage we got in Vegas before anyone in my family (especially my mother) finds out—but he won't sign the papers. You'd think the fact that I had no idea he was a member of my family's biggest rivals would have been enough to break the handfast. Erik Phillips. Yeah, he was no more some random witch than I am LeLe Collins, which has been my go-to fake bar name since I was in college.

Fine, I was using a false identity when we'd met too. I didn't say I was all clean and shiny in this. However, if a woman couldn't go to Vegas and live the life she wants instead of the one she has in reality, she'd lose it—or at least I would. There are all kinds of pressures that come with being the heir apparent to Izzy Sherwood. Most days it's fine, but there's always a limit, and I'd reached mine before hopping the jet to Vegas last year to meet up with the mystery guy I'd been talking to online for a year.

And that's when it happened. There were sparks. It felt like kismet. And I got carried away by the moment—me, the woman who plans her spontaneity and has planners for her planners. They're color coordinated, and I have a killer sticker collection as well as a whole rolling cart of colored pens. Just because I'm overly organized doesn't mean I don't like things to be pretty.

Speaking of pretty, this situation is not, but there's no way to get out of it without making a fuss in front of my entire family and exposing my one bout of impulsivity.

Keeping my smile in place so no one looking will realize I'm talking to my own personal albatross, I lower my voice so only Erik can hear me. "Well, we might as well get this over with."

He winks at me. "Whatever you say, LeLe."

His grin matches mine just for showiness, but there's more to it, an intensity in his blue eyes that sends a shiver down my spine. Damn it. He shouldn't be able to still do that to me, not after what he did. He drops his hand the size of a dinner plate to the small of my back, his palm and long fingers spanning the space and setting off a whole swarm of butterflies loose in my belly. The smug look on his handsome face shows that he knows exactly what he's doing.

It takes everything I have not to let my annoyance show to the rest of my family, who are sneaking looks at us.

Ugh.

He is such a giant pain in my ass, which he is well aware of. I know he goads me on purpose. Most people try to ruffle the iciest of the Sherwoods, as long as you don't count my mom. Almost no one succeeds. The exception? My sisters (come on, you know your siblings know exactly how to push every button you know about and half a million more you have no clue about) and Erik Svensen.

"You know I hate it when you call me that." He is the only one who does, because he obviously doesn't value his kneecaps.

"Fine." His hand drops a few millimeters, his fingertips almost but not quite brushing my ass. Typical Erik, tiptoeing along that line of acceptable and what will get him kneed in the balls. "I'll just call you wife instead. Is that better?"

"Not in the least." I side-eye him and take a small step forward, missing the sizzle from his touch as soon as I break contact.

He grins at me. "But it's what you are."

"Only because you won't sign the divorce papers." The ones I've sent multiple times with little yellow Post-it Notes marking everywhere his signature needs to go.

"I have absolutely no plans to do that," he says, not even bothering to pretend to be ashamed.

Yeah, no shock there. The first time I sent the paperwork, he opened the package and returned the papers unsigned. The next time, he signed his name as Santa Claus. The third time, the envelope came back unopened and stamped *return to sender*. The next set I sent via a flying monkey courier. All I'd gotten back were pics of Erik and the monkey living their best life in a beach resort somewhere tropical.

The why of his avoidance is easy. Erik Svensen loves a challenge, and I am a challenge. Not a person. Not a potential life partner. A challenge. An opportunity to show all of Witchingdom that he can do what no one thought possible—bring together the Svensen and Sherwood families.

Knocking my glare up a few notches, I keep my volume low as I tell him, "I'm not a prize to be won."

"No." He steps closer so he's just outside my personal bubble. "But you sure are a treasure to be cherished."

Ha! As if. I know better than to think he actually believes that.

His reputation with women is well-known. He's a natural-born flirt with women, men, and everyone else. There are at least fifty fan accounts on social media that document his every rumored romance. Not that I follow them. Okay. Fine. I do, but only so I can keep tabs on him to know where to send the divorce papers.

"Erik Svensen, you can't sweet-talk your way into my pants again."

And maybe if you say it enough, Leona Amber Sherwood, it'll actually be true.

Yeah, my inner horny self can just shut it about now.

"Now, LeLe,"—Erik reaches out and brushes his thumb across my wrist, his touch sending a jolt of desire straight to my core and exposing the otherwise invisible golden glow of the handfast chain printed on my skin—"we both know that's not true."

"You're the worst." But in the absolute best way if you're naked and in the mood to get your back blown out.

No!

I will not think about that now. I will not think about how we spent forty-eight hours in Vegas naked and utilizing every horizontal surface and quite a few vertical ones to fuck each other brainless. I don't think I've ever walked the same way after I came home. My body sure as hell hasn't forgotten. Just being this close to him again has my nipples perking up while my panties are already beyond damp in anticipation.

Why does this guy—and only this one—make me want to forget every good reason to keep my distance and only think about every bad reason to keep him close?

"But you bring out the best in me," he says, letting go of my wrist and flexing his fingers as if he feels the same electric spark whenever he touches me as I do. Then he takes a few steps toward Tilda and Gil, who still have the ancient spell book. "Come on, LeLe, let's get out of here before the Council gets it in their head that this is the perfect time to steal The Liber Umbrarum back."

My eyes go wide as the last word registers. "Back?" I sputter as I turn up the speed to catch up with Erik's long strides. "They want it back? You stole The Liber Umbrarum? From the Council?"

Of all the stupid, foolhardy, impulsive things to do, stealing from the Council is numbers one through ten on the list.

He stops next to me and shrugs. "All's fair in love and war, wife."

"Are we at war?" As my mom's second, I've heard the rumors, but for them to make any kind of public moves to take control of Witchingdom would change everything.

He dips his head down, his lips brushing the curve of my ear in a way guaranteed to drive me crazy and turn me on at the same time.

"When it comes to us, wife," he says, his voice velvet sandpaper on every one of my most sensitive spots, "I'm all about making love not war."

I let out a huff of frustration as I stare at him and his loose body language and smug grin as if nothing in the world—not even the Council—can touch him. Can he not take anything seriously? This is the Council we're talking about, the big baddie of the Witchingdom. Still, if he is insistent I go with him, that does give me some leverage—finally.

"If I go with you," I say, "you have to agree to sign the divorce papers."

"Of course," he says as if I'd just asked him if he wanted extra pepperoni on his pizza.

That was easy. *Too easy.* My inner warning bells are clanging loud enough I'm surprised he can't hear them. "For real?"

"LeLe"—he slips his arm around my waist like it's the most natural thing in the world, and we start walking toward my sister and her boyfriend—"let's take The Liber Umbrarum home and then I'll do whatever you want."

The sad part is, I know Erik is about as trustworthy as a tooth fairy around a six-year-old with a loose incisor, and yet . . . I can't help believing him.

He's my jinx.

I'm his curse.

Together, we're nothing but trouble, but, the fates help me, I'm in the mood to stir up that spell and see what happens next.

I'm not gonna regret this. What's the worst that could happen? It's not like I'm going to stay married to him. A few days, a week tops, with Erik and then I'll be a single woman again and everything will be the way it's supposed to be.

I can do this. It'll be fine. Really. I have absolutely nothing to worry about—especially falling in love with my secret husband.

Photo by Passion Pages / Annie Ray

USA Today and *Wall Street Journal* bestselling romance author Avery Flynn has three slightly wild children, loves a hockey-addicted husband, and is desperately hoping someone invents the coffee-IV drip. She lives outside of Washington, D.C., with her family, Dwight the cat, and a pack of five dogs all named after food. If she is not reading romance or bingeing reality TV, she is most definitely plotting to take over the world so she can banish Crocs from existence. Visit author's website at averyflynn.com.

Ready to find
your next great read?

Let us help.

Visit prh.com/nextread

Penguin
Random
House